CW00879724

WILLIAM ROBERT STANEK

CELEBRATING 250 BOOKS
40 YEARS OF WRITING

the PUBLISHER
& the WRITER

OVER 50
BESTSELLERS

OVER 20 MILLION
COPIES SOLD

TRANSLATED INTO OVER
57 LANGUAGES

In the Service of Dragons #2

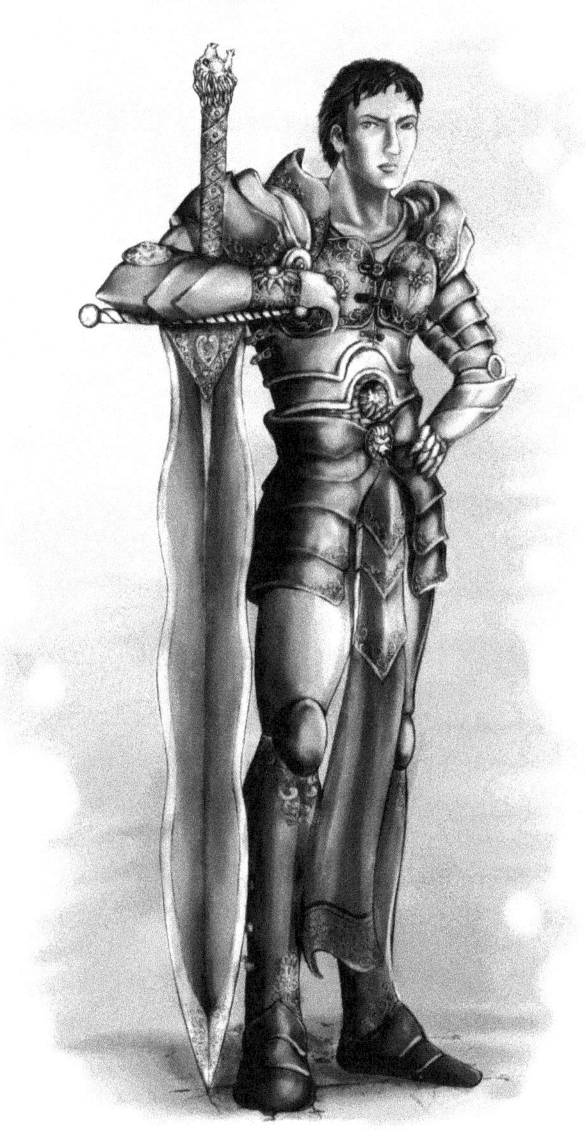

ROBERT STANEK

This is a work of fiction. All the characters, names, places and events portrayed in this book are either products of the author's imagination or are used fictitiously. Any resemblance to any actual locale, person or event is entirely coincidental.

In the Service of Dragons #2

20th Anniversary, Signature Illustrated Edition for Libraries

Learn more about the author at www.williamrstanek.com

First Printed in the United States of America.

Book 2

Table of Contents

1

Imtal palace and city were somber places over the many days that followed the announcement of the king's death. Three sisters with long black hair mourned and yearned for their father in the grand gardens. Midmorning found them seated around a table in the gazebo with Sister Catrin and Jasmine.

Jasmine, Catrin and Midori sat on one side and Calyin and Adrina were on the other. Two of Lord Serant's men stood behind Calyin. They would not leave even though they had been ordered to do so by Calyin herself. They had great respect for her wishes, yet followed only Lord Serant's orders where her safety was concerned. They judged the priestesses of the Mother as a threat and as such they would not even drop back a respectful distance where they could not hear the words being spoken.

"Today is the seventh day; let us not argue this day away," implored

Calyin. "Your fears are unfounded. There is no danger in Imtal. Look around you. What do you see? I see flowers being claimed by the coming of winter, losing their petals and withering to the ground. I see trees filled with autumn colors, bronze and gold and scarlet. Isn't it wonderful?"

"You are an eternal optimist. You would find good in a time like this," hissed Jasmine ominously.

"Calyin, we discussed this yesterday. You agreed then. Have you no sense of loyalty?"

"You speak of loyalty?" scoffed Calyin, "Loyalty is not something you suddenly find, but a thing that is built up over time. Do not throw it at me as if you have any sense of loyalty to this family. Your loyalty lies solely with the Mother."

Midori got a faraway look in her eyes. "You'll never know the depths of my loyalty," she whispered.

She said no more as Jasmine cautioned her.

"Honestly, tell me, what harm will come of it, Princess Calyin? For I can see none. Several days away will do the girl some good."

"What do you think, Adrina?" asked Calyin.

Adrina had her eyes turned out into the garden. She knew they argued over her as if she were some prize catch, yet she did not care.

"I am numb," she whispered, "I feel nothing."

She turned back to the fading greens of the garden. Calyin wrapped her arm around her shoulder and hugged her.

"It will pass," she said, "it will pass. Just let it all out. Go ahead, cry, cry until there are no more tears. Tears are good for the soul, they cleanse it."

"I can't cry; I don't feel," returned Adrina, wriggling away from her sister's hold.

"Do you see why a short respite will do her some good?" asked Midori in a stern voice. "She needs to get away from this dank place."

"Perhaps she will; perhaps she will return to the North with me when this is all cleared up and Prince Valam returns home."

"You are a fool!" shouted Jasmine. "The prince will not return!"

Calyin threw back her arms to restrain the guards, who had just pressed forward. Jasmine glared at the two men, unafraid.

"I am not afraid of death, you sons of mongrels. I would welcome it as surely as I welcome the night. Only good will come of my passing, only good. If you wish to take me now, do so, or back away, back away now, before I lay a curse upon you with my next breath that will blight your life until its end!"

The two took only one step back at first and then another as Jasmine continued to glare.

"Have you no respect?" asked Calyin. "This night we will lay my father to rest. Let us drop this paltry argument and talk no more of it until tomorrow. Tomorrow you can argue to your hearts' content."

Catrin whispered the only words she had said in days, words that only Jasmine and Midori heard. "The ignorant always believe tomorrow will come as did today," she said.

Midori was quick to find words. "Yes, perhaps you are right, sister. Perhaps we should wait and discuss this later. I think it is a good time to find lunch. Is anyone else as hungry as I?"

Adrina turned back.

"Let's not take it in the hall," she said, "there is a balcony in the tower beyond the wall. Father would often sit there at about this time."

The day passed slowly and it seemed that afternoon would never come. Some hours later, Calyin and Adrina were still on the balcony above the tower; remnants of a heavy, half eaten meal still rested on the table in front of them. Once the meal had been served, Adrina had chased off the attendants, telling them not to return until they were called, and so the uneaten food sat.

"High Province is grand this time of year," said Calyin. "I know I have told you this before, but I will tell you again. The choice is up to you. You needn't do anything if you don't want to. But please look at yourself. Your hair is a mess, you haven't bathed, and you hardly eat. Father is dead, Adrina. Nothing can bring him back and nothing that you could have done would have prevented his death."

Adrina averted her eyes as tears started to flow.

"Adrina," said Calyin, "it is time you mended your own soul. You cannot go on like this. I cannot go on like this. Cry, cry until there are no more tears within you. Let it all out, let it all out."

"You don't understand," said Adrina in a pathetic sounding voice, "you did not see his pain."

"Did you ever think that he is happier now? Can you truly say that he was happy since mother passed on? There was life and at rare times there was joy, but true happiness that runs deep within the soul was gone, long since gone. She was his life, his source of life, and without her life was void. No, I assure you, he is much happier now. He rests in the hall of the great ones, the kings and queens of all the lands that ever were, and she, his beloved queen and wife, rests beside him. He is happy, Adrina, he has found peace. Cry your tears of lament, but let go your remorse."

Lord Serant came looking for his wife and joined her in comforting her young sister: "You are young and you have a full life in front of you. Find inspiration in the day, joy in the light of the sun. Such sweetness in your beauty, such tenderness and grace. Find wonder in the simple pleasures of the world, in the wonders of youth."

"Find a young man's face and melt your heart within it," added Calyin, greeting her husband with a warm embrace.

"Oh, Calyin, I am so sorry," said Adrina, "it's just, it's just—"

"Shh, shh, hush now, dear. Say no more," gently soothed Calyin.

"So much happening at one time; it just overwhelmed me," Adrina said. "Do you think Valam is coming home?"

"We will have to wait and see; and if he does not, we can cope without him."

Adrina wiped the tears from her eyes. She thought of the irony of her father's death as the land was being reborn in spring and the flowers were returning to the gardens. She thought with bitterness of her upcoming nameday—a nameday that meant nothing without her father there to celebrate with her.

"Shall we find the bathhouse and put it to good use? A hot soothing bath would feel good about now, would it not? When father looks down from the heavens this night and sees his funeral bier pass through the city streets to the central square where he will be laid to rest, let him find us with our heads raised proud and our hearts filled with love, but our eyes void of tears. Then he will know that he can rest peacefully and without concern."

As Calyin finished, Adrina began to run her hands through her hair, fussing over the many tangles in it, a sign that she had at last begun to move on. Lord Serant, Calyin, and Adrina returned to the palace proper. The lord and lady's bodyguards, two to front and rear, moved with such skill that they seemed invisible; and to the three, it seemed that they were alone.

The bathing time was a private time for the two sisters. They relaxed in the warm waters, stretching sore muscles and washing their hair with herbal-scented soaps that Calyin had brought from the Northlands. Dusk was approaching as they stepped from the hot pool into the cool air. Calyin rejected the gown that had been pressed and readied for her, selecting new riding leathers instead. Adrina did likewise. Neither intended to ride in a coach this eve.

An anxious hour passed as they waited for a few last-minute items to be readied. The castle was suddenly alive with activity. Chancellor Yi rushed to and fro. Servants groomed horses. Guards polished armor and fanciful weaponry. The bier coach and its team were the last things readied. The guests and family crowded into the forward courtyard, assembling before the great gates of the outer wall. At the sounding of the first toll they mounted and waited.

Precisely at the time of the setting sun, the funeral procession was in place. At the sounding of the first knell, those present mounted and waited; at the sounding of the second, the gates slowly began to open, and at the sounding of the third, the procession began to move. Father Francis had embalmed King Andrew's body so that he looked as he had in life except that he now appeared at peace with himself.

The declaration was made in the manner decreed: the people must see their king once more in death as he was in life. In this way all bore witness that the king had indeed passed. With the sounding of the fourth knell, the gates were fully opened. First to exit were the honor guard, twelve men arrayed in black armor upon mounts of gray. They rode out in single file, followed by the open funeral bier.

The bier itself was quite simple, an ordinary oaken box painted black, fixed with long brass handles along head and foot and two thick silver poles running down the long sides. It was pulled by seven black horses. The royal family followed, each mounted on a pure white stallion. A cry of despair rose from the growing crowd, which had been summoned by the first toll; their king was truly dead.

The final group to depart the courtyard and slowly enter the city streets was the rear honor guard of a full complement of soldiers, fifty in all. They followed, outfitted in armor that shimmered in the falling light. The procession advanced one trumpet blast at a time toward the central square. With each sounding of the horn, more people crowded into the streets.

The path they took from palace to the square was not a direct route into the city's heart, rather an indirect route that wound its way along many of the long cobblestone paths of Imtal and then slowly, after a wide outward circle, began to creep inward.

The streets in all directions were filled now as people streamed out of their houses to pay their last respects. Many felt obliged to follow the bier and the thick line that stretched behind the procession grew and grew until its end could no longer be seen by those who would often look back in wonder. King Andrew had been a fair monarch and the Great Kingdom had prospered under his caring hand.

The eve of his passing had been a grievous event. Uncertainty now lay ahead for all the citizens of the realm. Where was the crowned prince? Had he not heard the cry for his return? Would the prosperous days of the past now end? What was ahead? These were the many questions that ran hushed through the crowd.

The procession turned inward now, beginning the slow creep toward the central square. Each sounding of the toll brought them one step closer. Adrina looked into the faces of the crowd. She could see that they also felt the sadness of this great loss. Princess Midori and her companions also rode with the royal family. They rode to Adrina's left.

Lord Serant had flatly refused to allow Princess Calyin to leave the castle without his personal guards. He rode with her at the rear of the procession, surrounded by the faithful ones who had accompanied them on the journey from High Province. Father Francis had tried to convince Lord Serant that the kingdom was not like his former home, the Western Territories; but Serant would not listen and eventually Father Francis had acquiesced.

The procession reached the grand central square. Even at peak market season when hundreds of stalls lined its depths and many thousands more came for the festivities and goods, the area was only half filled. But today, it was filled to capacity. The inner circle, however, had been kept empty by decree. Twelve blocks from the central square was a large encircled garden, a memorial to the previous kings of the Great Kingdom. It was here where new kings were crowned and old ones were honored and entombed.

The crowd parted to let the procession enter. As was the custom, the funeral procession circled the garden three times and then stopped. Each horseman dismounted one at a time, from the first to the last. The final decree of death was given and a long silence followed. The final toll sounded just as the last light of day shone on the square; and as its echoes fell away from the land, the sun sank below the horizon.

Tiny red sparks burst from sparse areas of the gathered throng. As the torchlight began to spread and its light slowly became agreeable, the members of the procession started to remount, as was customary. The twelve in black mounted, bowed their heads respectfully and waited. As the fiftieth man of the rear guard mounted, the dozen forward guards looked up, dismounted and went to the bier, forming two lines, four abreast, on either side of it while the four others waited.

Those who looked on bowed their heads now. The twelve took a momentary breath and then the chosen eight heaved the casket from the bier. As the casket was slowly carried toward Andrew's crypt, the remaining four men labored to push away the guarding stone. There was such a silence over the next few moments that the footsteps of the men descending into the vault carried across the square nearly to its ends. As the last of the onlookers bowed their heads, waiting for the last prayer to begin, a group of men broke from the crowd. They lunged into the midst of the royal family. Jasmine was knocked from her horse. Adrina had seen the attack and tried to scream. A hand covered her mouth and she was dragged from her horse. The attack had come and gone in an instant that left the viewers dazed.

2

The sound of clashing steel broke the silence. A cry of panic erupted from the bewildered crowd. All around the square soldiers clad in black emerged, tossing their deceitful robes of white onto the ground and raising their weapons high. They attacked everyone in sight, hacking and slashing even the innocent. Guards rushed to stop the onslaught. Many of them died before they could even draw their blades.

Lord Serant's bodyguards sprang into action. The small contingent flashed as a burst of white lightning into the surge of the dark, and it was temporarily thrust back. Wielding huge two-handed battle swords as a child would a toy dagger, these men were obvious masters, their skill and expertise unmatched on the field.

The dark warriors paid a grave price for their fall; however, Serant's guards were simply overwhelmed by the number of the enemy. For each they cut down, two warriors lunged forward in the fallen's stead. They did not shame their lord as the last man crumpled to the ground, a mortal wound in his side; they had given the others much needed time, a chance to prepare.

The dark warriors were non-selective in their blows. Their blades struck out in every direction. The dead and dying littered the square. Cries of pain and anguish filled the night, even above the din of clashing steel. Darkness began to fill the square as the torchlight was slowly smothered and with it came chaos, which the dark ones used to their advantage.

The innocent tried to flee the square, dragging those who could not make it on their own, but the dark warriors hacked them down as they fled. No one was allowed to leave the square. More of the dark-clothed warriors began filing in from the adjacent byways, as the two forces, one considerably smaller and determined, the other larger and stronger, faced each other.

The rear guard was fully mounted and sought to protect those they honored. Fifty brave souls crashed into the encroaching wave of dark. Their ornamental armor gleamed defiantly and proudly in the pale red light of the square. Their weaponry was varied and though it had all been meant for ceremonial purposes, it was highly functional and well crafted. They bore pikes and spears with great forked blades; some had full-handed swords, others lances, but all poured forth, driven on by anger and anguish to a ferocity that bit into the enemy and would eventually cause their downfall.

Father Francis was mounted next to Keeper Q'yer and the chancellor. They had a momentary reprieve while the dark warriors dropped back to regroup. The three weighed the odds; heavily outnumbered though they were, their protective guards were also on horseback. The enemy was on foot. Hopefully, the defense would last long enough for reinforcements to arrive from Imtal garrison.

The former lord of the Western Territories and empowered lord of High Province stared coldly at his assailants. He looked to Calyin, with one single thought on his mind. He must protect her. He had sworn an oath that he would forever watch over her; he would not fail. Anger also flowed through him. In his territories, though they were not as civilized as here, nothing like this could ever happen. He spat on the ground. If he survived, his honor would demand retribution. He vowed he would kill Chancellor Yi for his incompetence. One stroke of his blade would end the old man's life and provide partial compensation.

Sister Catrin knelt over her fallen sister. Jasmine had taken a nasty blow to the head and was unconscious. Midori and Catrin placed her upon her mount, then they also remounted. Midori cried out in anguish; Adrina had been taken from her so easily. One moment Adrina had been beside her; the next she was gone and Jasmine lay on the ground. The will of the Mother flowed inside Midori, its power strong and cleansing. A similar flow came to Sister Catrin, yet her anger was not washed away.

The short reprieve was over; the dark warriors had regrouped and now attacked from all sides. The mounted guard plunged again into their midst; their weapons danced in the dull light of the square. Horses trampled over the fallen as they moved outward. Although the attackers were greater in number, they were no match for the superior guard.

The small force seemed to be turning the battle around. Now the enemy was feeling the cold of the rapier. While horses trampled the fallen and claimed what remained of their threads of life, the riders lashed out, finding new victims. But even in the face of the vicious assault by the mounted guard, the enemy did not retreat again. They continued to pour forth almost as if they welcomed death.

Keeper Q'yer concentrated all the energy of his will into a single thought. He cried out to those at the palace and the city garrison for help. He beseeched them to find the urgency in his desperate words and hurry to the square. He did not know if they heard his call, only that his cry went forth. He would have to wait, as would the others, to know if the garrison soldiers would come.

Father Francis could feel the power of the Father within him; to disturb a ceremony of passing of a great one was an outrage. The call of the Mother also came to his mind. He looked to the sisters; he saw that Jasmine was unconscious. He stared beyond her to Midori, who nodded her head and thanked the Father. He reached out and embraced her center. The two were linked together. A warm feeling came over them both. Wild emotions of the joining of both the Mother-Earth and the Great-Father pulsed throughout their entire being. Great power was coming to the fore.

A whirlwind of thought flowed from one mind to the other. Father

Francis saw an image of Midori in his mind. They embraced each other, releasing the power as their bodies locked as one in spirit and in mind. A wall of flames shot from the earth, running in a wide arc until it formed a great circle, leaving only the rear guard and the dark warriors in the open. Oddly, the great wall of flames circled the road before the garden of entombment and coronation.

Keeper Q'yer slumped over in his saddle, all his energy spent, in the thrusting out of that one hopeful summons. The twang of release as scores of bowstrings settled back into place, combined with the whine of arrows flying through the air followed by cries of agony, rose above the cacophony of battle. The wall of flame had come just in time to save the inner group. The last of the mounted guard regrouped around the flames, although of fifty, only six remained. They raised their swords high one last time and charged, unafraid and willing to offer their lives for the ones they were devoted to. Arrows pelted them from all sides, and before the first man swung he died.

The five continued on undaunted. Among them were a bladesman, two pikemen, a former huntsman who wielded a double-bladed spear, and a swordmaster first-class. None of them knew this as they shot forth to certain death, each focused on a single line of sight.

For one man, it was the tower of a city church that he wished to reach before he died. For another it was a tavern that lay six blocks north along the eastern side of the square; he could not see it though he knew it was there. For still another it was his home and his wife and child that lay beyond the eastern side of the square.

Not one of the small company reached his goal, yet as each died in his turn, the simple goals seemed to lose their purpose, and as the last man fell, he looked back at the wall of fire, wishing those within luck and survival.

3

Adrina felt powerful hands cover her mouth. She tried to scream, but only a voiceless gasp passed her lips. Awestruck, she was swept into the crowd, buried beneath a long flowing black cloak. She looked out with eyes that saw only a dream, not that which was real; and she could do nothing as she was carried away. She could hear the din of a battle as if very far away, veiled from her eyes and masked from her ears by the silencing cloak.

Sounds of agony, her own agony, filled her ears. Once out of the crowd her captors met another group. At first she saw only many black leather boots as she peered downward through the folds of the cloak. The hand was still pressed against her mouth as she was lifted from the veil. Now she saw the masked faces of the small band that had taken her. They paused only to bind and gag her. Once the blindfold was in place, her world returned to blackness. Terror filled her mind and she began to shake uncontrollably.

The blackness began to envelop her, and for a time the princess passed into unconsciousness. This was a quiet time for her as her agony and terror subsided. Unaware that she was being hurried through the back paths and alleyways of Imtal to a waiting group of horsemen, Adrina slept. At some point she was placed onto the back of a horse and led wildly along cobblestone paths although the princess was unaware of this.

The jostling of the horse aroused her and she opened her eyes to find that she was still shrouded in the black cloak. As she regained consciousness, she realized what had happened to her. She waited now, not terrified any longer, but not at ease either. At any moment she expected the palace guard to come to her rescue. She struggled against her bonds to no avail, listening for the thunder of many hooves and the boom of angry voices, signs that her rescuers were near.

She heard hooves pounding across the hard stone streets and she knew they were still inside the city although she did not know where. But she did not hear the thunder of a hundred pairs of hooves striking the ground as she had expected; she heard only those of the small band that led her away into the darkness. Suddenly, her horse was reined to a halt, and she was lifted from it.

A quiet time passed as leather soles marched along another set of back alleyways. Heavy hands were around her thighs and she kicked, punched, and clawed trying to break free. Shouts filled the air. She heard voices screaming. The hands held her strongly now as the man bolted away. Her head bobbed up and down until it ached as her captor ran madly.

Voices followed, and Adrina realized that her rescuers were close. She felt hopeful, but then without warning she was cast to the ground; her head struck a solid stone wall and then her face hit the cold, cold rock. She lay motionless. Her world seemed still to be moving, swirling around her. Perhaps close by, or perhaps far away, Adrina heard the voices again. They screamed more wildly as panic engulfed them. Her head started to throb and a moist flow began to trickle across her forehead, running warmly until it touched the cold stone, forming a tiny pool beneath her head, which she was unable to move.

Colors of red and gray swam before her eyes. She heard the distant sound of clashing steel, which might have been right beside her; she could not tell. She started to wriggle and writhe as the throbbing in her head was joined by a dull, numbing pain that inched its way up her legs. Pain hit her quickly, sharp and excruciating, as a heavy boot found her gut. Adrina rasped and coughed.

Something fell beside her, prostrate on the cold ground beside her. She groped outward with her hands, finding a cold limp thing that she did not at first recognize as an arm. The numbing pain swept up her legs into her arms and once more she found she could not move. Her hands fell still. The tiny pool beneath her had grown until it was a small puddle that circled her head. With her head pressed against the unforgiving stone, the liquid streamed around her face; she felt it on her chin and then suddenly it touched her lips. It tasted bitter and salty against her tongue.

Hands found her again, heaving her limp form up and pressing her against the stone wall, forcing her to sit upright, her head hanging limply. A dull yellow came before her closed lids as the blindfold was lifted momentarily. The gash at the back of her head was checked and bandaged; with its binding, the moist, warm trickle ended. A dull white light flooded into her eyes as her pupils were checked. A distant voice sounding in her ears whispered, "She lives."

Hands found her again, groping along the back of her head. The tingling that accompanied the numbing returned and then suddenly the pain was gone, the throbbing subsided, and Adrina found semi-coherence. No longer was her head against the cold unforgiving stone. Something warm was touched to it. For a long while, she didn't note that she was again draped over a broad shoulder, firm hands clasped to her thighs.

Minutes passed silently and then a grinding noise filled her ears, followed by a pungent aroma that assaulted her nostrils. The smell made her sick and she vomited, the gag in her mouth causing her to choke on her vomit. The sour taste made her rasp and choke more violently. Spittle oozed from her mouth. The movement stopped. Her head whirled as she was brought upright; a damp cold came to her buttocks. The blindfold was removed. A soft hand touched her face and she heard a whisper: "Do not scream and I'll remove your gag. We are friends, not enemies."

Adrina spat the chunks of the vomit from her mouth. She struggled to clasp a hand to her nose to shield her nostrils from the foul stench that surrounded her. She couldn't move; her hands were still tied tightly. She started to scream and the gag quickly filled her mouth. The soft voice returned and whispered kind words that she half listened to.

The gag was removed again. Adrina did not attempt to scream. She considered the words of her captor, which sounded sincere. She doubted she could believe those around her were anything but enemies, but at least the gag was gone from her mouth. She spat more of the vomit from her mouth. She could inhale through her mouth now, and the gag was gone. The smell around her was horrible, like sewage.

She was lifted and placed back onto the firm shoulder. They had not gone far when they stopped once more. Adrina could hear many voices whispering in hushed tones. One voice stood out from all the others, stronger, firmer, commanding. It was this voice that Adrina sought to key in on, to hear the words the man spoke. She heard bits and pieces of his words and from those pieces she gathered that the group was splitting up and was to regroup outside the city. She thought of escape.

They began to walk again. The splashing of water led Adrina to conclude that they must be in the sewers. It was the only place where she had ever smelled this repugnant odor. The slow, trudging march through the thick waters lasted for what seemed hours. The stench in this sector was magnified by the dank waters around them. Even the strong-hearted among the mysterious figures that held her hacked and coughed, breathing harshly in the putrid aroma of the deteriorating sludge, the waste that had been spewed from the immense city far above.

Long tunnels stretched from the ceiling above. Some spewed more putrid bilge, which landed in sputters and splashes. Others lay dormant, constructed long ago to filter natural lighting and fresh air into the dank tunnels; however, only meager puffs of fresh air found their way into these depths today. Torchlight guided their way, sometimes reflecting its amber hue in the dark stone walls about them. At certain places along this route, dark shapes slithered in and out of the muck, becoming increasingly frequent as the mysterious figures led her deeper into the heart of the sewers.

The sludge, which had become knee deep, began to recede slowly. Adrina only knew its depth because as she clung fearfully to the figure that carried her, her long flowing hair was no longer dragging through the slime. She relaxed her neck, clinging less to the broad-backed figure. The splashing subsided as they reached a dry section of the tunnel. Adrina sighed as they stopped and she was again brought upright. Thinking this was her chance to flee, she tried to run, but only made it a few steps before heavy hands found her.

Tears were in her eyes, her hair still dripped. She felt it though she did not see it. Shivers traveled down her back as she felt things moving through her hair. She let loose a wailing scream that seemed to vibrate in the tunnels until a heavy, cuffed hand gripped her mouth and cut the scream short.

A strong, deep voice told her, "I shall release your bonds. Do not scream, and do not try to escape. We do not wish to harm you."

Adrina started to scream in response but bit her tongue instead. She desperately wanted the bonds to be removed from her wrists. Her arms were numb and her hands sore. The bonds were released from her hands and feet, but the blindfold was returned to her eyes. She was told not to remove it or the restraints would be returned.

She wondered what was happening. She relaxed her sore muscles and rubbed her bruised wrists, snapping her hands immediately afterwards to her hair. Hands grabbed her by the forearms as she did this, pulling her somewhat harshly. Her immediate reaction was to pull away as her arms were being bent back, but the hand was soft although strong, and Adrina wasn't afraid.

"Oh, does this hurt?" said another, touching Adrina's rope-burned wrists. Adrina had barely perceived the pain in her wrists while she was struggling, but now she felt it severely.

A tingling sensation ran through her hands and fingers; suddenly the pain dissipated and then was gone.

"There, now," whispered the soft voice. "See, we are friends."

Adrina thought she recognized the voice. It was a voice from the past, but it could not be the voice of the one she was thinking of.

"I will remove your blindfold only if you promise that you will not try to run. There is nowhere to flee down here and you will only hurt yourself if you flee. And we do not mean to harm you," spoke the strong voice.

Fingers returned to her messy, wet hair. "Here let me smooth this out for you," said the soft voice.

The blindfold was again removed. The torches had been extinguished and only the dull filtered light, eerie and off-yellow, came into the odd circular chamber. The light hurt her eyes and it took quite some time for them to adjust to it. When they did, she was startled beyond compare.

4

Chancellor Yi looked with agony into the flames, absently stroking the long line of his mount's mane from the head down to the withers to settle it as much as himself. His eyes shifted slightly to the right to Lord Serant and he hung his head in shame. He had been so stupid. He should have been more vigilant and seen what was coming; then he could have prevented the barbaric scene he had witnessed only moments ago, a scene he knew took place beyond his obscured view.

The sound of a multitude of horses thundering into the square drowned out all other sounds. Screams erupted from the black-hearted warriors. The clash of steel and the crunch of bone and armor beneath hooves were heard once more. The city garrison, in full force, had finally arrived. Chancellor Yi raised his head slightly higher. He had hope again.

Though engulfed horrifically in the orange-red flames, a dark warrior came bursting into their circle. Despite the fire surrounding him, he continued his forward lunge; his sword lashed out over and over, wildly, without direction. Lord Serant swiftly threw a dagger into him, which landed in the man's chest with a hefty thud. Disappearing within the flames, the man collapsed to the ground and died, shuddering from one last spasm before he went. The putrid scent of burning flesh spread quickly and soon permeated the air about those waiting for a chance at freedom or maybe even death.

In desperation the dark warriors were attempting anything to attain their goal. Their escape route was cut off, so now only death remained. They were not afraid to die. They were dying for a cause, their cause. They were the chosen; they must breach the flames. Using the dead and the dying as shields, they attempted to break through the flames with the capacity to fight. Several made it through, only to be hacked down immediately by Lord Serant's determined blade. Not discouraged by failure, in surges they poured into the flames, still bearing the dead and the wounded before them.

Chancellor Yi spurred his horse forward into one such group as they broke through. He knocked two of them back into the flames, and the remainder fell to the ground. Lord Serant cut down upon those remaining as they stood. His sword was lightning, deadly quick and accurate.

Outside the wall, the dark warriors were making another offensive. They clustered around their leader as the dark lord issued his commands, ordering them to continue their assault through the flames; and in the name of their lord, the dark warriors strove to do so. They would breach the flames and kill those inside at all cost, even their lives. They surged towards the wall.

Palace and city garrison soldiers alike poured into the square in unbroken lines of bowmen, pikemen, swordsmen and horsemen. The bowmen quickly pinpointed the locations of the enemy bowmen and returned their volleys with equal fervor, soon outnumbering them. Mounted soldiers followed by pikemen swept through the enemy ranks, forcing their retreat. The swordsmen had the role of clean-up, easily dispatching the wounded and the fallen.

The spirit of the Great-Father and Mother-Earth weakened as their hosts' willpower and stamina drained. Father Francis and Sister Midorishi could maintain the wall no longer; their will was spent. The flames sputtered then slowly dissipated. Soldiers of the kingdom now outnumbered the ranks of the attackers. The tide was being turned and soon the last of the dark warriors would be eradicated.

With the fall of the wall, a flicker of hope swept over the dark masses. The dark lord entreated them, and in a last desperate attempt, they plunged toward the central group. The kingdom soldiers watched in horror; they had not expected the mystical wall of flames to fall away. They could not reach the others soon enough. The dark warriors were only a few feet from their goal.

Lord Serant spurred his mount forward and struck down with full force into the first group. His blow cleanly took off the head of his victim. As he followed through with his swing, he hit a second man in the ribs and penetrated his chest. Both men fell, one dead immediately, the other waiting to die. Lord Serant and the dark lord locked eyes for an instant. Each saw the power in the other's eyes. He led his charge directly toward the opposing lord, nullifying the presence of the enemy around him with his blade as he reached toward his goal. Four more fell in his wake.

Sister Catrin unsheathed her ceremonial dagger. She looked to Midori and Jasmine, who clearly could not defend themselves. She quickly scanned the field. Only a few of the dark warriors remained as a threat, but aid would not come soon enough. The garrison soldiers needed to push through the few remaining ranks in order to reach them. She waited calmly for their approach, controlling her breathing, and then lunged at her would-be assailants.

Lord Serant swung and met cold, hard steel. Still mounted, he kicked out first left and then right to knock back the dark warriors that attempted to strike from the side. His antagonist quickly thrust again with an extremely adept maneuver that took Lord Serant's mount full in the side. His horse crumpled to the ground. Lord Serant half jumped and half fell from the horse. He rolled and instantly poised his sword for a block.

Sister Catrin's dagger found its mark deep in the heart of the first warrior. In answer, the second rammed his blade deep into her chest. A pained expression of combined horror and disbelief overtook her normally calm features. She turned and looked into the attacker's eyes. A teardrop trailed down her cheek as the strength of her life waned with every droplet of her blood that spilled upon the dirt. With her dagger yet poised, she fell upon him; in a moment neither moved.

The dark lord lunged full upon Lord Serant. Their two weapons locked together, each testing the strength of the other. Lord Serant pushed upward with all his might. The dark lord fell back, giving Serant time to recover his stance. He parried right and then blocked left, hacking forward. The two locked blades again.

The mounted guard pressed forward and quickly put an end to the lives of the last few resisters who had clung around their lord and had sought to deliver a deathblow to Lord Serant. The clean-up task was left to the swordsmen again. It was their duty to insure that all enemy were dead. As they picked their way through the bodies, they were sure no one was left alive.

"Who are you?" yelled Lord Serant through gritted teeth.

"I am Lord Konstantin of the Bandit Kingdoms. I spit on your dead!"

"You do not deserve to die with honor!"

Silence began to fill the square. Now only one dark warrior, the dark lord, himself, persisted. The soldiers watched this final duel, unsure if they should aid Lord Serant. Switching his weapon briefly into one hand, Lord Serant waved them back with his free fist as they approached. Instead of interfering, a group of kingdom soldiers circled the two, so the dark lord had nowhere to flee. They patiently awaited Lord Serant's signal that they should aid him, resolved to wait and watch until that time.

Lord Serant skillfully waved his blade. He struck repeatedly, but always he met the other's defense. A heavy mask of perspiration covered his face and dripped from forehead to chin. Fatigue set in, but determination drove him on. He would force the other to yield first. The dark lord sought to draw a second blade, a dagger, from his calf-high riding boot and throw it at Lord Serant, but Serant was quick to move and it missed him. The dagger struck one of the soldiers who watched. His eyes were wide and staring as he fell, his hands clutching the blade embedded in his chest.

Now Serant was enraged; he went wild with his sword, smashing down upon his enemy, driving him to his knees. Lord Serant cleft the blade from the dark lord's hand in one clean blow. His face flushed with anger, he held his blade at the other's throat.

Lord Serant held the blade pressed to the man's throat for several seconds contemplating killing him outright. He concluded that perhaps they could bleed the dark lord of information before they sentenced him to death, and upon Lord Serant's signal the kingdom soldiers swarmed.

Retrieving a tiny, finger-sized blade from a hidden spot in the small of his back, Lord Konstantin sought to kill himself but was denied the privilege. It took six men to hold him still while they bound his wrists and ankles, and he cursed vehemently until he was gagged.

"I am only the first! I am only the first!" he cried. "There are others! There are others! You will die! You will all die!"

Lord Serant looked to his beloved Calyin. She was safe, and he was content. His other companions were also safe; the danger was past. The priests of the city temple arrived, and he could see them tending to the wounded around the square. He walked over to his Calyin and knelt beside her in prayer. Calyin reached out her hand to him and he rose to his feet; together they went to check on the others.

All the Great Kingdom would doubly feel this time of mourning. Not only had the citizens lost their king, but also many a brave soldier and many innocent men, women and children. The heart of the kingdom had been invaded; honor and faith must be restored. As the setting of the sun was to begin a time of mourning, so would the rising of tomorrow's sun begin a time of retribution. The cry for retaliation would be heard and answered by all. The kingdom would stand without heir, but it would not fall.

The thunder of many hooves despoiled the silence. Lord Konstantin lit a smile to his lips. His eyes filled with glee; he knew who came. The palace guards were quick to their mounts and stood ready. Bowmen took up positions aiming for the many entrances to the square, waiting. Swordsmen mustered behind the shieldbearers and pikemen regained their line-defensive formations, standing at the ready, marching forward under their captain's orders. Lord Serant drew his sword from its scabbard sadly and waited for the next offensive.

5

Once Princess Adrina's eyes adjusted to the dull light, she was able to see the faces of her mysterious captors who claimed they were friends and not enemies, yet she had heard with her own ears their struggle with the guardsmen who sought to rescue her. A giant of a man stared into her eyes and gentle fingers still worked through the snarls in her hair. The voice she heard from behind her was soft and kind and the one before, though deep and strong, was warm and charming.

"Do not let my size frighten you," he said.

"Only the two of you?" asked Adrina, thinking of escape.

The giant's eyes went wild with sudden fury. He raised a silencing hand to his lips, then it seemed as if he were listening to sounds that only he could hear. Adrina held silent as indicated. In the moments that followed, she considered running, thinking naively that she could easily outpace the two tired travelers. She didn't act on that notion, though; she waited, somehow interested, drawn in by the behemoth before her. The large man indicated that it was all right to speak freely and Adrina sighed. She didn't know what had brought on his sudden concern, but whatever it had been, she had seen that he seemed more concerned with her safety than anything else.

"Why?" she bluntly asked.

She looked around the room, which was small and rounded. The two were alone now; the other had seemingly slipped silently away into the shadows.

"Where did she go?"

"She will return momentarily," replied the large man.

"Why me? Why did you kidnap me?" repeated Adrina.

"We did what we had to do."

"Why? How many had to die because of that?" accused Adrina.

When he did not answer, she became angry and said again harshly, "How many?"

She angrily approached him and began to hit him, releasing all her pent up frustration upon him. Her hands slapped him again and again. He did not flinch, nor did he stop her. Tears were flowing down her cheeks when her fists came to rest against his abdomen.

He looked down upon her, not knowing what to do or say.

"It— was— not—" he stopped, unable to finish.

He took her in his arms and held her. Another's soft hand unexpectedly wiped away her tears as the large man embraced her. The fear faded away. She heard a voice say, "There was nothing we could do to help them. It was their fate. Your fate is with us. We were only trying to save you."

"Why me? There were so many others," sobbed Adrina.

"We did what we could. If we had delayed to save others, we too would have—" the other paused, and did not finish the sentence.

There was evident pain in that other voice, the soft feminine voice. It echoed in her mind. She was sure she knew the voice from somewhere. Her thoughts skipped, but it could not be. Her mind wandered back to another time. A face of a distant memory became alive inside her thoughts. She turned and faced the other. As she looked into the other's eyes, memories flooded into her mind.

"It cannot be," she said as she fainted.

She awoke a short time later with the same face staring into her eyes. She started to say the name that flowed through her mind, but a gentle finger touched her lips and stopped her. The other shook her head, indicating yes.

Adrina did not understand.

"How?" she started to say; again the other stopped her.

"This is Amir," quickly said the other, pointing to the giant. "I am the one without name. I am without past." And to herself she added, "Everything comes full circle at the end."

Adrina registered the coldness with which the words were said. She wondered what had happened to make the other so bitter. She didn't understand how the other was here, but she accepted it. The other was here and alive; the Great-Father and Mother worked in mysterious ways.

"We must go now and meet the others. We have little time left," Amir said, looking about anxiously.

"I just want to know why?" cried out Adrina. "Why me and not anyone else? Are they all dead?"

"You are the last," said Amir, avoiding the rest of Adrina's questions.

"The last?"

"The last of the children. We have come to take you home."

Adrina started to say something else and was silenced again.

"Quickly now," urged Amir, "we have no more time. Say no more but know that our intentions are earnest and that we did not initiate the attack in the square. We rescued you from those that would do you harm, so follow quickly now; time is short, and say nothing until I say it is safe. Do you understand?"

Adrina nodded her head.

"How many were back there?" Amir directed this at the Little One.

"Only two persist. They guess nothing more; they do not know we are here for sure."

Amir glared angrily down one of the dark tunnels, wishing that he had ended the lives he had earlier spared. He looked to Adrina and then to the other, shrugging his shoulders; lifting a short blade from his belt, he darted into the dark tunnel, his form quickly swallowed by the gray of the tunnel, only his shadow remained visible for a time before all trace of him was completely absorbed. Five minutes passed with no audible sounds reaching the two waiting, not even the muffled echoes of the giant's footsteps; then in an instant they heard a stifled shriek followed by the faint echo of sloshing water. Several minutes later, a shape came from out of the darkness.

The Little One jumped in front of Adrina, arms spread wide. Catching each breath, they waited. Amir would not move so heavily in the water. The shape loomed closer, its shadowed form not appearing to be that of a humanoid but that of a beast. Blades were not tools the Little One thought fondly of, but she had been stripped of what she once was. Only her healing powers were intact; she had no other resource at her disposal, and it was with deep remorse that she lifted from her boot the tiny blade that Amir had given her, her last line of defense.

The silhouette of the approaching creature showed that it had many legs and arms, its twisted form was enormous, seeming to fill the whole of the tunnel. Adrina was pushed farther away and the Little One crept forward, waiting to lunge on the approaching beast. Still, the two stared into the shadowy darkness, the sound of splashing water increasing. The Little One signaled for Adrina to crouch low and wait; her small blade shone dully in the pale yellow light of the sewer chamber. She lifted the blade. Just as she was about to spring, she paused. Squinting, she focused her eyes, searching out the strange form.

"Amir?" she hissed.

There was a splash and then a thud. A large figure lunged out of the darkness. The Little One lashed out. The figure dodged the well-timed blow and grabbed the small arm and held it firm.

"What are you doing?" whispered Amir.

"I thought you were—I am sorry—I misjudged."

Amir grinned.

"You are surprisingly strong," he stated, seeming pleased by the assessment.

Amir returned for the two bodies he had carried through the tunnels, one slung over each shoulder, dropping them again onto the floor of the small chamber. Adrina cringed and looked away, but even as she flinched and closed her eyes, the dead eyes imprinted themselves upon her subconscious. Grated drainage shafts lay chest high on each of the four walls; Amir selected one and removed its grating. He grabbed one of the corpses, latching onto a thick tuft of hair and a large leather belt, and stuffed the darkly clad man into the shaft. Similarly, he rammed the second man into the shaft, fixing the grating into place afterwards.

Adrina had seen that the two were obviously not kingdom soldiers, for which she was relieved; still she was horrified for a moment, her mouth wide in a long incredulous gasp. Amir said nothing, nor did he show any indication of remorse. He had simply done what had to be done, nothing more. No words were spoken, only simple hand gestures that indicated that she should follow and the other should trail.

Silently, Adrina followed the giant Amir from the sewers under Imtal, still not understanding the trust she was developing for the mysterious giant. The sewer muck was quickly around her ankles as they entered the first tunnel, traversing its length before coming to another larger tunnel, one that was filled with even more sewage. The stench became overwhelming once more, yet just as she thought she could go on no more, they came to another open dry area. Here the trio stopped.

"These tunnels before us will lead us out of the sewers," stated Amir in a light tone, "there is fresh air ahead and plenty of it, so you must only hold out for a short while yet. The tunnels will grow drier as we work our way slowly towards the catacombs. Once there, stay close. Do not lag behind and stand ready. Again, we move in silence; there is danger ahead. Watch for my hand signals and all will be fine."

"How do I know that you speak the truth and you are not leading me to my enemies?" objected Adrina, throwing out words to register the large man's reaction.

"I speak only in full truths," replied Amir, "It is obvious to me that you have found trust in me and my companion. Be safe in the knowledge that we lead you away from danger and not towards it. One called Noman will explain all. We must hurry now. There is little time left."

They forged ahead through the maze of underground tunnels. Adrina had no idea where she was, but apparently Amir did. He led them, turning at junctures in the path without a moment's hesitation. The tunnels grew steadily drier as Amir said they would. The stench also receded with the dank waters. The trio kept silent, solely relying on Amir's hand signals to speak where words would otherwise have been needed.

Fixing her eyes on his great back, Adrina was very attentive to his movements. She followed where he led, stopped when he stopped, veered left or right as he signaled. For a time, once they reached dry tunnels, it seemed as if they were descending into the earth and then the downward slopes gradually leveled out.

Though it was not on the tunnel floors, a dampness returned. It was held in the air around the three, which suddenly grew cool. The lines of perspiration streaming down her back and face collected the cool air and Adrina began to shiver. She clutched her arms to her chest to stave off the cold, blowing warm air into her hands. The floor that had been hard, firm rock became earthen and the tunnel floor began to pitch upward. Soon the damp chill was left behind, replaced by dry stale air.

After many hours of traversing the dark tunnels, Amir called a full halt. They had come to a large chamber that was semi-lit from above. Water could be heard dripping from the ceiling into a basin on the tunnel floor.

"What is that? That stuff is worse than the stench of the sewers," groaned Adrina.

Amir lifted Adrina to her feet.

"Come quickly; the others wait ahead."

Adrina stood unsteadily for a moment and then as the dizziness passed, she nodded her head, gesturing that she was ready to proceed.

6

Hundreds of darkly clad warriors pushed their way into the square. They bore the brunt of the waves of arrows pouring down upon them from the garrison bowmen. Behind them came horsemen clad in heavy mail; even the beasts of this evil guard were armored. The mounted horsemen pushed the footmen forward, and slowly they made progress.

The garrison bowmen were forced to be more selective in their volleys as the palace mounted guard charged the enemy ranks and intermixed with them. In gallant groups of ten they charged the approaching footmen. On horseback they had considerably more maneuverability than their foes, yet the enemy quickly learned how to sever rider from horse. Instead of striking at the man on the horse as they charged, they attacked the horse. As the horse fell, the rider was easily dealt a deadly blow. Few riders were able to recover as their mounts crumpled beneath them. Many were pinned beneath their horses and could only lie struggling to get free as their foes claimed their lives.

The enemy horsemen seemed to be lagging purposefully behind, waiting until the footmen had taken the brunt of the defensive. Lord Serant ushered Calyin and the others into a protective circle within the folds of the shieldbearers. He would not leave Calyin's side any more.

He waited and watched. The numbers on each side were quickly balancing out. Enemy bowmen were taking up positions and returning the volleys of the garrison bowmen. Serant ordered the garrison bowmen to make a strategic retreat; he needed to save their ability to strike into the enemy's heart for later.

Pikemen with their long shafted blades followed in the wake of their mounted comrades. Easily they drove the enemy back for a time. The dark warriors' swords were no match against the great length of the pike. The long blades pierced the enemies' hearts before they could get close enough to strike. The advantage was clearly on the side of good, at least momentarily.

A thick rain of arrows fell in surges against the pikemen, falling on both friend and foe; those who attacked did not care as long as their enemies died. Lord Serant could see the enemy commanders ordering the bowmen to shoot; and in spiteful retaliation, he ground the heel of his boot into the enemy lord's back near the base of the skull. He understood why they attacked thus. It was a desperate foe who didn't care if he killed his own as long as he was the victor in the end.

"How many more come?" demanded Lord Serant of Lord Konstantin, grabbing the man by the scruff of the hair, his boot still in place.

The vile lord's only response was to work a ball of spittle up in his mouth and launch it at Lord Serant. The westerner did not flinch as the spittle struck his right cheek and dripped downward. Calmly, he cuffed Lord Konstantin with a heavy hand.

"Chancellor, here is your chance to redeem yourself," said Lord Serant, with evident animosity. He knew the chancellor was wounded, but he needed someone who could follow detailed orders well. He saw a blind spot in the enemy ranks and he intended to take advantage of it.

"They need someone to follow; can you lead them?"

"Yes."

"Good!" said Lord Serant, smiling.

He hurriedly explained his elaborate plan to infiltrate the enemies' rear flank and then issued a group of swordsmen to accompany the chancellor. Lord Serant ordered the bowmen to lay a screen of arrows into the heart of the enemy. Afterward, he mustered all but a handful of his remaining soldiers. They awaited his signal to charge into the enemy ranks. His words were inspiring; they were welcome to the soldiers' ears. This was a man of power for whom they would willingly die. The end was close at hand.

On his command, those not already engaged in combat streamed forth. Their goal was the enemies' mounted guard, and they cut a direct line for it through what remained of the enemy footmen's ranks. The charge was timed with the chancellor's sneak attack to the rear, the line where the enemy officers gathered. The twang of bowstrings and the crashing of steel rose from a clamor to pandemonium once more.

The kingdom soldiers' charge was short lived as the enemies' mounted horde swept forth. The black beasts whinnied and reared up as they raced forth, trampling the first brave few who reached their ranks. The shield ring was brought closer as the enemy leaders directed fire against Lord Serant's position. Even behind the wall of tower shields, arrows found their marks, picking off those that shielded their lord and the other dignitaries with their own bodies.

Lord Serant ordered his holdouts to charge, followed by his bowmen who were to shoot on the run. For a brief time, it seemed as if they had the enemy surrounded and were closing in, but the superior horsemen had been holding back again and they crashed forth with a vengeance. The last of the pikemen fell; the swordsmen continued their charge, followed by a mixed contingent of bowmen and bladesmen.

The hope that had lasted briefly ended with the fall of the chancellor's group. Their strike had apparently been ineffective. A new battle cry rang out across the square; a new banner was raised in the field. More mounted warriors streamed into the square from the western sector.

Their presence sent terror into the hearts of those that saw them; the kingdom soldiers, though discouraged, continued their assault. The end was near, very near. Lord Serant vowed he would fight until his last breath. He ordered the shield bearers to move out and all who could still wield a weapon, even his precious Calyin, followed.

Lord Serant spat on the dark warrior lord who was bound helpless beneath his scornful heel. His eyes filled with glee as he saw horror and disappointment on Lord Serant's face. He held no regrets for this day. He had served his master well. Lifting his great sword from its sheath, Lord Serant left Lord Konstantin where he lay face down in a puddle of blood. He would not offer the dark lord the dignity of a swift death, hoping instead that his fellows thought him lost in the chaos of the field, knowing that in time the man would bleed to death, but that death would come slowly and with much pain.

Horsemen filed into the square from the west and the north now, wreaking havoc as they came. The sheer numbers were unfathomable to his mind; how could the enemy have such a vast reserve? How had so many been able to infiltrate this far into the Great Kingdom unseen? He was appalled. As he ran, he handed Calyin a dagger from his belt, his last; the look in his eyes spoke volumes, a lifetime's worth of dreams that would never come true, also of love, deep, lasting love. Calyin smiled and took the dagger. She was also ready to die.

"Look!" yelled Calyin, her voice wild and captivating, "Look!"

Lord Serant raised his eyes and cocked his head; surprise swept over him. He saw, yet he did not believe. A change had taken place; the banner once raised was gone. Another one stood proudly in its place, one that he clearly recognized. The dark warriors also realized the trick, but it was too late. Their horsemen were cut down as they watched.

The only defense left to them was to flee, but opposing horsemen were already upon them, coming in from all sides now. All possibility of escape was cut off. Mounted soldiers continued to pour into the square. The will of the enemy to fight was sucked from them in one swift move. They huddled around their leaders, who issued orders the soldiers no longer followed.

Thousands clustered around the hundreds that frantically sought to escape. Sorrowful whinnies of dying beasts rose above the cries of the desperate men. More banners were raised on the field as the fleet horsemen surged into the square. Moonrise had come long ago, full and ominous, though the combatants had not noticed its arrival and beneath this full yellow globe and an unmarred starlit sky, the battle came to an end.

A small group of riders circled back to those who had stopped their charge dead still and looked on in awe. Two flag bearers rode to left and right of this small group, carrying the spectacular gold and silver banner of freedom whose symbols were oddly enough the scimitar, the eclipsed moon and the free man's crest.

"Greetings, on this deceitful night," yelled a rider who approached, "I am Lord Geoffrey of—"

"—Solntse. But how did you know?" interrupted Lord Serant.

"I had a strange visitor a number of day's ago. He told me the waxing gibbous moon brought ill tidings and to rouse our garrison and set wings to our feet. 'Reach Imtal before the full moon wanes,' he beckoned, and thankfully I heeded his words."

"You don't know how indebted to you I am, good sir. I thank you and all the free men who have come to our aid!" yelled Lord Serant.

For a moment the two men looked silently about the square. Many expressions crossed their faces as the soldiers of Solntse and those few of the Imtal palace and garrison that lived scoured the square in search of survivors, both friend and foe alike. The scene was one of death and destruction. The dark warriors had left their mark deep on the kingdom. The blood of many had flowed through the central square. Many brave soldiers had lost their lives. Those who had insisted that the strife would never reach them were quite mistaken.

In the days to come they would scour the countryside in search of those responsible for collaborating with the enemy. The guilty would be found and dutifully punished, and then they would turn their anger outward upon the leaders of the insurgency. Lord Serant had little doubt that this search would lead them south, but first reparations must be made. Imtal garrison must be rebuilt, a new palace guard would have to be selected, and the heir to the throne must return.

Watching the proceedings from the glowing orb in his hand, Xith was pleased. The company he had sought to build was together and Great Kingdom had once again survived the test of the darkness. Yet Xith knew all too well that notions of good and evil were too simple an interpretation for what was taking place. The cosmos didn't understand the concepts of good and evil—to the cosmos there was only the cycle of renewal. When one age ended, another began. That is the way of it and it did not matter whether that age was good or evil in someone's eyes for there was always another interpretation, always another point of view.

Satisfied, Xith focused his thoughts on the warrior elf and the kingdom prince and their faces appeared in the glowing orb. He blew onto the orb, casting wind to the sails of their ships and taking them easily past the dark storm that approached. He wondered then what would happen to them when they discovered that everything they thought they knew was a lie and that only in the lies would they find the truth. This saddened him and this sadness turned his thoughts to Vilmos, the boy the company was built to protect. The boy who would become the one against which the forces of darkness and light would align and then single-mindedly seek to destroy.

7

“Jasmine, please don’t leave us,” cried Sister Midori-shi. She looked to Sister Catrin-ni, who knelt on the other side of Jasmine. The two stared deep into Jasmine’s eyes. They could see that her spirit yearned to be gathered by the Great-Father.

For a moment they both looked around the square. The scene was one of death and destruction. The assassins had left their mark deep on the kingdom. The blood of many had flowed through the central square. Many brave soldiers had lost their lives this eve.

All would remember this day. Those who had insisted that the war would never reach them were quite mistaken. The distant war in the Eastern Reaches had been brought to them. The kingdom had been plunged into the midst of a war they were unprepared to fight.

The peace that had existed for centuries was completely gone. Their king had been assassinated. A princess of the kingdom had been kidnapped. But worst of all, an army of assassins had invaded their homeland. They had infiltrated all the way into the vary heart of the kingdom, the capital city of Imtal.

Father Francis returned after checking on the others of the royal party. The guards were clearing the wounded and the dead from the field. A strange thought was clawing at the back of his mind. An emotion before unknown to him permeated his other thoughts. He tried to meditate them from his mind, but they remained.

He looked to the dark-haired woman across the square and for the first time the impact of her beauty fell upon him. He that was of the Great-Father and her that had given herself to the Mother-Earth. The thoughts in his mind would not be denied acknowledgment. They demanded to be allowed existence. He could suppress them no more. He had shared the union of the Mother and Father with this one. The natural love of the two for each other and for all things was inside him.

He wondered if she, too, felt the pull of emotions upon her. He wished to go to her, but he could not. He had acknowledged his feelings for her, yet they could not be allowed. He decided he would return to the palace with Lord Serant and Princess Calyin, and leave the past behind him.

Lord Serant defiantly looked around the square. He still clutched the hilt of his sword tightly. His beloved Calyin stood at his side. She reached out and took his free hand in hers. She tightly clasped it. Finally, he sheathed his weapon and the two embraced.

Tears flowed down Calyin's cheeks. Lord Serant gazed into her eyes and wiped her tears away. "I will forever protect you, my love," he whispered into her ear.

His eyes saw the body of Chancellor Yi, which lay behind Calyin. Lord Serant had found the chancellor to be most foolish. Nothing like this carnage could have happened in the Western Territories. The lands might be barbaric, but he was safe there. No one could have so easily entered his capital and attempted to slay him.

Slowly the square emptied of all save three who refused to leave. Captain Brodst continued to attempt to persuade them to leave though they would not listen. He understood why they would not leave. He knew the beliefs of the priestesses of the Mother.

If it were Jasmine's time to pass, she would. Nothing they could do would save her. Now, he stood patiently watching them. He ordered more patrols to search the city street by street. The gates of the city were sealed, so Princess Adrina must still be inside the city, and if they searched long enough, they would have to find her.

Midori and Catrin joined hands with Jasmine; one last time the three would become one. The two could feel the yearning of Jasmine's spirit. They knew the Mother called her to join with her. At the last all were gathered home by the Father save the priestesses of the Mother. They alone were given the privilege; their devotion had allowed them to join with the Mother.

The connection was complete. They could feel the Father watch them from above. They sensed a smile on his lips. A blazing light filled the center of their thoughts. They knew this was the presence of the Mother, strong within them.

Captain Brodst watched the scene. He was greatly intrigued by it. He did not know whether he should continue to watch or not. He knew very well the secrecy of the priestesses. He knew no male had ever witnessed what was now taking place before him.

This was more than the passing of the first of the Mother; it was also a ritual of choosing. One of the other two would become the first, and the other would become the second. As he watched, joy filled his mind such as he had never known but the joy soon became so overpowering that it overwhelmed him. He could watch no more; he could not walk away either. He was held transfixed and looked out at the world around him as if from afar.

In silence the three priestesses were connected. The image of the Mother grew clearer in their minds. Slowly a face defined itself. This was the face of the Mother; it spoke of power and beauty, but more than that a feeling of all encompassing love flowed from that image.

Energy surged rapidly through them. A white light emanated from them and swirled rapidly around them. Jasmine's body began to shimmer and then faded out of existence. All of her thoughts became joined with Catrin's and Midori's. Her thoughts became their memories, and thus Jasmine's spirit passed to rest with the Mother.

They could see Jasmine make the journey to the Mother's garden. A feeling of immense happiness flowed to them. They could also sense the other priestesses who rested there welcoming Jasmine home.

As the Mother bade them farewell, they begged her to stay and cried out into the night. "Wait," they implored, "Wait!" "Which of us is to be the first?" they asked. But the Mother did not heed their words and soon it was just the two of them, facing each other, hands joined. Not far off stood the transfixed captain. He could no more look away than a fly could escape a spider's web.

An old memory came to Catrin and Midori, and with it realization of what they must do and how the ceremony of choosing must begin. They set their minds to the struggle of will quickly losing track of time and space. Now, they existed solely in a whirlwind of thought and will. Both stretched out from their center with every ounce of their being to gather the flow to them, but both encountered vast difficulties.

Indefinite thoughts spun into their consciousness. Some were pieces of past experiences, some of the present, and all were intertwined with the future. The normal order of passage said Sister Catrin should become the first, as she was now the second, but the final test of servitude was still to be passed. The victor would become as one with the Mother.

Slowly the thoughts began to define. They became single thoughts, forming a multitude of future paths, turning points in the future. The two were forced to make decisions. They must choose the correct path to follow from the many. The choosing went on and on until it seemed it would never end.

Midori screamed in agony, collapsed. Captain Brodst was startled and looked to where Midori was sprawled, motionless on the ground. He tried to run to her aid, but could not. He could only watch in horror.

He could see the pain clearly etched on her face. His heart pounded rapidly as he was drawn to watch. He could not take his eyes off her face. He felt complete sympathy for her, utter empathy if that were possible. In that moment he longed for the Delinna Alder he had once known and in that moment he envied no man more than Father Francis. For Father Francis had shared with her a closeness which was denied to him, a oneness which he would never know again. His heart felt the wound of old as raw as it ever was.

As he watched, the image of Catrin appeared near Midori. Catrin quickly knelt beside her friend. Tears began to trickle down her cheeks. "I have failed you," she whispered. The low sound seemed to cut into the silence and echoed throughout the square.

The image faded again. Now, the two sat across from each other, hands joined once more. Without a sound, they rose and walked towards the captain. The three then departed the square, each thinking different thoughts as they did so. Captain Brodst was eager to return to the palace to interrogate the enemy leader, Lord Konstantin. Other thoughts tempted his mind. They flowed through and permeated his conscious. He would willingly greet this war as a chance to prove his military prowess and the strength of the kingdom, yet at the same time he regretted its coming to the fore, the countless unnecessary deaths of the innocent caught in the struggle for power.

Sister Catrin thought about the trial. It had torn her mind asunder and shattered her ego. She had taken the wrong path. She had chosen herself over the welfare of her companion. She had failed the test.

Midori looked back with retrospect on her life. She understood how she had become first priestess although her conscience could not accept it. She still saw the impetuous child within her. "Why me? I am not worthy—what of the second, or of the third?" she whispered quietly to herself. "Accept the gift my child. The choice was correctly made," said a voice echoing in her mind. Midori clearly recognized the voice; it was a voice from her childhood. "Mother!" cried Midori. "Good-bye, my child—" said the voice as it faded.

A city patrol intercepted the trio on the way to the palace and escorted them the remainder of the trek. Captain Brodst gave the guardsmen a black stare, but accepted their escort. The palace was bustling with activity when they returned. Captain Brodst was wondering if the entire city garrison were inside the palace when Lord Serant approached him.

"Captain Brodst, it is good you are all safe. Come, Princess Calyin and Father Francis await your arrival in the council room."

The two began to speed toward the council chambers with Midori and Catrin closely following. They found Princess Calyin, Father Francis, Chancellor Volnej and Keeper Q'yer seated and waiting for them. Princess Calyin sat at the head of the table, with a vacant place to her right, and Chancellor Volnej seated himself to her immediate left, in the seat of honor reserved for the first adviser. Father Francis was seated to Volnej's left with Keeper Q'yer directly across from him. Lord Serant took his place to the right of Calyin and the two priestesses took their appropriate places as guests near the opposite end of the table.

Calyin signaled for the guards to seal the door; then the meeting started. Calyin greeted each of those present in an abrupt manner, cutting quickly to the point of their presence here, which was obvious to those present but must be stated for the record. The hall seemed strangely empty compared to the great meetings she remembered from her youth.

Captain Brodst nervously searched the hilt of his sword beneath the table, his eyes never leaving the two seats at the head of the table, those reserved for the king and queen. The second head chair had always been placed away from the table as a remembrance of honor. King Andrew had ruled alone since his queen had died. The captain was not pleased to see it placed back at the table. Princess Calyin with Lord Serant in the king's place now occupied the chair.

"This is an outrage! How dare you?" shouted Captain Brodst as he jumped up and drew his blade. Lord Serant's response was immediate; he likewise drew his sword and launched himself at the captain. Calyin was also quick to her feet and placed herself between them. "Stop!" she yelled with all the strength of her voice. "You both will seat yourselves now!" she commanded, her anger lividly displayed on her fiery red face and glaring ice-cold eyes. The two stood defiantly in the face of her fury, which was quite difficult considering Calyin's persuasive glare, a trait that ran in the family. "Please," she pleaded. "We will get nowhere like this. The safety and unity of the kingdom are at stake here. We cannot fight among ourselves."

"Please!" she begged again.

Lord Serant held his blade firm. He would not be the first to back down. Hesitantly, Captain Brodst seated himself back at the table, and then Lord Serant did the same. Princess Calyin calmly began, "Captain Brodst, please hear me out. Yes, my lord and husband is seated in the king's position and I am properly seated to his left. It is for the good of the kingdom that we assume these positions. The one thing we do *not* need now is division. We need clear unity. I am the next in the royal line and as my husband, Lord Serant *will* rule by my side. When King Andrew died, the Council of Keepers along with the High Council decided this. It is as it must be until Prince Valam's return. *The Kingdom will stand united!*" Calyin spoke those words not only for Captain Brodst's benefit, but also for all those in the room. Lord Serant had been the only one to come to her aid; the others had remained seated, indifferent or unsure, themselves, what was happening.

"We do not need civil war within the kingdom itself! We need to wait and watch until we are sure where the conspiracy leads us. We must try to stop it before it gets out of hand. To do that we must show that order, not chaos rules! Together we have a chance!"

8

"Ne mozhet byt'! Ehto Brat-Seth i Kapitan-Cagan! Kak ehto?"

The words flowed into Seth's mind in the way of the brotherhood. They sounded strangely foreign to him. He had been in the world of men for too long. It took him a moment to re-orient his thoughts; then he understood the meaning of the words.

Subconsciously he thought back to another time and a far distant place. Pictures of the council of the Great Kingdom filled his mind. It was in this room that he had lost his Galan forever. Now, she was just an image in his mind. He had loved her even though it was against the general rules of the brotherhood. But they could never be together; fate had divided them.

The elder one ran to Seth and embraced him. It took a moment for Seth to gather his thoughts. He stared deeply into the eyes of his old friend. "Ehto ty?" said Brother Liyan with his mind.

"Dejstvitel'no v camom dele. Ehto menya, Brat-Liyan," Seth answered aloud in the words of his kind. He then added in the words of men, "Yes, it is truly I, Brother Liyan!"

Brother Liyan didn't understand; why had Seth spoken aloud? Most of the brotherhood spoke with their minds. Only a select few spoke aloud. They were the ones who refused the gifts of the Great-Father. In this way, they sought to increase their suffering in this world. When you spoke aloud it set you apart from everyone; your mind was open and free, revealing the cause of your shame. Liyan dwelled so much on the fact that Seth had spoken aloud he had not even heard Seth's words, words in the tongue of man.

"Pochemy?" he started to ask, but Seth stopped him. He searched Seth's mind for the words, suddenly realizing the thing that had eluded his thoughts. In a moment, he rephrased his question, "What has happened?" yet as he spoke the words, he came to know the answer, and sadness flowed through him. He understood Brother Seth's wrongdoing. He did not feel pity for him or see his shame.

"Pupil, you have much to learn of life and living. Come, I know one who will greatly rejoice at your return. You shall bring light at a time of darkness. And hope will be felt by all!" Brother Liyan directed the words only into Seth's mind.

Brother Liyan paused a moment to regard the remainder of the group. He extended a hand to his old friend Cagan. "It is good to be home at last!" exclaimed Cagan. Brother Liyan was not surprised by the fact that Cagan spoke aloud. The captain had freely chosen to speak thus long ago; now it was a sign of the strength of his will.

Will is in all things. It flows through the land, the plants, and animals. In the very center of your being is your will. The strength of your will defines your place in creation. The stronger your will, the higher place you will occupy when you complete the final journey to the Father.

The others in the group Liyan did not recognize. They were of the world of men. He studied each in turn. They did not appear much different from his kind. They had a sincerity to them that spoke of inner strength.

Valam waited a moment for Seth to introduce them. He could clearly see that Seth was lost in other thoughts and understood the reasons. His natural openness compelled him to introduce himself, though he didn't know if it were proper.

Seth had explained to him the formalities of introduction of his kind. Although he still didn't understand which type he should use for which occasion. "I am Prince Valam of the royal order, first heir to the throne of the Great Kingdom, largest of the kingdoms, holder of the alliance," he said brashly in the tongue of Seth's people.

Brother Liyan held back a smile. Valam had spoken the introduction well. He wondered if men could access the power of their will. It was such a natural thing for him; the thought that they couldn't had never occurred to him before. He shook the idea from his mind and introduced himself. "I am Brother Liyan, wisest of the High Council of the Eastern Reaches, first adviser to the Queen-Mother."

As he spoke, Liyan studied the tall brooding prince with his clear, bright eyes. The prince carried with him an artifact of old though Liyan doubted the other knew the true origins of the blade. But the blade was not the source of the prince's power rather it was an inner strength of character that Liyan could readily sense. The prince was clearly a fair and just man.

Evgej looked worriedly to Valam. He had only recently begun to learn the other tongue. Valam quickly introduced his friend. "This is Captain Evgej, swordmaster first class, city garrison of Quashan', capital city of South Province."

"Welcome to East Reach," Liyan said as he acknowledged the fair-haired captain. Noticing the bow and horn Evgej carried in addition to the great sword slung across his back, Liyan marked the man as a hunter and the steady, unflinching eyes said the captain was a man of strength as well.

Liyan smiled broadly as he turned to study the rest of the prince's men. "A most intriguing company," Liyan whispered into Seth's mind, adding as he turned back to the prince, "Does he know?"

"I have been teaching him the art of will should—"

"—Preparing him, yes," directed Liyan. "You have done well. He has the inner strength required." Liyan looked the prince up and down, repeated, "Does he know?"

"He does not," Seth said aloud.

Desiring to be polite, Valam and Evgej said nothing of what seemed a rather one-sided conversation. Noticing the prince's increasing unease, Cagan was quick to direct him to other issues. "River sails," he said indicating the arrival of the river sloops.

To Cagan there was nothing more beautiful or graceful in the water than a sloop with her mainsail, single mast and jib sail and he couldn't take his eyes off the line of ships gliding easily across the waters of the Gildway. A tear came to his eyes. "Home," he whispered to the wind.

"How far by ship?" asked Valam. He was eager to depart for Leklorall. The group had spent several days of much needed rest recuperating after the long sea journey. The patrol that had discovered them had left them in the capable hands of the village elders of Marudal—the city of Cagan's birth. The patrol had departed that same day to bring word to the High Council of the arrival, and when they returned Brother Liyan was with them.

"This day, a night and a day, no more," said Cagan as he watched the sloops dock to the river piers. "We've to sail north through the Ester and then on to the Clarwater. Leklorall is an island city in the center of the great lake."

"Where are her sailors?" asked Valam looking to the closest sloop.

Cagan grinned knowingly. "A captain and his mate are all that are needed. The ship does most of the sailing on her own. She is grand is she not."

"The symbols on the line of the stern?" asked Valam.

Cagan pointed to each ship in turn and spoke their names. Indicating the ship docked before them, he said, "Maru. She is my favorite. She asks of you."

"The ship speaks?" asked Valam incredulously.

"To me, yes," said Cagan running his hand along the side of the ship. "The Maru is named after Marudall. It was my father who built her and the blood of my line is within her."

Valam started to respond but Evgej clasped a hand to his shoulder and spoke first, "The men await your command. It is time to board the ships and depart, my prince."

Valam turned expectantly to Seth. "My men—"

"—will receive the finest all of East Reach has to offer this night," Seth said. "On the morrow, the march to Riven End begins where the High Elves and your people will join the Gray—all as we've discussed."

"And when the second group arrives?"

"All will be well, my prince," said Captain Mikhal approaching from the line of men standing at the ready behind the prince. "Tsandra of the Brown has been accommodating at every turn. Our needs are met. The men are in goods spirits and well. The journey has only strengthened their resolve and mine. I will see you in Riven End when it is time."

"Riven End then, be well," said Valam.

"And you, my prince."

Captain Mikhal walked back to the line of men and began issuing orders. Cagan departed to make final preparations. Valam and Evgej turned their attention back to Brother Liyan and Seth. Seth for his part did not hide his excitement. He longed to once more see his home and the Queen-Mother. Brother Liyan had not given him any message from her. He wondered if something were wrong, or if Liyan had come to personally insure he was alive and had really returned.

His thoughts skipped back again to the council chamber of the kingdom. He had poured his entire being into maintaining the mind link. He had seen the Father coming to bring him to rest beside him. Galan's pleading cry still echoed through his mind. In the instant the contact was broken he should have passed. Galan though had given herself in his stead and he felt the weight of guilt heavy upon him. Guilt because he lived and breathed and she did not.

As he boarded the Maru, Cagan swept his gaze up and down the river and beyond to Maru Bay. His great love for the water had been tainted by the storm that had brought them here. All his life he had been a sailor. He had never encountered a storm so severe; he could not outrun her. He had fought desperately to keep control over his ship and had lost.

The immense power of the storm was self-evident. He had also felt the will of the Father within it. The Father had guided them to this shore. Both he and Seth had felt it, though he did not comprehend why; he knew Seth had.

Fate rested well with Seth. Twice now, he had survived when he should not have. Slowly he was lost to his thoughts, as they began to sail away. As he often did when troubled, he returned to his early teachings. It was in them he could piece together the things that occurred around him.

"Always remember, pupil, when your mind is troubled and you cannot find your center, return to that which separates you, distinguishes you from everyone else, your thoughts. For they are truly your own—they are you."

Brother Liyan stood on the deck of the Maru alongside Seth. He could see Seth's distant stare and knew Seth's mind was troubled. Physically, Seth had changed only slightly in the time he had been gone, but within, Liyan could sense a vast growth. Liyan gently probed Seth's thoughts. Seth sensed this and invited Liyan into his mind. Seth took Liyan on a tour of the past, and together they relived its many paths.

Time progressed rapidly in swirling images. Liyan saw vividly the Battle of Quashan'. He saw Seth hold the last threads of Galan's life against the will of the Father, a feat that defied their laws. He saw the great council of the kingdom and then felt sadness fall like an anvil upon him. He saw Galan give all that she was for Seth. With a single selfless act, Galan willingly destroyed everything she was. She utterly ceased to exist.

Seth's mind leapt and raced through the times at the palace. His love for Galan was clearly revealed. Liyan understood it. He wanted to tell Seth it was not wrong but could not interrupt the vision.

He then witnessed how Seth met the brash Evgej during the journey to South Province. Seth stopped the vision with the reunion with Cagan and his sorrowful cry to the Father for his forgivencss; it was then that he discovered the fatal error he made. From that night on, Seth vowed never to speak with his mind again.

The group stood in silence, the gentle rocking of the ship soothing their senses. Valam studied the countryside in the fading light of the late afternoon. An area of low grassy hills filled the view from the coast. In the distance to the North he could see only the expanse of the river. All in all, he saw no apparent difference between here and his home.

His mood grew from light to dark when he began to think of the purpose of their journey. They came in answer to a plea by the Queen-Mother of East Reach. The peaceful times of the past would soon be replaced with the ravages of war.

He had never doubted the urgency of the situation; through Seth, he had come to understand what was taking place. Sathar had returned from the dark journey, beginning the ancient prophecy that marked the ending of everything they knew. There were many, though, who did doubt. They opposed the sending of soldiers to these distant shores. The Battle of Quashan' they said was proof that there was greater need in the kingdoms than in the reaches.

"Men often wait until it is too late—you must not wait." Valam remembered those words distinctly. After many long months of planning, they had finally departed. Even many of the soldiers who had volunteered doubted the reality of the distant war. The many weeks aboard the ships, however, had somehow changed their views. They began to realize with certainty the truth of their situation. They could not back out now, and this knowledge cleared their minds. The war existed, if only in their thoughts.

Valam whispered a prayer to the Father. The storm that had swept them into the rocks hopefully had spared the others. Valam was confident that the second group had entirely missed the storm, but the first group that followed their guidance could easily have been lost. Nonetheless, he continued saying his silent prayer for a moment longer.

Seth moved alongside Valam and Evgej. "What do you think about my homeland?" he asked pointedly, striving to break the glum moods of his companions.

"It appears much the same as the lands of the kingdom."

"More like the grassy foothills of South Province I'd say."

"On the morrow, we should reach the Clarwater; there I am sure you will see vast differences."

9

Adrina followed the giant, Amir, and the one she had once known, whom Amir had dubbed as "Little One," as she had told none her name, from the sewers under Imtal. She still could not hold back the tears. She no longer cried for the ones she thought lost in the battle in the central square; now her sorrow was for the one who had told her with such bitterness that she had no name, no past and was nothing. She cried for a friend lost. She cried for Galan.

The two of them had rescued her from the massacre on the square. Only recently Adrina had learned that she was the object of the assassins' quest. They had been sent to kill her, but she did not understand why. Most of the upper officials of the Great Kingdom had been on the square, why her? Amir had assured her that one called Noman would explain everything to her when they joined his group, but for the time being she muddled over that single question and thoughts of a time not long ago, times of happiness inside the palace proper. She longed for Seth and Valam to return to her, and most of all she wanted to see Galan whole once more. She wished she could share Galan's burden.

Still, they wandered through the maze of underground tunnels. Adrina had no idea where she was, but apparently Amir did. He continued to lead them, turning in many directions without a moment's hesitation. After many hours of traversing the damp, poorly lit tunnels, they stopped. Adrina was near exhaustion, perspiration dripped heavily from her forehead. "Good, we have stopped," said Adrina. No one responded.

They had come to a large chamber that was semi-lit from above. Water could be heard dripping from the ceiling into the pool of water on the tunnel floor. Adrina was about to say something else, when a gentle hand touched her lips and she stopped.

Amir stood poised in front of Adrina and the Little One, his right hand lightly fingering the two-handed sword in his sheath. In less than one beat of Adrina's heart, Amir drew his sword. Instantly a bright blue-white light filled the room. Amir's sword rested on the neck of a darkly tanned man clad in black.

The man slowly withdrew the hood from over his head. Amir said smartly as he re-sheathed his sword, "I knew it was you Ayrian. I could smell your presence two tunnels away. But I had to be sure."

Ayrian tried to hold back a laugh, but could not, "It is a wonder you didn't lob my head off."

"Yes, I could have blamed it on the light."

"Or lack thereof, my friend."

Adrina didn't understand the pun. The others, however, had understood it; even Galan almost broke a smile. Amir turned around to introduce Ayrian to Adrina.

"Princess Adrina Alder, I would like to introduce Ayrian, Eagle Lord of the Gray Clan."

"Eagle Lord?"

"Princess," said Ayrian as he reached out and kissed Adrina's hand. Adrina was shocked by Ayrian's appearance. At first she thought he wore a costume of feathers since the light in the chamber was shadowy, but Ayrian assured her the talons and feathers were indeed real.

"Come, the others await your arrival," said Ayrian as he retreated down a tunnel. The tunnel came to a dead end at a blank wall of stone. Ayrian took the hilt of his sword and rapped heavily on the wall. A moment later the sound seemed to echo and Ayrian disappeared through the wall. The others soon followed with a bewildered Adrina being led by Amir.

A short, withered-looking man who Adrina recognized immediately as Xith stood on the other side of the wall. His face was clenched in strain. His outstretched hands were engaged in a frenzy of movement. He moaned a sigh of relief when the last of the group stood in the chamber. Standing beside the anguished man stood a younger man, as amazed at the feat as Adrina had been.

Adrina realized that Xith was performing magic, which was expressly forbidden. All magic was evil. Another stepped from the shadows and approached Adrina. "No! You are quite wrong there, princess. It is neither wrong, nor evil, for without its existence all would be lost."

"How did you—but the teachings—! That is why darkness has entered the kingdom!"

"I am Noman," said the gray-looking gentleman. "We have waited a long time for you and the others." His voice was weak on the last words. In his mind he thought, "Now there are three, and seven."

"Do not fear us," said Xith. Adrina looked to the squat man outfitted in brown robes. "We could not allow the others to take you. We need you. Together with the others, you are the key, the next generation of hope and light in a world succumbing to darkness."

Adrina was again shocked; she had not heard the last part of Xith's statement, only the talk of hope and light.

"There is no light in darkness," disagreed Adrina.

The one whom Adrina had known by another name took her hand and nodded her head indicating yes.

"There is always light," she whispered.

"Do not worry about that," Noman said, subjecting Adrina to the soothing guiles of the voice. "Come here, my child, you are safe now. No harm will befall you in our care."

Noman reached out and took her other hand.

"Once it is safe, we will take you home; until that time you will remain in our care. Come, there are others you should meet. Xith, Amir, Ayrian—" called out Noman.

"But the darkness," protested Adrina.

"The darkness came of its own accord. It was time—the time for an ending of the old and a beginning for the new."

"End? Beginning?"

"In time you will understand the nature of what takes place."

"You are the one that—"

"Yes," answered Noman; for an instant, he thought Adrina recalled their previous meeting. He had told her too much. As he watched her eyes, her features, and her thoughts, he knew she didn't remember and was relieved. A flicker of thought passed before his eyes, images he had taken from Adrina.

Noman began to introduce his other companions. The short elder, Xith, last of the Watchers; Vilmos, the sandy-haired youth who appeared somehow older than the boy she had first met on the way to Alderan; and Nijal, of Solntse. Noman stopped Adrina's questions about Vilmos and further attempts at conversation by insisting they must leave. "*I will not go*!" yelled Adrina, "I demand to know what is happening. My *place* is in the palace!"

"Not if you are *killed* it isn't! We have no time. *Come*!"

Adrina held her ground. She with all her kindness and tenderness had one fault: she liked to get her own way. At times her youthfulness showed clearly, especially in her temper.

"Where are we?"

"We are in the caves of the Braddabaggon, just outside the city."

"But how? We were just in the sewers beneath the city."

"Those were the ancient catacombs beneath the sewers that we were in," corrected Amir.

"What catacombs?"

"Come, princess, we can talk about this at a later time."

Adrina still held her ground, a belligerent look steeling her features. Amir picked Adrina up, threw her over his shoulder, and carried her away. The air in the chamber, though deadly still, suddenly became cool. Amir placed Adrina back on her feet and an instant later darkness seemed to sweep into the room from an adjacent tunnel.

A brilliant blue light burst aglow in the room. The ball of light danced between Xith's fingers, fury clearly showing on his face. Vilmos stood next to Xith, with the same blue light dancing in his hand. Sounds of movement filled the air.

Darkly clad figures poured into the chamber from all sides. Amir charged into their midst. His deadly sword wildly wrought havoc among them. With one sweep of his blade, two lay beneath his feet, the last sound of their lives one syllable of a cry to battle.

Nijal followed Amir's gesture and charged. His skill with his weapon could not match the lighting speed and legendary skill of Amir, but he also dealt punishment to the enemy. In endless numbers the attackers poured into the room.

Ayrian crouched low to the ground. Rapidly, his form was transfixed. With one powerful beat of his mighty wings he shot into the tunnel. His form was slightly different from usual. Here in the tunnels he could not use his immense form. This slightly touched his pride, as one of the truly beautiful things about his kind was their overwhelming power in giant form. For now, he settled on a much smaller size. He stalked the enemy from above. His agility more than compensated for the restriction of the small space. With his razor-sharp talons he tore the foe apart.

Together, Xith and Vilmos unleashed their combined energy. Smoke and flames filled the second tunnel. Pitiful cries of agony rolled into the chamber. The smell of burning flesh became pungent, permeating the air all around them. Vilmos and Xith set their minds to the task again, clearing their centers and focusing the energies they felt there. They stole power from the very air and rock around them, devouring it and then reshaping it to their whims.

Noman had sensed the imminent attack, but he thought they would have more time to escape. He cursed his shortsightedness. An image filled his mind. "No!" he cried. He could not counter it completely. He turned around, but it was too late. Galan, who had been standing towards the front of the room read his thoughts and leapt on top of Adrina, shielding the girl with her own body.

A tongue of crimson flames streamed into the room. Vilmos and Xith were in the direct path of the fire. Xith tried to shout a warning to Vilmos, but the red and blue flames met and in a swirl of raging energy they burst outward. The resulting explosion rocked the room, and the impact collapsed the ceiling of the second tunnel, which in turn caused the ceiling of the chamber they were in to give.

The assailants sought to seal them all in the chamber and surged forward over the bodies of their fallen comrades. The blast had knocked Nijal flat on his face. Even Amir had been shaken by the blast. Amir helped his companion right himself, narrowly blocking a crippling blow. Amir thrust his sword full into the attacker. His blade sank deep and the rogue crumpled lifeless to the ground, the rogue's sword lightly glancing Amir's arm as he went down. Desperately Amir and Nijal plunged full force into the tunnel.

Ayrian was midway down the tunnel when the explosion hit. His animal instincts were alert. He sensed the grave danger. At once he took the giant form. He had no room to fly and fell heavily to the tunnel floor, crushing several foes beneath him with his talons. The wide-eyed assailants stopped the attack on him as they stared at him in awe. They were unsure whether to attack or retreat. Ayrian took the chance and with beak and talon ripped into the two who stood before him. The pieces of their bodies dropped about him.

Wearily, Noman regained his feet. He shook his aching head. Xith and Vilmos lay unconscious near him. In the instant that Noman realized he could not stop the explosion, he built up all the energy he could gather before it was too late. He cast it outward as a single wall of force into the explosion, but the shock wave was not overcome.

Quickly, he leaned down, grabbed Xith and Vilmos by their tunics, and began to pull them from the room. The room slowly crumbled behind them. He reached safety just as the room totally caved in. "Oh, Father!" he sighed painfully, looking back into the room. It was buried in rubble.

Sweat streamed down Nijal's face. He was near exhaustion, but he still fought on. His reactions became slower with each blow and block. His only inspiration was the seemingly endless strength of the giant beside him. As the two hacked their way down the corridor, several times Amir blocked blows Nijal could no longer defend against.

The number of assassins replacing their fallen comrades was decreasing. Their morale was being dealt a staggering blow. For each that charged into the tunnel two of his companions fell; that is, if they could make it past Ayrian. So far, none of the replacements had; Ayrian was extremely enraged.

Slowly the assailants began to retreat; those trapped between Amir, Nijal and Ayrian were easily dispatched. Soon the last one fell and Nijal, with Amir's aid, staggered back down the tunnel, crawling through the debris in the chamber toward the others. Ayrian changed back to his humanoid form and joined them. They found Noman looking sadly into a pile of debris. Xith and Vilmos were unconscious on the floor beside him.

Amir knelt next to his master and stared into Noman's eyes. Ever since he had joined Noman in the City of the Sky, Amir had striven to emulate Noman. Noman rarely showed emotions and was never at a loss for words. The one thing Amir could always count on was Noman's stability; his natural charisma always issued forth, strength, wisdom, and inner peace being his main qualities. Amir had lived with Noman over 600 years. He had never known Noman to know doubt or fear, but he did now.

Amir leaned close to Noman and whispered into his ear. "Look inside of you. What do you see? Can you find your center? Look outward; do you not see the world? Caress it in your hands Shape it. Become one with it. Now can you not see your true enemy?" Amir repeated one of the basic lessons Noman taught him long, long ago. "One's true enemy is himself. First, you must conquer your own spirit."

The words infuriated Noman. A multitude of thoughts spun through his mind. He sorted them out and understood. "Quickly!" he yelled, "We must try to clear the debris. There may yet be time."

Amir and Ayrian carried Xith and Vilmos down to the middle of the hall so they would be out of the way. "Go, Nijal. Someone must watch the tunnel entrance," said Amir kindly. Nijal did not argue. He was too tired to argue. He didn't know if he could defend them from further attacks though he would try if need be. Sword in hand, he retreated down the corridor.

Noman stood and looked deep into the rubble. His eyes were closed, and he was deep in a trance. He searched with his mind. His eyes jumped wide open, his heart pumped rapidly with elation. He had found them. The words exploded from his lips: "One lives!"

Noman slowly felt the energy returning to him. He let it build. "Begin!" Amir and Ayrian began pulling the stone from the pile of debris. Noman released his energy in a wave. While the two tunneled, he held the stones around them from further collapse. Never again would Noman forget his sacred vow; he was guardian of the children. He existed for this single purpose.

It was Amir who uncovered the last rocks covering the Little One's body. He could not look at her. He wanted to remember her radiant beauty as it had been. Her body had been crushed brutally beneath the weight of the rocks. Solemnly he handed her to Ayrian behind him.

Amir gathered Adrina into his arms and crawled from the tunnel. Adrina appeared unscathed by the rocks; her body had been mostly shielded beneath the other. Noman's first thoughts were of Adrina. He had sensed her life force strongly beneath the rubble. Amir still held her gently in his arms, unsure if he should place her on the ground. Noman assured him it was all right.

"Adrina," called Noman loudly, "can you hear me?" He did not expect a response but he wanted to be sure before he reset her broken bones. Noman re-checked her injuries; her left hand was severely damaged and her right leg was broken, but she would survive. A part of him rejoiced.

Now he could turn his attentions to the other. He could still feel the will within her. It grew weaker and weaker. He could not do anything to save her, but he could ease her suffering. Her spirit fought to survive, to linger a second more. She was not yet ready to pass, but she was losing the fight.

Noman surged his will into the center of her dwindling will. He knew what her spirit fought for. He would take the risk and tell her. "She is Alive!" he yelled into her mind. He retreated his will from her. A solitary emotion reached him as her spirit passed to rest with the Great-Father—happiness, extreme happiness.

10

With the arrival of evening the air above decks grew cool, causing Seth, Valam, Evgej, and Liyan to retreat below decks. Liyan and Seth began a discussion about the progression of the enemy campaign, breaking any chance of a change of moods.

"King Mark has not yet crossed the Crags?"

"The people of the wood, his people, and the River Elves have joined as one. The Silver folk have all but succumbed. He has taken Winthall and Sumer. Those that remain have fled Tamer. Some gather near the Sea of Edengar. Others take refuge in the Shadow Mountains.

"The Valley folk joined him unwillingly after the fall of Hakdell. The port city of Elorendale is home to his reserve fleet. Our contacts say the masters of wood and stone and sail from all the West are building weapons of war there the likes of which have never before been seen in the land."

"And we have done nothing?"

"We have offered all the aid we could, but it was not enough. The mountains are a boundary to both our forces. We cannot risk sending any more of our forces through the passes to those few of our allies that remain. We will need all our strength here. A few of those remaining in the west are in the process of retreating to us in the east. Most will stay; it is a matter of honor to remain and die in their homeland."

"*Remain* and *die*?" asked Evgej. "What honor is there in that?"

"It is the same as I would do for my queen and our land. It is the sacrifice of oneself for the greater good," said Seth.

"As it would be for me also. For now we are locked in a stalemate. We wait for King Mark's forces to cross the mountains. We expect he will strike Avenwood and Rivenwood first. It is there we plan to engage him. He will wait until all those behind him lie dead, then he will come."

"His forces will continue to grow in strength, while you wait—"

"So do ours. The time will come soon enough."

"Yes, *soon*," answered Seth distantly.

"But have you not considered bringing the battle to him? It could turn the tide against him."

"Ahh, Evgej, you must consider the forces in opposition. It could not be that easy. We would not invade another's lands. It is not our way."

"But you are at *war*!"

"Yes, there is honor even in times of war."

"Your enemy does not seem to be following any code of honor."

"For our people it is personal. It is our way. It is the way the Great-Father and Mother-Earth gave us."

"But they would not wish you to be destroyed for your honor's sake."

"We are peaceful by nature. We still could not. If we are to be destroyed, then it is by *their* will alone that we shall go."

"In the Blood Wars—"

"It was not our doing," said Seth, interrupting.

"Are these mountains neutral territory?" asked Valam, who had been listening intently to the flow of the conversation.

"Yes."

"How many passes are there through the mountains?"

"There are but two that are wide enough for an army."

"Hmm—" Valam raised his eyebrows as he said it.

The discussion continued, at times growing heated and at times progressing slowly, but always flowing with the emotion of the four men who spoke and listened with greater wisdom than most.

Late in the afternoon the next day, the island city of Leklorall lay on the horizon, growing larger with each passing moment. The size of the city baffled Valam's mind. No city of the kingdom compared to it, not even the free city of Solntse. Even at this great distance he could see spiraling towers that shot up into the sky, which amazed him.

Earlier in the day, they had finally come to Lake Clarwater. They were completing the remainder of the journey with an escort of many more ships than they had begun with. Valam and Evgej stood motionless watching the sailmaster, who sat cross-legged at the rear of the sloop, eyes closed and hands resting calmly on his lap. The sloop was moving by itself or so it seemed. Seth had explained, "It is really quite simple—" Evgej had cut him off saying, "But the current flows in the opposite direction!"

"The direction is of no importance. The sailmaster instructs the ship and the ship listens. Quite simple."

The answer to this question still wandered through the back of Valam's mind as they floated up to the docks near the palace. The palace was a glowing array of twisting structures and turrets that formed an outward and upward spiral. "She is indeed magnificent!" exclaimed Valam and Evgej almost simultaneously.

A cry of welcome sounded from their greeters. A multitude clad in many colors lined the pathway through the central courtyard, yelling and cheering. As Seth passed those who wore the red of his order, they began chanting rapidly in their tongue, a song of the returning champion.

As they mounted the long sweeping staircase into the palace, strange, mystical instruments greeted their every step with a simple series of musical sounds that together created a peaceful, flowing melody. Upon reaching the last stair, the double doors to the court slowly opened inward. The raised dais to the throne was suspended in mid-air by a series of pillars that followed the contour of the sloping floor. In a semi-circle behind the dais were tiers of seats; many elves filled the chairs, each dressed in a different color representing their order. The only exception was a single line of gray representing those of Liyan's order seated to the rear and those clad in the red of Seth's order that were posted throughout the room.

In the center of the dais, seated upon a transparent, delicately carved throne was the Queen-Mother. Valam recognized her from the images of the mind-link. She was even more beautiful in person. She radiated pure perfection. A feeling of kindness and love flowed into his mind. For the first time in his life Valam was in total awe. When Seth introduced him, Valam could do nothing but gracefully kneel and lightly kiss her hand. He was at a complete loss for words. The Queen-Mother had the same tantalizing effect on Evgej. He, too, was at a loss for words, as he stared deeply into her eyes.

A cry of rejoicing and release from remorse burst into their minds. "*My Son*!" cried the Queen-Mother, reaching out to all with her mind. A smile touched the queen's lips as she regarded Seth. The two exchanged a wordless conversation, only obvious to the observers by the change of expressions that filled their two faces—sadness, hope, joy, thanks, and love.

11

The meeting progressed very well after Captain Brodst apologized for his rashness. After all resolutions were made, they parted for the evening, having come to decisions on many topics. The decree went forth that same night. An assemblage of the High Council, the Council of Keepers, and the leaders from all members of the alliance was being called. All nobles would be welcome. They would also seek the advice of the Priests of the Father, the Priestesses of the Mother, and the Priests of the Dark Flame. The decree also said that anyone not in attendance by the declared time would be held in contempt of the alliance and face persecution accordingly, an insurance policy against the Minor Kingdom's probable ban.

Lord Edwar Serant and Captain Ansh Brodst departed for the detainment area where the assassin lord was being held. Lord Serant admired the captain's strength of mind, but he scoffed at his foolish arrogance. It was one thing to be arrogant if you could justify that arrogance, clearly another to claim it when the right to proclaim it had not been earned. He could see a promise of great things to come in Brodst; with a nurturing of his talents, then perhaps he could proclaim arrogance.

They entered the detention chamber and directed the guards to wait outside. Lord Konstantin was shackled by his hands and feet to the wall, still blindfolded and gagged. Once the blindfold and gag were removed, Lord Konstantin went wild with rage. He thrashed violently, causing the chains to gouge into his wrists and ankles. He did not care. His curses and thrashing only increased with the pain. He enjoyed it.

Lord Serant was the first to begin the interrogation. "Who sent you?" he demanded of the prisoner. He quickly received the answer: spittle in his face. Captain Brodst removed a whip from the wall and lashed it harshly against the assassin lord's face. Lord Konstantin's response was a deep howling cackle. Blood trickled down his face profusely, which he licked with his tongue. He smiled hideously.

Lord Serant repeated his question, "Who sent you?" When they received no answer, Captain Brodst struck the assassin with the whip repeatedly. Lord Konstantin didn't give them the satisfaction of hearing his pain-filled screams; with each blow his laughter increased, until it reached the threshold of insanity.

Captain Brodst looked quizzically to Lord Serant, wondering if he should continue. Serant shrugged his shoulders and said quietly, "No." He then motioned to the captain to grasp the assassin's hands. The chains were just long enough; Lord Konstantin might be able to try something. Serant did not want to risk the chance. Captain Brodst firmly held the prisoner's hands, while Serant grasped the prisoner by the throat.

"We will get the information we seek out of you one way or another. Death will come. But one way is quicker than the other. I do not mind waiting, and since you seem to be enjoying it, we will continue this just as long as need be. So, I will ask you one more time. Who sent you?"

"He that did."

Lord Serant drew his sword and held it before the assassin's eyes, so he could look at its coldness. "I'm sure that you would enjoy it if I were to kill you now, but I will not. I am a very patient man. Why did you come?"

"I think that is quite obvious." His tone was one of steel. His eyes seemed to stare through Lord Serant as if he did not exist.

Serant decided to let the captain try to persuade the man to talk. Captain Brodst ordered the guards to retrieve some hot logs from the kitchen's fire. When they returned, he heated a dagger until it was crimson. "Strip him!" Brodst ran the blade lightly along the assassin's bare legs, just enough so Lord Konstantin could feel the intensity of the heat.

"Who sent you? I will ask only one more time in case you were distracted by my blade. Who sent you?"

The prisoner offered no retort. Captain Brodst pressed the flat side of the dagger full against the other's leg. He held it there while he repeated his question. Repeatedly he recapitulated his words and his actions with no reply.

"Guards, get in here!" yelled Serant, as his patience thinned. He saw that the prisoner was tended to and then he and Captain Brodst departed the room, neither very pleased. Lord Serant did have an idea that he hoped might work. After a brief discussion while they walked towards the conference room, the two decided it would be a good idea to consult Father Francis and Keeper Q'yer.

They found the two in Father Jacob's old study, engaged in a heated conversation. "Ah, Father Francis and Keeper Q'yer, just the two we were looking for. Sorry to interrupt you," spoke Lord Serant as he entered the room.

"How may we help you, my lord?"

"It is about the assassin, Lord Konstantin. He will not talk. He does not fear death or pain. In fact, I think he rather enjoys it. Can you use the power of the Father to enter his mind and learn his secrets?"

"I am afraid I know not of such things. Keeper?"

"I have seen nothing of it in our histories, but in the ancient books I have read of such a thing. It is something Brother Seth could have done."

"Seth?" Lord Serant asked, before he could recall the name. He had never met Seth, but he had heard the stories about him. "Is there then no other way?"

"I think I have an idea. I'll give him a taste of the death that he so dearly seeks. The Father does not welcome those who do not earn their place with him. They are sent to the darkness of the pit, a cold, unforgiving place."

The four then returned to the dungeon, which was an area of the castle that had been mostly unused for a very long time. The musty smell of mildew and dank waters assaulted their nostrils as they descended the stairs. All in all, the section was very small, including only six adjacent cells, but it had always been plenty spacious for Imtal. It was rare that any of the cells had an occupant.

Father Francis began his deep concentration. His head began to sway back and forth as a trance overtook him. He faced the assassin lord and asked, "Do you wish death? It is what I offer. Take it." His voice was compelling. "Take it," he enticed. "Take it—take it."

"Yes!" screamed the prisoner, "Yes!"

Father Francis had been waiting for his total acceptance. "Then take it!" he bellowed.

Lord Konstantin yelled for joy. His eyes and mouth were wide as he embraced death. The after life was everything he ever dreamed it would be and the dark lord's promises seemed to ring true. The land abounded with riches and treasures—all there for his taking. An army of faithful servants waited for his beckon call. But as he sought to claim the riches the area around him suddenly became dark and cold. He began to shiver uncontrollably. The army of the faithful became a great host of white specters that danced all around him. Their agony greeted him. They eagerly waited to drink the warmth of his newly passed spirit.

Horror began to fill the assassin's mind. "This is not death!"

"Oh, but it is!" assured Father Francis.

"This is not what my master promised!"

"Oh, but it is. Join us," said a multitude of withered voices. "Join us."

"No! I've changed my mind. I do not want to die. Please, please, please, oh please," begged Lord Konstantin.

Father Francis let the rogue's mind linger for a time in the land of the damned. "Tell us what we want to know. Who sent you? Why have you come?"

"No. Please, I do not—"

"Who sent you? Why have you come?"

"I do not know who hired me."

"Liar!" yelled Father Francis as he plunged the assassin back into the pit.

"No, really. I was hired—paid in advance."

Father Francis left Lord Konstantin dangling above the pit. Slowly he lowered him in, while he repeated the questions.

"They called themselves the coalition. The leader's name was Antare. He told me that for each I killed he would give me a count of gold, save for the girl. He would triple the sum for her, but only if she were alive. If she were dead we would only get the original payment and nothing extra."

"If you lie!" tempted Father Francis, clearly angry.

"It is the truth!"

Father Francis released Lord Konstantin's spirit. He could hold it no more. "Thank you for your help, Father," he whispered as he came out of the trance. Captain Brodst steadied the priest as he gathered his wits. "I am fine. I am fine."

"You are a miracle worker; whatever you did worked magnificently! I am ever grateful," said Lord Serant.

"Do not thank me. Thank the Great-Father."

Lord Konstantin was still trying to sort out what had happened when his tormentors left the room. He had been tricked by the foul priest's treachery. "I will kill you—I will kill you all," he yelled as the gag was returned to his mouth.

"I have never heard of one called Antare," said Lord Serant as they walked down the hall.

"It is not a person, but a place," said Keeper Q'yer, "It is an ancient word. I have seen it mentioned in the great book. If you permit me, I will return to the council and seek their help."

"Of course, Keeper, go."

"I will return when I discover something." Keeper Q'yer struck his staff against the hard stones of the floor and spoke the words of power, "Starod sil, otkry ot zemlya i pozhar, veter i vod!" As the new head of the keepers, he enjoyed the privilege of using the old devices though the process of teleportation eluded him. Keeper Martin was the one who had taught him how to use it. Most of the other keepers feared using the device and wished it destroyed, but Keeper Martin protested, as had others before him. Keeper Martin had actually been the first one to use it in generations.

Keeper Q'yer thought back to the time when Martin had first discovered the device. Keeper Martin had stayed up for days searching the old tomes for clues on its use. He had found them. His pleas to the council Keeper Q'yer vividly recalled. "It has survived even the purging—it was kept here for a purpose! And this is that purpose!" By using it, Keeper Martin's wisdom was clearly shown. It was thus that he gained the respect of the council and eventually became its head.

Keeper Q'yer remembered those days with fondness. From those times he and Martin had also come to know each other, and their friendship had grown. All these thoughts flashed through his mind as he returned to the council.

"But why would they want Adrina?" asked Lord Serant.

"That is a good question—it troubles me."

"Could you try that again?"

"I do not think I could trick his mind again. Only willingly could I take him there."

"Then we shall have to try another way, but for now let him sulk. Maybe just the fear of going there will loosen his tongue again."

"Good. I am famished."

"Me, too. It is long past dinner. Will you join us, Father?"

"I'm sorry, but no. I will join you two later. I cannot eat when my mind is troubled."

The two watched Father Francis leave then left for the kitchen. Lord Serant was also caught up with his thoughts; maybe he had judged Captain Brodst too harshly. He was beginning to enjoy his company. The two feasted well on the food they found in the kitchen. Lord Serant grabbed a large hunk of meat and Captain Brodst a cask of ale. They were engaged in light conversation and drinking when Isador found them.

The old nanny, who had brought up all three of King Andrew's daughters, was fuming. Lord Serant had heard many things about her temperament. He suspected it was where Calyin got her temper.

"Lord Serant, Princess Calyin has sent me to retrieve you. She wishes to speak with you."

Lord Serant looked to Captain Brodst for help. Captain Brodst smiled broadly and said, "I must be going also. I have many things to do yet today. Sorry, Lord Serant."

"Tomorrow morning, then."

Isador led Lord Serant to Calyin's quarters and then dismissed herself. "Oh Edwar, I was so worried," said Calyin as she ran into his arms. His presence calmed her shivers. "Calyin, there is nothing to fear. I—we are safe here. Nothing will harm you or me—nothing." She answered by holding him tighter; feeling his warmth reassured her that he was all right.

Gently he carried her to the bed and tucked her in. He lay there beside her, soothing her until she fell asleep. However, he was still wide-awake. He had doubts that he could not tell her about. He admired her strength too much. They each got their strength from the other. Even at times like this, he could feel it in her.

For hours he lay there unable to sleep until finally he got up to go for a walk. He slipped out quietly, pulling the covers tight around his beloved Calyin before he went. He strolled the halls of the palace, eventually finding himself at the terrace overlooking the garden. Captain Brodst was also there, staring into the night sky.

"Hello, Lord Serant," spoke the startled captain.

"May I join you?"

"Of course; you needn't ask for permission."

Lord Serant sat down in a chair opposite the captain. They silently enjoyed the night, neither wishing to disturb the other's thoughts. The hours passed and soon they were welcoming the dawn of early morning.

Captain Brodst stood and stretched. Lord Serant followed and stretched his stiff muscles. Brodst looked mischievously to Serant and raised his eyebrows. They both knew what the other was thinking, had been thinking about all during the night. "Come, let's go see if we can stir that wretch's tongue!" said Lord Serant.

They hurried back down the winding stairs toward the cells and had the guard unlock and open the door for them. "Wake up!" they yelled in unison. The assassin did not move. "Wake up!" The assassin did not move. Captain Brodst picked up a bucket of water and threw it into the prisoner's face.

Lord Konstantin hung there limply like one dead. Serant removed the gag from the man's mouth. The prisoner did not respond. He still hung there limply in the chains. Lord Serant then removed the blindfold; still, there was no response. He then slapped Lord Konstantin's face, again and again.

The two watched the prisoner. He offered no signs that he was alive. He seemed not to be breathing. Lord Serant jabbed him with the hilt of his sword several times. The man did not move.

Lord Serant walked towards the door and beckoned for the captain to join him. He whispered quietly to Captain Brodst, while he kept a watch on their prisoner with his peripheral vision, "This could be a trick of some sort. Be careful. Don't get too close to him. I'll send a guard to get Father Francis."

Serant called to one of the guards and sent him after the father. Cautiously Lord Serant approached Konstantin. He looked at the chains; they were secure. He pressed his ear against the man's chest; he could hear no heart beat. The man was indeed dead.

"Guard, get in here!"

"Yes, my lord," said the guard entering the room.

"Have you been watching this man?"

"Yes, as you ordered."

"He is dead!"

"That cannot be. He was alive—believe me. He was cursing and yelling."

"Release him now!"

The guard began to release the prisoner's bonds, hands first. Lord Serant and the captain unsheathed their swords, ready for action. The assassin slumped limply to the floor. The guard unlocked the feet shackles and turned around. He looked at their poised weapons and started to babble out an apology, "I am sorry! It was not my fault. Please, don't kill me!"

"Kill who?" asked Father Francis entering the cell.

"No, there will be no killing," said Lord Serant turning to face the father.

The assassin lunged from the floor, grabbing Lord Serant's sword arm and thrusting it up and backward. Lord Serant had been taken completely by surprise. His arm offered no resistance as the blade cut deep. He slumped to the floor.

The assassin wasted not a moment. He continued his upward motion. In one quick move, he jumped high, kicking out with full force, his foot striking Captain Brodst cleanly. The captain followed Lord Serant to the floor.

The assassin turned mid-air simultaneously timed with the kick and lashed out with his hand. His blow met the other's neck, crushing his wind pipe. Father Francis stumbled, shocked, and fell to the floor.

The entire sequence of events happened in an instant. The assassin had fully made use of the element of surprise. He had encountered absolutely no resistance. A smile touched his lips as he awkwardly landed on the floor, twisting his ankle slightly as he did so. It took him a moment to recover his balance; the last lunge had been a desperate gambit but had been successful. He was, indeed, pleased with himself.

He felt a coldness sweep through him. The air seemed to turn suddenly icy cold. He looked down as a guard, the only other person in the room, pulled a blood-covered sword from within his belly. Lord Konstantin died before the smile left his face.

Several guards burst into the room, weapons drawn and ready. They were shocked when they only saw a lone survivor, kneeling over Captain Brodst's body. "Get help! Now!" bellowed the guard with a lump of sadness in his throat. The guards ran from the room to find help. The other, Pyetr, second son of Captain Brodst, crumpled to the floor again clutching his father's hand. His thoughts began to fill with rage. He had not wanted to become a guard. He hated fighting. Fighting was senseless; killing was senseless. He stood and removed his helmet, breastplate and sword. He let them drop noisily to the floor.

He looked to the men lying on the floor. He could do nothing to save them. He felt so helpless. All his life he had been nothing except a fighter. He had never learned about saving a person's life, only taking it.

He bent down and checked each. He found no signs they were alive and had no idea what to do, so in frustration he turned and fled the room. He ran smack into Chancellor Volnej, who was just turning into the room. "Please save them," Pyetr said staring straight into the chancellor's eyes. He then turned around and ran, as fast as he could, down the corridor.

The chancellor, followed by Princess Calyin, Midori, and Sister Catrin rushed into the room. A single expression of horror on each of their faces. Calyin raced to where Lord Serant lay on the floor. Suddenly, she felt so alone and insecure. Her eyes fell to the sword her lord still clutched, buried deep within his chest. She tried to retain a strong front but could not.

Calyin pleaded desperately for Midori to save him. Midori looked sympathetically to her and said, "If there is one who could save him now it is I, sister. You must let him go."

"But—?" cried Calyin, disbelieving the words she heard.

"It is in the Mother's hands; her will providing, he will survive. Could you please wait outside? I will do everything in my power to save him. I promise."

Reluctantly, Calyin left the room. Chancellor Volnej also followed Calyin out of the room, closing the door after himself.

Catrin gently closed Father Francis' eyes. "He has passed," she said in a reverent tone to Midori. Though she had only known the father a short while, she had come to respect him. She knew that Midori also had a great fondness of him though she hid it well. The union of the Mother and Father had also joined Midori and Father Francis. The emotions could not be denied. Midori would miss him as one would miss one very dear to them, as one would miss their love, though the only true love Midori could feel now was the all encompassing love for the Mother.

With a heavy heart, Catrin checked Captain Brodst. She was very thankful to find that he was alive. "He lives. The blow only knocked him out."

"Lord Serant also lives though his heartbeat grows faint. We must hurry!"

Midori examined how the sword had entered Lord Serant's chest. She had to remove it carefully, or he could die. She unclasped his hands from the hilt and gently removed it, being extremely careful to insure that it followed the same path out that it had taken in.

Blood began to flow rapidly from the gaping wound. Quickly Catrin removed Lord Serant's robe and Midori placed the palm of her hands onto his chest. Catrin then touched her index fingers to Lord Serant's temples, gently stimulating them.

Together the two began the solemn prayer of healing. Midori reached out to the Mother for her help in saving Lord Serant's life. The flow of blood began to slow as Midori's mental chanting grew in intensity. Time moved rapidly between the apexes of her fingers. The wound began to close, a light scab formed, the scab disappeared, and the wound was totally closed. Midori's chanting ceased and she removed her hands from Lord Serant's chest. Catrin continued massaging his temples with her fingers until Midori was completely finished. "Rest well," Catrin spoke as she removed her fingers. Midori added in a whisper, "The Mother has plans for you yet."

Midori then went to Captain Brodst and examined his head injury. If the blow had been placed any closer to the pressure point behind his ear, it would have killed him instantly; however, it had only knocked him unconscious. It would take her only a moment to reduce the swelling from the blow. She found the proper pressure points, then applied her right hand to the wound. When she finished, Catrin opened the door and let the others back into the room.

Calyin was the first to enter. She ran to her lord's side and caressed his face, grateful he was alive. "Thank you!" she said to Midori, "Thank you!"

"Have them taken to their rooms. Let them have plenty of rest and they will be fine. If you'll excuse me," said Midori as she hurried from the room. Catrin luckily had followed Midori out, for as she walked into the corridor Midori stumbled and fell. Catrin caught her and walked her back to her quarters.

Midori refused to rest, but Catrin insisted. Midori still had not fully recovered from the ordeal at the square and had spent her reserve strength for the healing. Catrin could see the fatigue written in Midori's eyes. She knew the look well because she was fighting hard to hide it also. After she made sure Midori did indeed rest, which took some very fast-talking and much persuasion, she also took a much-needed rest.

Calyin had the captain and her lord placed in the same room so she could check on them both at the same time. But for now, she would be forced to return to the affairs of state. Chancellor Volnej was very prudent in helping her so she didn't overwork herself. A great many things needed to be prepared and quickly.

* * *

The homecoming ceremony was a joyous occasion. The festival lasted long into the evening. Though Valam enjoyed every moment of it, he was glad when he could rest. Each of his companions had been given separate rooms, so he was alone to contemplate his thoughts.

Seth had introduced them to so many of the Brotherhood he could not hope to recall their names. Valam was simply fascinated by the complexity of the workings of Seth's society. Each order was given a specific duty and a set of rules they were to follow. The entire system was based upon honor and personal integrity.

Many times, Valam and Seth had discussed the system back in the kingdom and on the journey, but it became real only when he could see it working. Seth had told him the Brotherhood consisted of seven main orders, the Gray, the Red, the White, the Yellow, the Black, the Blue and the Brown. The hardest thing for him to do was to stop comparing the orders to things in the kingdom.

His thoughts shifted as he began to fade off to sleep. He struggled to stay awake but could not. The day had been tiring, and he was soon fast asleep.

Evgej had sneaked off with Cagan during the banquet. They had both needed to get away from the merriment. They did not feel like having fun; more than anything, they needed to be alone. Evgej found himself aboard a ship, the last place he had thought he would ever willingly return to. It was Cagan's old ship, a small, sleek, beauty.

"I used to come out here late at night, like now, and sail up the river to nowhere in particular, with nothing but a slight breeze and the water for company. It was so tranquil."

"Well, what do we wait for?" said Evgej with a sparkle in his eye. The sea had a captivating effect on him. Instead of getting seasick, now he felt good, revived. The river trip here had only rekindled his desire for the water. He had never thought he would miss it, but he had. Cagan said it was because he had the heart of a sailor, and perhaps he did.

Without a further thought, Cagan untied the boat and raised the sail. The small craft drank in the shallow breeze well. Cagan and Evgej began to glide peacefully across Lake Clarwater and soon the waters of the Gildway were before them.

Evgej watched Cagan handle the tiller and the sail of the boat. He began to understand how Cagan controlled it. "May I try?"

"Sure, go right ahead."

"How is this?"

"Good, just keep the rudder steady. It is used to control the course we take. Turn it slowly, not sharply. Turn it left and the boat will veer to the right and vice versa."

"I understand. The force of the rudder against the water moves the boat in the opposite direction."

"Don't lose the wind. See how the sail sags? Keep it tight, and the boat will move faster. Watch out for the—"

Cagan had given the warning too late. The wind caught the sail from the opposite side, sweeping the sail sharply to the right. It hit the unsuspecting Evgej squarely in the shoulder and propelled him into the water.

It took Evgej a moment to recollect his orientation; by that time, Cagan had already released the sail and fastened a line around himself and had jumped into the water after him. Cagan was just in time. Evgej was going under for the third time when the crafty sailmaster grabbed him and held him above water.

Cagan was about to push Evgej back into the boat when he heard something. He put a hand over Evgej's mouth and pointed to the riverbank. The two remained still, holding tightly to the boat. Neither dared to look towards the shore, afraid of what they might see.

They heard movement from the bank again. A voice yelled, "It is a boat. I don't see anyone aboard."

"Are you sure?" asked another in a deep masculine voice.

"Yes. It is drifting."

"Well, swim out and retrieve it so we can examine it."

"The water is freezing. You swim out to it."

"I am your senior. Go and get it."

Cagan and Evgej could hear the splash of someone entering the water. Evgej groped for his sword, but it was gone. "What a time to lose my sword!" he thought to himself; then he remembered that he had left it in his room when he had bathed for the banquet. He felt stupid. He always wore the sword, no matter where he went.

The water was indeed very cold. Evgej was beginning to feel its chilling effect sweeping through him. "Hold on to the boat and *swim*," whispered Cagan in Evgej's ear. They heard shouting from the shore. The two guards were arguing back and forth between themselves over whose fault it was that the boat slipped by. As the current carried the boat further downstream, Evgej heard them come to a decision to blame it on the current and not to tell anyone what had happened.

After they were a long distance away, the two climbed back into the boat, waited for a time, and then began the return trip. They were relieved when they docked safely along the pier. Water still dripped from their clothes as they walked back toward the palace. They found a very angry Brother Liyan awaiting their return. "Are you mad? Did you not hear my call?" The two stared questioningly at each other then turned to look innocently at Liyan. "Did you forget we are at war?"

"We stayed near the capital," offered Evgej. Liyan finally noticed their wet clothes and departed without saying anything further. Cagan playfully said to Evgej, "Well, we made it back safely did we not?"

"A little wet, yes, but safely."

Liyan looked back toward them with a disgusted expression on his face. Evgej could not help but laugh, despite his heavy mood. Liyan whispered into Cagan's thoughts, "You are lucky that the guards were ours and not the enemies."

"You knew?" mouthed Cagan back to Liyan.

"Yes," responded Liyan flatly.

Morning found Seth, Valam, Evgej, Cagan, and Liyan seated around an enormous conference table, awaiting the arrival of the council and the Queen-Mother. The council soon arrived, led by Brother Liyan. They were followed by the remainder of the leaders of each of the main orders. Once they were all seated in their proper positions, the Queen-Mother entered. All bowed their heads until she was seated, as was customary in council.

"Brother Liyan of the order of the Gray and the distinguished members of the high council. Welcome! Brother Seth of the order of the Red. Welcome! Your return has brought a smile to my lips. Thank you. Brother Ylad' of the order of the White, Brother Nikol of the order of the Yellow, Brother Tsandra of the order of the Brown, Brother Ontyv of the order of the Black, Brother Samyuehl of the order of the Blue, Sailmaster Cagan. We welcome your wisdom to the council. And lastly, our special visitors, Prince Valam of the Great Kingdom. Captain Evgej of Quashan' in the South Province, it is a great honor to have you join us!

"Only the Great-Father and Mother-Earth can answer the many riddles of the prophecy. The prophecy is the greatest gift they ever gave their children. It was a gift for all the children of the Mother and Father. They risked the very balance of the universe to give us the gift. A gift of future hope. They gave us the clues to interpret and understand the warning of the future. We have spent centuries pondering its many pieces. In the past, we have all misread portions of it. The betrayal of the Blood Wars depicts this quite vividly. The dark forces used the prophecy against us. Brother slew brother. The mistakes of the past will be no more. We will make no such mistakes this time!"

The Queen-Mother spoke with a power and elegance that enticed the listeners. When she spoke, all eyes were fixed on her, catching every gesture and every rise and fall in her voice. The sound of her words still resonated throughout the room, perhaps the reason she chose to speak her words aloud.

Valam's attention, however, had been lost to another. Seth had to elbow Valam sharply before he snapped out of it. Valam followed Evgej's lead and stood and bowed, making his introduction. Only his many years in his father's court had allowed him to recover his grace in full measure.

His eyes were still transfixed to the same point they had occupied as he bowed and then seated himself. Though no one else seemed to notice his awkwardness, Tsandra of the Brown had, for she was the object of Valam's powerful gaze. She could see the emotion in his eyes as he looked upon her and didn't understand why.

The reason for Valam's fixed stare was two-fold. He had expected to see a large, powerfully built male as the leader of the warrior order, not an extremely enchanting, petite female. The other reason was her striking resemblance to the Queen-Mother. When Valam finally regained his wits, he managed to force himself to look away from her; however, occasionally during the remainder of the meeting, he found his gaze wandering back to rest upon her face.

The meeting was meant to initiate Valam and Evgej to the ways and histories of the Brotherhood and to unite all the leaders with the ways of men so they could work together as a whole. For Valam, it was nothing new. He had already given his full trust to Seth, as had Evgej. The real problem was getting the others to accept the presence of Men. Even though the kingdomers came in response to the Queen-Mother's call for help, long ago Men and Elves had been enemies. Time had proven the bitter deception that both societies had succumbed to. Each had repented for its blindness, but until now neither side had ever again communicated with the other.

"Seth?" asked Valam as they walked through the great halls leaving the conference room. "Could you tell me more about the Brown Order? How does it survive if it only exists in time of war?"

"It has."

"But how?"

"Remember when I told you how one was chosen at birth to enter the Brotherhood?"

"I don't," said Evgej, who had been listening quietly. "Sorry, but I would like to better understand," he quickly explained, noting Valam's glare.

"It is okay. It is easier if I digress and describe the entire method. Besides, I think you are both better prepared to understand it. Before, I only outlined it. Let us sit here for a moment."

Seth brought them to a small balcony overlooking the courtyard of the palace. "The choosing takes place at birth. It was Ontyv, himself, who chose me. Very few are chosen, and even fewer pass the final tests of servitude. The tests determine which order you will belong to. If you fail one portion of the test, you fail the entire test."

"What happens if you fail?"

"You journey to the Great-Father. Not only how well you perform the tests comprises the final outcome, but how you reach those decisions as well as how quickly you act on those decisions. To understand the choosing you must also fully understand the purpose of each order. The orders of the Gray and White are forbidden to apprentices. They are comprised only of elders, for only through time can you gain sufficient wisdom to justify the honor. And only one who was once a member of the White may become a member of the Gray. I know of only two exceptions to that rule in the entirety of the Brotherhood's existence, one very long ago and one recently. The order of Gray consists of only ten members. A new one is chosen only when an existing one has passed. The White consists of a number equal to ten times the number of the Gray, which is not always 100."

"But how can it be otherwise?"

"That is how it is written."

"Why?"

"I think I can answer that question," Brother Liyan said walking onto the balcony.

"Good," said Seth, welcoming Liyan, "I could use your knowledge of the histories."

"Each member of the Gray is delegated eight consorts to study and work with him. The others stay here in the capital for training new initiates and keeping records and many other tasks. The true number is always more than 100. But there have been times when the council consisted of less than ten members and there have been times when more than ten were needed. They use their wisdom to enlighten and teach our people. They keep records of our histories, and they give council. The order of the Red also is very small; new members are added infrequently. To fully understand the honor of being chosen to this order you must understand that its place is equal to that of the order of the Gray, for there is no greater office than to serve in the protection of the Queen-Mother.

"In matters pertaining to the Queen, the order of the Red has supreme authority even over that of the Gray. The Red is comprised of those who were destined to wear the white and eventually the gray. The orders of the Yellow and Black were the largest orders until the Brown was restored. The Yellow preserve the peace and harmony among our people by showing us our past and present errors and teaching us to love the Great-Father and Mother-Earth. The Black bring us into the world and carry us from it. They keep us pure and whole.

"The Brown order differs from all the others in that it did not always exist. It was born from war, and as it was born another order died, something our kind had never experienced. We had always stayed out of the affairs of others. Leaders of this order are chosen from birth and preserve the ways of war by passing it down through the generations. A true warrior and leader is also a rarity. They are born for no other purpose than to practice the art of death. In times of peace the Brown order is a private sect. In our eyes they cease to exist. In war, they return and cry out for our people to join them. It is also an honor to be allowed to serve thus. The Brown differs from the others again, in that those not of the Brotherhood are allowed to join. They serve until they are no longer needed."

"Was Tsandra then born into it?"

"The truth in your heart shows through, Valam," said Seth. "Yes, she was."

"How can you tell the difference?"

It was then that Seth realized something he and Liyan had taken for granted. "By the robes—"

"The belts!" exclaimed Evgej.

"Yes, in all orders the first wears a belt of silver and the others don those of the color of their order except in the brown order. The white belt signifies those of the original order."

"What of the Blue order? I have only seen one of that order—

Samyuehl."

"There are currently only two of this order, as it has always been. It is near Samyuehl's time; then Ry'al will take his place, and there will be only one until it is again time for another."

"But how do you know when it is time?"

"It is not our choice. It is the choice of the Mother-Earth."

"But what—"

"Come, it is time to join the others for supper."

The four were just in time to join the other leaders for the evening meal. For Valam and Evgej it was similar to eating in the great hall of the Kingdom, except for the immense proportions of this hall. It was composed of three tiers with an open center. In the center stood an oval-shaped stone table where those of high office dined.

The Queen-Mother was seated at the head of the table. Before they began to eat, her words of praise to the Father and Mother drifted pleasantly through the minds of all present. Evgej mused that the hall held the population of the entire city. "Almost—" whispered Brother Liyan to Evgej's mind.

"Sorry, I'll try not to think aloud any more," spoke Evgej cheerfully. Liyan smiled and answered, "No it was my fault. I have to learn how to deal with an open mind."

"But I thought there were some who talked aloud and purposely opened their thoughts."

"That is different. They contain their thoughts within the arena of their own center, but the center is always open if one wishes to access it. Seth taught you how to block your thoughts also, yes?"

"Well, as a child does, yes, but not a complete mind block."

"Children eventually become adults. You will learn how on your own in time. Practice."

"What do you think, Valam?" asked Evgej. Liyan and Seth simultaneously pointed to where Valam's gaze was fixed. Evgej looked and understood Valam's silence. He half held back a smile and continued eating his food.

"It is impolite to stare," Tsandra directed into Valam's mind teasingly. She felt the presence of his watching each time they were near. Valam only shrugged his shoulders and smiled. It was then that Tsandra remembered that Valam could not project his thoughts.

She directed back into his mind, "Sorry." After a pause for a moment of careful thinking, Tsandra thought of something. It was a game she had learned long ago. She and her mother used to play it. Thoughts of her mother brought sadness.

She pushed the thoughts away and thought to Valam, "This is a game I used to play very long ago. If I say something, to answer just think the thought to yourself." After she said it, she realized that was the only way Valam could think, to himself.

"How is that a game?" Valam thought to himself, "This is dumb. I'm talking to myself in my own mind!"

"I heard that," came the answering reply into his mind.

"Well, how is it a game?"

Tsandra considered it for a time. "It is sort of—abstractly, that is—except my mother would block the thoughts and I would have to try to find out what she was thinking. At first she would only concentrate lightly on closing the thoughts and then more and so on."

"Try this." Valam used the trick Seth had taught him. He gathered his thoughts in his mind and encircled them with an empty thought, thus closing his mind.

Tsandra's reply came an instant later. It was a feeling of embarrassment. Valam could almost picture her blush in his mind. "You should try harder and never think thoughts you do not want others to know."

"Sorry."

"Has he told you yet of the sword?" she asked indicating Liyan.

Valam didn't understand. "The sword?"

Tsandra felt Liyan's watchful gaze upon her and said no more. "Next time," she whispered to his mind. "I must be going—and you really should eat now." There was laughter in the fading echoes of her voice.

***

"Amir, she has passed. You must let her go," urged Noman. Amir reluctantly released his Little One's hand. "She rests with the Father," Noman assured him. The giant carefully picked up Adrina and followed Noman out of the tunnel.

"Have you seen anything?" Noman asked Nijal.

"Nothing," he answered weakly.

"Good!"

Noman watched Ayrian take flight to go retrieve the horses. "Hurry!" Noman whispered after him. Noman then proceeded to tear off his outer robe and rip it into strips, so he could make wraps for the splints for Adrina's hand and leg. When he finished, he lightly touched her to check on the life within her. He felt it warm within her and was glad.

Amir and Nijal stood watch over her while Noman went back to check on Xith and Vilmos. He praised their good fortune. Once they regained consciousness, they would recover rapidly. For now it was better to conserve his strength. He could not afford to spend his supply striving to reach their minds. He was forced to wait until they reached a safer place.

The night faded; Ayrian had not returned. Noman began to worry. He could sense the foulness in the late night air. Amir took Nijal's place in guarding the mouth of the tunnel. The others sat silently watching their companions, wishing they would speedily recover.

Darkness began to give way to the early morning twilight. Ayrian still had not returned. Noman was forced to make a very hard decision. They could leave in the light of the day. In the open, either the garrison would find them or the assassins would and on foot they could not flee. The garrison finding them would seem a blessing, but it would not be. Noman had seen the crossing of these two paths. Both would lead to their downfall, one quick and the other slow with even darker consequences. The other choice was to wait out the day, and if Ayrian still had not returned, then leave. They would be sitting in a ready-made trap. The enemy already knew they were here. Nevertheless, Noman decided after careful deliberation that they must wait. At least here they had some cover.

With the daylight came the heat of a summer day although spring was at hand. The stench of bodies became unbearable. Amir could not sit idly any longer. He had to do something. He looked to Nijal for help, but he was sleeping deeply from fatigue. Amir decided to do the dirty work by himself. First he moved Galan's body out of the way, and then he began piling bodies to the rear of the shaft.

It was a task he did not enjoy doing. It did, however, relieve the tediousness of waiting. He hated waiting. The scent reminded him of the smell of the battlefields of his past. He softly cursed that time. "Is this what I have waited for?" he asked himself.

He reached down to pick up the next body in a long line of them. He noticed something different about it. It was clad in only a robe, different from the others who wore light leathers. He called Noman over to him.

Noman studied the body closely. He could not believe what he saw.

Near the body lay a wooden walking stick. Noman picked it up in disgust and examined it. "It is what I feared." He closed his eyes and wandered back through his mind. He replayed the images of the explosion in his thoughts. He then re-examined the staff.

He had not seen where the negative energy had come from. He had sensed the coming explosion and had responded. Until now, he thought it had been an accident on Vilmos' part by mixing negative and positive energy. The expression on his face was not a pleasant one. The situation suddenly appeared worse. A magic-user, even one who used devices, was to be feared.

The staff was a device from the past. Noman had thought all those devices destroyed. He leaned down and loosened the man's robe. His worst nightmare was confirmed by the small symbol inked above the man's heart. In disgust, Noman spat into the dead man's face and walked away without saying a word to Amir.

Amir had also seen the mark, a tiny black-inked torch. He roared his anger, picked up the deceased by the hair and with one clean sweep of his sword beheaded him. The anger released, he sheathed his blade and went back to his tedious task.

Xith opened his eyes and attempted to focus them. "Ooh! My head aches!" he said rubbing his forehead. "Xith!" yelled Noman, elated. "What hit me?" Xith asked, queasily.

"Negative energy."

"Ouch!" expressed Xith as he tried to sit up. Painstakingly, he completed the chore. His body ached all over. "What of the others?"

"Adrina is injured and unconscious, but is well. Vilmos is also unconscious."

Xith looked around the cave. "Ayrian?"

"He is missing for the moment."

"And—"

Noman shook his head no before Xith could finish asking. "She died saving Adrina."

"I feel so tired." Xith closed his eyes and fell into a deep slumber.

The remainder of the afternoon passed slowly. Amir, Noman and Nijal eagerly awaited nightfall. They had all given up hope of Ayrian's returning. They knew if he could have returned he would have long ago. They did not wish ill upon him, but hoped his end had come quickly and without the pain of torture.

Xith awoke again as the darkness of night crept in. He startled Nijal, when he walked up behind him and touched his shoulder. "Xi—" Nijal started to say. "Shh!" said Xith staring out into the night from the tunnel entrance. "Has he returned?"

"No. How did you—?"

Xith walked back into the cave. "It is good you have recovered," said

Noman.

"When do we leave?"

"As soon as the night gathers full."

"Have you tried to awaken them?"

"No. I have been saving my strength and waiting for you."

"Yes, we cannot bear the burden of two."

Noman knelt next to Vilmos and touched his left hand to Vilmos' forehead and his right to Xith's. Xith focused inward to his center. He reached outward through Noman to Vilmos' mind. "Vilmos, look to your center—find it—focus on it—concentrate—feel it flow through you—drink it in—bathe in it."

"It is so dark. I can't find my way out."

"Vilmos?" said Xith looking outward through Vilmos' center, "It is only a dream. Create a light within your mind and awaken."

"No, you do not understand. He is with me. He won't let me escape."

"He is dead, Vilmos—it is not real."

"Oh Xith, leave quickly. He comes—I cannot hold him off any longer."

"Vilmos, no! Fight it! It is only a dream!" Xith surged his will outward into Vilmos. Energy surged back into Xith's body through Noman. The shock was enormous. Noman was forced to break the link.

Vilmos opened his eyes and stared wildly at Noman. "Noman, restore the link now!" The voice was Xith's, but the sound issued from Vilmos. Suddenly, for the first time, Noman saw Xith's limp, pale body slumped beside Vilmos. Without hesitation, Noman restored the link.

The link was restored, but Xith was still entranced. He was connected to Vilmos. He saw what Vilmos saw. The vision was captivating. He had to turn away from it. The longer he watched, the stronger the vision became.

It beckoned for him to stay. Xith could feel the pull on him. The strength to resist it was rapidly disappearing. "No," cried out a faint voice from somewhere in the distance. "No!" came Xith's answering call.

Noman faltered as the connection broke suddenly. Xith stumbled backward as he pulled away, wildly staring at Vilmos. Vilmos shook his head slowly from side to side, trying to shake the images of the dream out of his mind. The images, nonetheless, remained distinctly etched into his memory.

"Vilmos you must *never* allow yourself to have those dreams again. Push the thoughts from your mind!"

"But how?" appealed Vilmos, as he sat up. He had completely forgotten the events of the previous day. Scenes from the nightmare were perpetually repeating in his thoughts. Dreams were frightening for Vilmos, especially because when he dreamed them, they had a bad habit of becoming reality.

"We will discuss it later; for now we must concentrate on getting as far away from here as we can. How do you feel?"

"A little weak and I have a terrible headache, but I'll make it."

Vilmos stood and stretched his aching muscles. He felt very unwell; still, he would not say anything about it. His head throbbed as if he had smacked into a wall. He tried to concentrate his thoughts. It was a difficult feat at best, yet with perseverance he shook the disorientation from his mind.

He concentrated his thoughts on one thing: the energy flow that Xith had so painstakingly taught him. He lightly reached out for the energy; what he found was different from usual but returned a sensation that he had forgotten.

It also brought memories from the past. Though he saw them through another's eyes, they were his own. The wild energy of creation flowed fully through him. He had once felt a shadowing of this power back in the Barrens where Xith said the wild magic danced more freely although he had never felt it pulse so strongly within him, or had he?

His strength quickly returned. He tried to stop the energy flow. He could not. He was caught by it. He wondered if Xith or Noman could sense the power within him. He looked questioningly to them; they offered no response. What could it hurt, Vilmos asked himself.

Xith turned to Vilmos. "Vilmos, are you truly all right?" he asked.

“Yes, I’m fine.”

“Good, go join Amir and Nijal at the front of the tunnel.”

When Vilmos reached the far end, Noman showed Xith the staff Amir found on the assassin. They both understood the reality of the situation that they had uncovered. They hoped they were not too late to stop it.

“We have no choice but to go to Tsitadel’.”

“Is there no other way?”

“I am afraid there is no other way, old friend.”

“What of the child?”

“It is a risk, granted, but one we must take.”

“Have you seen the Paths?”

“Yes, but they are faint in the distance now. I have seen a vision, but you must say nothing about it. It has been set in motion as we have feared.”

“Then are we too late?”

“Let us hope we are not. It is time. We must leave.”

“What of Adrina?”

“The time is not right. She must sleep peacefully for now.”

The two joined the others and prepared to begin the journey. “Do we journey north?" asked Amir.

"You know where we shall go; do not despair," said Noman, softly speaking the last part so only Amir could hear it. Noman then knelt beside Adrina and readied her for the trek. "Sleep, my child," he said quietly as he kissed her forehead.

Noman motioned for Amir to carry Adrina. "Let us walk calmly through this night," Xith said into the light evening breeze. Amir gently picked up Adrina and the group departed into the blackness of the night.

12

With each passing day, Lord Serant's strength increased. He felt that he was well, but Calyin had left orders with Isador that he was to remain in bed. Captain Brodst had recovered almost completely, yet Calyin also forbade him to return to his duties until the seventh day. Her argument was that he needed more rest and would get it.

Captain Brodst had tried in vain to resist, but as Lord Serant had told him, "No one ever really wins an argument with Calyin. Even if you win, you lose, so it is best just to go along with what she says." Lord Serant was very thankful for his company; at least he was not cooped up in bed with no one to talk to. The topics of their conversations varied though eventually they would end up discussing the words of the assassin lord.

When Isador would leave after breakfast, Captain Brodst would quickly close the door and help Serant out of bed. The two would escape to a little balcony just off the room. They would bask in the sunlight of the day, enjoying the cool breezes that often blew in from the north.

Just before lunch, they would move back into their "little cell" as they called it. Isador would bring lunch, and when she couldn't endure their protests any longer would leave. They would then sneak back out to the balcony.

Calyin often found them out there when she checked in on them. She'd look at Lord Serant's broad smile and her cross mood would ease. The questions they asked her were always the same, "Has Keeper Q'yer returned yet?" "Any word from the alliance?" "What of the council?" Calyin's response was also always the same, "If they had I would have told you first thing." Both Lord Serant and the captain doubted that she would have, which is why they continually asked the questions.

Six days had passed. On the eve of the seventh, Calyin had sent Midori to check on their progress. Serant pleaded with her to tell Calyin he was fully recovered. Midori knew better; her healing powers were strong, but the internal damage needed time to mend on its own.

The next morning, Captain Brodst tried everything he could think of to convince Isador that Lord Serant was well, but his words were wasted. He had even talked to Calyin who told him her decision was final. The captain dreaded seeing the look on Serant's face when he told him what Calyin had said. He tried to rationalize it by telling himself several times that it was, after all, for the best. Lord Serant must be totally recovered by the next seventh day as they could not afford the risk if he had not fully regained his strength. The kingdom depended on it.

Just as he expected, Lord Serant had an anxious expression on his face, which was readily followed by a frown. "Sorry, I tried, but you know Calyin. Don't worry. I'll come back this evening. I'll sneak a jug in. Okay?" Captain Brodst said with a smile as he gathered the remainder of his things and prepared to leave. He was surprised when he opened the door to find Calyin just about to come in. His face turned red with embarrassment as he walked past. There was nothing he could keep secret from her. He was hoping to be far down the corridor before she could say something to stop him, but he was not so fortunate.

"A jug! Is that all you ever think of? He does not need any of that."

"It is for medicinal purposes."

"I am sure it is. Has a week in bed tried your patience so much?"

Calyin whirled around to face Serant and unleash her disappointment at him. Lord Serant looked to Brodst for some assistance from Calyin's wrath. Captain Brodst was still hoping to sneak out past Calyin, so he offered no help. "Captain Brodst, I wish to talk with you also!" Reluctantly the captain walked back into the room.

"I would like you both to meet Father Joshua. He has just arrived this morning from the priesthood."

For the first time, Lord Serant and Captain Brodst noticed the middle-aged, dark skinned man who stood quietly behind Calyin. Captain

Brodst tried to compare him to other priests he had known, but could not. Father Jacob and Father Francis had been much, much older. This man was younger. He didn't have a gray hair in his curly black locks.

"Welcome, Father Joshua; I am Lord Serant," said Serant as he attempted to stand and shake the father's hand. Father Joshua was quick to move and shook Serant's hand before he could stand. "Yes, I know much about you, my lord. I was born and raised in the Western Territories until the priesthood found me. It is an honor to meet you."

"Good to have you with us, Father Joshua. I am Captain Brodst."

"A pleasure to meet you also, Captain."

The four talked for a time, and then Captain Brodst excused himself. He said he had to catch up on the week's duties; the real reason was that seeing Father Joshua had reminded him of something he had forgotten. He mouthed the words to Serant, "I'll come back later," and winked. Calyin saw the gesture and glared at him as he departed.

Captain Brodst returned to his old quarters and placed his clothes inside. A short time later he found what he was looking for in the eastern tower. "Guard!" he bellowed as he approached, "You will come to attention when I approach!"

The guard, who had been standing watch, instantly snapped to attention. The captain paced back and forth behind him, loudly cracking his heels in the stone. "You are at the wrong post. Do you know what the punishment is?"

A long silence followed. The guard knew better than to speak while at attention without being granted permission. He could not understand why he was being treated thus. He had done nothing wrong. He had only heard the jingle of officer's bells a little too late. He wished he could see the man's face, for he could not recognize the voice.

"About face, Sergeant Brodst!"

"Sergeant—" Pyetr exclaimed as he completed the order, turning to face the captain. His expression changed to one of shock when he saw the broad smile on Captain Brodst's face. Pyetr lowered his head in shame under the captain's gaze.

"I owe you my life and so does Lord Serant. Your deed did not go unnoticed. I know we have had our differences in the past, but I think it is time for a change. Remove that plate and helmet. No sergeant of mine wears that. Go get suitable chain and send someone else to the eastern tower; then return to my office."

"Thank you!" Pyetr said as he bolted away. "No, thank *you*!" shouted Captain Brodst after him. He watched Pyetr retreat along the wall. Seeing Pyetr excited and happy for once made him feel good. It had been so long since he had seen a smile cross his face.

They had not spoken except for official matters for years. He had thought Pyetr had closed him out of his life forever. He was glad to find that he hadn't. His thoughts returned to the time they had last really talked to one another. It had been an argument.

Pyetr had not wanted to serve in the garrison. Captain Brodst had told him he would join just as his own father before him had told him he must do. He had been so determined to force Pyetr into the military that he had ignored the reasons that Pyetr loathed weapons and armor.

The captain's wife, Pyetr's mother, had died by the sword. Captain Brodst recalled the day clearly in his memory. He had heard Pyetr's cries and screams and had come running. He found her with a dagger clutched in her hands. "I am sorry, my husband," she cried as she plunged the dagger up and into her, piercing her heart before the captain could stop her. She had crumpled into his arms, dead before he even caught her. He had never known why she had done it. He could only think of one reason, but he could not believe it. He would not believe it.

From that day on, Pyetr had never spoken again to him. Pyetr, who had been only a child then, and he blamed his mother's death on his father. The two had never spoken again.

Captain Brodst walked back to his office and waited for Pyetr's return. He set aside his other pressing duties and passed the time in reminiscence. The joyous times of the past returned to his mind.

A knock sounded on the door and Pyetr entered. He was outfitted in shining mail and a sparkling red tunic. The captain smiled his approval at Pyetr's choice. Pyetr stood rigidly at attention, awaiting the captain's further orders. Captain Brodst offered him a chair, but Pyetr refused. "I would prefer to stand if the captain does not mind."

Captain Brodst frowned, but agreed. All his hopes that the two would ever communicate like father and son were shattered; still, he held a straight face as he studied Pyetr. Somewhere he would find a spark within Pyetr and he would light it.

"Well, Sergeant, I would like you to begin some extensive training with Swordmaster Timmer. I would also like for you to select a few of the best from the guard and have them also start training with the swordmaster."

"How many is a few, sir?"

"I will leave the decision to your discretion. We lost many of the royal guard when the city was besieged. The gaps need to be refilled. But I want the best. I don't care where you get them as long as they are expert soldiers and trustworthy."

"Yes sir, will we be joining the royal guard then?"

"You're dismissed. I will see you tomorrow morning."

Pyetr turned on his heel and departed. The captain looked around his office. It was the same old place it had always been. The small vacation had been good for him. He left to make his daily rounds and to check on the affairs of the palace. He found to his surprise that everything was in order, which appeared too good to be true.

He returned to his office after an exhausting day of searching for something, anything that was out of place. He found nothing. He was disappointed. He sat at his desk for the remainder of the day, feeling perplexed and dejected.

"Sorry—" said the chancellor, who entered without knocking.

"Chancellor Volnej, it is okay. Come in, come in, you are most welcome."

"Did you find everything satisfactory?"

"Yes, very much so."

"Good! I was hoping you would. Your assistant is a very thorough man."

"Assistant? I don't have an assistant."

"A tall young fellow with brownish hair and green eyes, like yours. He always wears a light helmet and heavy armor like a—"

"Guard?"

"Yes. Like a guard."

"Oh, yes, yes, how silly of me. I remember. It's just that I had just appointed him and after the attack, I forgot. What did you come by for anyway?"

"Actually, I was just looking for my walking stick. I haven't been able to find it all day. I stopped by here yesterday evening, so—oh, there it is—well, I'll leave you to return to your thoughts."

"Good-bye, Chancellor Volnej," said Captain Brodst, already lost in thought. He knew whom the chancellor was referring to; it could have been only one person. He was unsure whether to be angry or happy. He resolved to be confused.

Late in the evening, he went to the kitchen and acquired a jug of ale and headed for Lord Serant's room. He winked to the post guards and rapped lightly on the door. To his surprise, Calyin opened the door. "Why, do come in, Captain Brodst. I was rather expecting you."

The captain quickly sneaked the bottle to one of the guards. Calyin looked puzzled when he walked into the room empty-handed. She could have sworn he had something in his hand.

Captain Brodst stifled a sigh when he saw Calyin's confounded look. He was pleased with himself for getting out of trouble so easily. He was extremely surprised to see that he and Calyin weren't Lord Serant's only late night visitors. Father Joshua, Sister Midori, Sister Catrin, Chancellor Volnej, and Keeper Q'yer were all seated around Lord Serant.

"Don't worry, captain, you didn't miss a thing. Keeper Q'yer arrived only minutes ago. I was going to send for you, but Calyin wouldn't let me," said Lord Serant, smiling slyly.

"Oh, really, I wonder why?"

"She said that you'd be along any moment because Isador saw you pilfering something from the kitchen."

"Me? Certainly not."

"Oh, I agree entirely. I told her drinking was against your ethics."

"Oh yes, I never drink on an empty stomach, never."

"See. I told you Calyin."

The sound of laughter filled the room, chasing away the gloom that had hung over the room a moment before, but it died quickly and was replaced by the same feelings of foreboding. Keeper Q'yer began to tell a story of the past, a story of a great kingdom that had once flourished and spread across the land but was now forever gone, forgotten.

"I have found the object of our search. It was in the first book of Dalphan the Wanderer. Antare was a place, as I had thought. It was only mentioned once in all the tomes of our library. On a single page of Dalphan's book, which read, '...and so we watched our capital burn, Antare it was called. With it died the dreams and hopes of our nation. The fire spread throughout the lands and swallowed them, forever destroying them, returning them to the place from which they were born. It was here at the end, at the gathering, that I betrayed my brothers.' Do you see what is occurring?"

The room was solemnly calm. "The decision of the Council of Keepers was unanimous. We cannot afford the risk. At the end, all things come full circle. We bring our own destruction."

"It is too late, Keeper. It has already been set in motion."

"Do you speak the words of the Mother or do you really wish it so?"

"Midori speaks those words truthfully. She is quite correct. I can feel it as does she. It will be here that the paths converge. We cannot stop it."

"Are you both mad? There is time, I tell you!"

"Let's discuss this rationally, Keeper Q'yer, Father Joshua, Sister Midori. We know what will take place. We can direct our efforts toward a logical solution."

"There is no logic in nature, Lord Serant."

"If I may interrupt, I agree with Lord Serant. If we plan this correctly, there must be a way out; as you said there is no logic in nature, and I well know there cannot be good without evil, so there must be a way out. We will have to find it."

"Definitely, Captain, well spoken! We know all the facts from the past. We can learn from our ancestors' mistakes. Let's just follow the facts step by step and guide ourselves through them. We will prove we have learned something in two thousand years."

13

"You really should start eating your food. It is quite delicious."

Valam looked down at his plate for the first time since he and Tsandra had begun their conversation. Valam thought, "How can I talk and eat at the same time?"

He had not expected a response, but Tsandra gave him one anyway. "Quite simply, just like this. You can think with your mouth full, can't you?" Tsandra stated the question sincerely, but Valam thought it was a joke. He almost choked on his food before he gulped down a glass of wine. "I guess you can't," commented Tsandra as she watched him.

The remainder of the meal proceeded without conversation. Valam was embarrassed to find Seth and Evgej staring at him as he finally took in their presence and that of everyone else around him again. When the dinner assemblage broke up, Valam almost expected Tsandra to come over and talk to him, but she didn't. In silence, he walked beside Evgej from the hall, with Cagan, Seth, and Liyan not far behind.

"The war still seems so very distant," said Valam as he stopped mid-stride, "so different."

"Yes, at times I even wonder if it exists, yet I know it does," answered Seth.

They slowly, subconsciously, walked towards the balcony they had occupied earlier in the evening, while they talked.

"Tomorrow also seems so distant. Do you think we will be able to reach Keeper Martin and Father Jacob?"

"Yes. We will reach them. Our outposts tell us that King Mark's forces have not yet passed the Western Ranges. They and the plains are still the boundaries that separate us. If your men have indeed landed on the position Brother Seth chose, they should be well away from the mountains. We have sent our scouts out all along the coast. We will receive word soon."

"This King Mark you speak of. He is the one that completed the journey?"

"No it was Sathar."

"Then why does the enemy align under King Mark if Sathar is the true leader?"

Liyan looked to Seth questioningly and directed to only him and Cagan, "You did not tell them?" Seth shook his head solemnly. Liyan then looked to Cagan, who repeated Seth's gesture of no. Liyan's heart sank as he fought an inner battle. He had to tell them, but something stopped him, held him back from saying anything further.

"It is all right, Brother Liyan." The voice came from behind them. It fell crisply, beautifully into the air of the night. Valam heard the voice and turned, his heart racing. It was not the one he thought of. All eyes moved to stare upon the radiance of the Queen-Mother.

"My Queen-Mother," said Seth quickly. He looked around for her normal entourage of escorts, but she was alone. He gasped aloud, "My Queen you should not be alone."

"Shh," she said, taking a seat next to him. "I will tell you of Sathar and the dark journey. I know much of your kind, Prince Valam." The Queen-Mother paused to choose her words carefully, yet simply. "In your Great Kingdom, who do men follow? They follow other men, do they not? What do they fight for?" She paused again to let Valam consider her words. "They fight for their beliefs, do they not? Their beliefs come from their God, do they not? King Mark is just a tool. He is the one that our enemy gathers under, but Sathar is the one they fight for. Do you understand?" Valam felt the words fall upon him. He fully understood them, though he wished he did not. "What, then, is the dark journey?" he began to think. Before the words escaped his lips, the Queen-Mother answered his question. "It is a passage to a plane in opposition to our own. As ours exists in life, it exists in death. One who completes the journey now lives in both worlds, neither dead nor alive."

She continued, "How can we defeat him, you want to ask. The final words of the prophecy answer that question. When he that is cursed finds his way back from the dark journey, the end of all we have known is finally upon us. Only from our vigilance in the watch shall we learn of his return. Only with our knowledge shall we have the means to defeat him. But only through our faith shall we truly overcome him at the last."

The word faith rang through their minds endlessly. The Queen-Mother paused for a moment and then began again, "We must also understand the entire message of the prophecy. As I have previously stated, the mistakes of the past will not be repeated. During the Blood Wars the original writings of the prophet were thought lost. They were not."

"You have them?" screamed Valam, anger etched deeply into the pulsing veins of his face. Evgej also felt the rush of anger within him. "That reaction is the exact reason we have kept it secret for so long. When you hear the rest of my words you will understand. It was for the good of all that we have kept their existence a secret even amongst our own people. Only the great council and I, and now you, know the truth."

The same thoughts filled Evgej and Valam's minds. They began to look around the balcony and the surrounding area. "Do not worry. My thoughts only go as far as your minds. No one else can hear my words. Brother Seth and Brother Liyan maintain a thought barrier encircling us all. There is nothing to fear. Portions of the prophecy that were restored are incomplete. Several key paragraphs were deleted when it was rescribed. How? Ask the questions of your mind, but the answer is unimportant. The gift had to be so delicately balanced that it could not give one side of the struggle an advantage. It contained clues of equal value for both sides if they would heed the warning. The two paths have run parallel throughout time, both in equal balance with each other. They will converge at the time marked. The end will become the beginning and the beginning will become the end. All of this you know, but the secret we have preserved is who they are. The majority of the prophecy speaks of how he will return amongst us. He that has surpassed the dark journey. He that is evil will bring the past with the future. But the last lines of the paragraph read: he that was formed from the vortex of three shall also return. One shall raise the banner of the east. One shall raise the banner of the west. Together they shall rule over all. The next paragraph you should also know well. It is the curse of the prophecy. Evil works in many types of shading. Their union cannot be stopped. They will return through their dark magic. They are the harbingers of death and destruction. This is their curse. The last lines should have been this. The child that is yet to be, child of east and west, is the bearer of light and remembrance, and in him, child of past and present, the bearer of darkness will come full circle in the end. He, the bringer of death, child of darkness, also hides the angel of life and the key. He is the third."

Valam had spent months studying the prophecy and the related writings in his youth. Anger surged through him as he silently shouted these words within his mind, "Why have you brought us here? You did not need us!!"

"But Prince Valam, we do need you!" said the Queen-Mother sorrowfully. For Valam it was the second time he had shared her deep feelings of remorse and sorrow. This time, however, the tears flowed from his eyes, not hers.

"We need time. We must find the other; we will bring the child of the future to him."

"I still don't understand why you needed us to come here."

"Let me re-read this line to you so that you may understand. The child that is yet to be, heir of east and west, is the bearer of light and remembrance. We need *you*, Valam."

"Are you serious? Then why did all the others have to come? They shall die for nothing. They have traveled all this way for nothing."

"It is not for nothing. You have arrived here safely—that is what matters."

"Me?"

"We could not take the risk that a lone ship would be caught. Do you recall the storm that brought your ship to us?"

"No!" cried Valam, "Oh, Father, No! What of those that died on the journey and those that will die in the fields?"

"They have passed for a greater cause. It was the only way. If I could have made the journey I would have, but I could not leave. Sathar would have sensed it. He would have sent everything against us. We at least have hope now."

Valam sat quietly thinking and staring into the darkness of the night. Seth felt sorry for his friend; it had to be. He could sense the mixed feelings of those present. He nodded to Cagan and Evgej and they followed his lead from the balcony. Valam and the Queen-Mother were alone.

The Queen-Mother stood and stared at Valam. She studied him from his jet-black hair down past his broad shoulders to his muscular arms. She could sense the feelings within him and understood them. "Valam," she said as she seated herself next to him, "they are not here for nothing. We also need them. The capital cannot fall until after the child is born. We will do everything we can to see that it doesn't. Our child is the child yet to be. Do you not understand?"

For the first time Valam fully comprehended the actions that would follow. He, too, could sense emotions within her. "But I do not love you. How could I? How could I?"

"How could you father a child? Easier than you would think. I know the feelings you seek to hide. Do not hide them. Allow them to come."

"You are the Queen-Mother. How can you?"

"I do what I must. You judge too harshly. I have love within me for all things, for everyone. I can see feelings of love within you. Yes, Tsandra is beautiful and perfect and you feel sorrow for her for reasons you cannot understand, but where lie your real thoughts, whom do you compare her to, for whom do you secretly yearn? The thoughts in your own mind do not lie."

She grasped Valam firmly by the hand and led him from the balcony. "I still do not understand. Why me?"

"You are the first heir to the throne of the Great Kingdom, and I am Queen of the East. I have seen you in my many dreams, Valam. I have seen you and me together. I have seen our child, the child that is yet to be."

The Queen-Mother led him along many long corridors. Finally, they came to a long, narrow staircase along one of the tiny back hallways. The stairs were steep and seemed to wind their way forever upward.

Together they climbed. The Queen-Mother climbed backwards, staring deeply into Valam's eyes. She held both of his hands warmly within her own, weaving an intricate, sensuous pattern with her forefingers in his palms.

Valam was still having difficulty dealing with the reality of the situation. It seemed like a dream to him, a very wonderful dream. He began to wonder if he were, in fact, dreaming. "You are not dreaming, my prince," came the melodic whisper into his mind.

As they climbed, Valam felt the sensation of movement beneath his feet, as if the tower were swaying back and forth, ushering them upward. He could feel a breeze gently blowing; the air, though cool, was warm and soothing to his skin.

The staircase ended in a small alcove with no apparent door. Valam started to yell a warning as the queen backed into the wall, but the wall faded as she stepped into it. The room on the other side was plush and richly decorated. The queen softly pulled Valam over to the large westerly window. The view from the pinnacle was breathtaking. He could look out across the whole of the city all the way to the eastern gates.

The sun hanging on the far horizon added to the impact of the view. The two stood tightly pressed against each other and watched with wonder the beautiful, simple spectacle of the setting sun.

A blanket of darkness swept over the room as the last shadows of daylight dimmed from the sky. Gradually, caressingly, the Queen-Mother moved her lips to Valam's. Their lips remained locked as they slowly sank to the floor.

The wildness and warmth of passion began to carry them away. All worries about today or tomorrow were gone. They were in a world of their own creation. They alone dwelt on its shores. They alone drank in its captivating spell.

The two became one in thought and body. Their dreams and wishes flowed freely between them, surrounding and protecting them. They shed their inner light and became themselves. The Queen-Mother became nothing but a woman and the prince became nothing but a man. They were a man and a woman entangled and united in each other's caresses and affections.

They awoke in each other's arms to the sounds of a clear, beautiful day.

Valam stared into the queen's liquid blue eyes. She stared back into his. They shared one last moment in each other's warmth. Valam kissed her deeply and passionately, then stood and put on his clothes. The Queen-Mother got out of bed and dressed also.

Valam watched her silken beauty with admiration, as she admired him. Sunlight poured through an eastern window. Valam took her hand and they went to the window to welcome the coming day. The scene was as beautiful as the previous day's sunset.

"How long will it be before you find out if you are with child? Maybe it was not the correct time?" said Valam, hoping, searching for anything to prevent the inevitable. "I am the Queen-Mother. If I wish for a child, it will be. It is. The time is when I wish it. I can feel the life begin."

"Are you sure?"

"Yes, quite."

"Then it is over."

"Yes, it is."

In that twinkling, the inevitable had arrived. She became the queen, and he became the prince. He was Prince Valam of the Great Kingdom, and she was the Queen-Mother of the Eastern Reaches. Valam turned from the window and walked to the stairs. He did not look back as he descended.

The Queen-Mother watched him leave within her mind. She did not have to look to see him go; she knew he had. She continued to stare out the window at the dawning day, hiding her sorrow in the alleys of her mind.

Her thoughts began to waver and fade. Emotions within her churned with a torrent of rage and wildness unknown to her. An image slowly formed in her mind's eye. She was with Valam as he wound his way downwards from the tower and into the adjacent hall.

Valam aimlessly strolled down many halls, finally finding Evgej's room. He knocked and then entered. Evgej was startled as Valam walked in; he awoke and dressed just moments before Valam arrived.

Evgej misread the expression on Valam's face and asked him how the night had gone. Valam's answer was a scowl. Evgej was lost in confusion. He had understood what the queen had asked Valam, or at least he thought he did. "How could anyone be in such a mood after that? It was a dream come true," he said to himself.

He replayed the events in his mind. He was sure that he had understood completely. "Hey, Valam, I'm famished. Let's go get something to eat."

"I'm not really hungry. I'll go with you anyway. We have a lot to prepare with Seth so we can leave today."

"Leave today? Why? We can wait for a couple more days."

"No. We have an obligation to fulfill, and I am hungry after all. Let's go and eat, then we can find Seth," added Valam quickly, to change the subject.

After they had both eaten, they went in search of Seth. They could not understand where everyone had gone. The great hall was empty. In the kitchens there were only the cooks and no help.

They went first to Seth and Cagan's quarters to find no one there. They looked everywhere, and came up empty. As they returned to the first floor, they heard sounds from outside. Valam rushed to the nearest window and peered out.

What he saw astounded him—a virtual sea of brown. The brown robes filled the courtyards as far as he could see. He strained his neck out the window to the left and the right. The view was the same.

Valam grabbed Evgej and pulled him to the window. Evgej gaped in awe. "Let's get down there quick," said Valam. With Evgej immediately behind him, he raced through the corridors toward the outer doors.

The two stopped dead as they rounded a corner into the audience hall. It was filled with those of Seth's order, standing rigidly facing the outer doors. Evgej spotted Seth at the fore of the group and pointed to him.

"Seth, what is it? What is happening?"

Seth pretended not to notice their presence. Valam and Evgej approached him, yelling his name and still he did not move from his position or acknowledge them. "In the name of the Father, Seth, what is it?"

"See for yourself," said Seth, opening one of the great doors slightly.

"Yes, I have seen them. Why are they here?"

"They are here because of the Queen-Mother."

"Why, though? What is happening?"

"You cannot see. It is brother against brother. Tsandra has called them here."

"Tsandra?"

"Yes, Tsandra."

"Where is she? I will talk to her. She will listen to me."

"She is out there," answered Seth pointing into the crowd, "She will not listen to you."

"Why does she do this?"

"The Queen-Mother is in Shalan's tower. She will not come out. Tsandra says she has seen a vision, that the Queen-Mother was hurt and crying. Crying out for help."

"Just tell her the Queen-Mother isn't hurt, that she is perfectly fine."

"If it were that simple, believe me, I would have already done that. It is not that simple. She thinks someone has injured the queen."

"Where is the Queen-Mother?"

"She is in the tower."

"Why haven't you sent for her?"

"Valam, as I stated before, the solution is not simple. No one is allowed in the tower but the Queen-Mother."

"I was in the tower! I will go to her."

"Valam, no! Don't ever say that again. You couldn't have been in that tower. Only the Queen-Mother can enter or leave it."

"It is just a tower, a pile of stone, Seth, think—"

"Valam, no! It is not just a pile of stone. It is the symbol of our people. It is the heart and soul of our kind. Only the Queen-Mother can enter the heart and soul of her people. Even my thoughts cannot reach her inside the tower. There she is closer to the Father and Mother. Our combined wills could not reach her."

"Nonsense! I will go and talk to Tsandra."

"No, Valam," yelled Seth as Valam plunged through the door. "It is you that Tsandra seeks to punish. It was you she saw injure the queen. It is you I protect."

Evgej followed close behind Valam out the door. Valam ran down the stairs and straight into the crowd. Evgej attempted to stop him, but it was too late; he could only follow Valam into the midst of the brown clad warriors.

"Tsandra, no. You are wrong. It is a mistake!" shouted Valam. Tsandra screamed out with her mind and pointed to Valam. The crowd descended upon him. Evgej and Valam stood back to back, fending off the crowd, and for a moment they stood gallant; then they were swallowed by a wave of bodies.

Seth was halfway out the door to aid Valam and Evgej when he heard Tsandra's invocation. He challenged with one of his own, but it was too late. He saw the mob engulf the two. Seth screamed out to his order and they followed him without hesitation into the brown.

The two forces clashed. A small red tide swept into an ocean of brown. It was brother against brother. Seth continued to cry out to Tsandra; she would not answer his pleas.

An explosion rocked the courtyard. All quarreling stopped. All eyes turned to look upon Shalan's tower as it disintegrated before their eyes. The heart and soul of the people was forever gone. They began to look around to one another, realizing what they had done. They were horrified.

A star of energy descended upon the crowd. It soared to the spot where Valam lay. The mass made room for it, creating a wide circle around the fallen two. The light cleared and took on form; it became the queen.

"Oh Father, Mother! What have I done?" cried the Queen-Mother into the gathered minds. "Samyuehl!" she pleaded. "Samyuehl, come quickly." She knelt beside Valam and took his hand to her wet cheeks.

"What have I done?" echoed Tsandra. She removed her dagger from its sheath and held it to her breast. "Gather me home, Father," she said, plunging the blade inward.

"Tsandra, no, don't!" shouted Seth as he leapt upon her. He thrust his will into her mind and she released her grasp on the dagger. It fell harmlessly to the ground. Seth firmly held Tsandra's arms as she struggled to attain freedom. He held her until she stopped trying to resist, whispering thoughts silently into her mind to calm her.

An opening cleared as a man in blue rushed into the courtyard. He moved tall and proud for a man of his years. His features spoke of one cold as steel, but his heart spoke of one tender and kind.

"Is it too late?"

"No, my queen," simply answered Samyuehl. He closed his mind and concentrated his thoughts. He gathered them into a whirlwind and hurled them out into the land, performing a feat that only he could do. He was Samyuehl, first of the order of the Blue. His powers of healing were equaled by none save the Mother-Earth.

Throughout time, the gift had been passed from heir to heir and so the gift was preserved. He was the conduit of life for his land and his people. His powers were created and joined from that life. He drank it in and formed it within him. He guided it through his center outward.

A ray of light radiated from him onto Valam and Evgej. It encompassed them and soothed them. The color returned to their limp bodies. Their many lacerations and bruises began to mend as their spilled blood returned to its proper place within them.

The light intensified and the wounds were gone. Their lives were restored. All was as it should be. Tsandra stopped resisting Seth and faced her mistake. Her great devotion to the queen had led her from the true path. She would never allow herself to make such a mistake again. She would re-earn the respect of her followers, and she would regain the wisdom of her position. She would carry this incident within her as a banner against those who were the true enemies of her kind.

Valam was the first to open his eyes. He rested his eyes on the Queen-Mother and smiled. Slowly his lips moved, though no sound escaped them. Several times, they formed these words, "I am sorry, my love." His eyes closed as his lips ceased to move.

Evgej eased to a sitting position and shook his head warily from side to side. When his vision cleared, he stood and turned to Valam to help him up. In one beat of his heart, his mouth fell open in shock and he picked Valam up in his arms and cradled him closely.

"Oh, no, no!" he yelled, "Oh please, someone help him." He looked first to Seth and upon seeing the sorrow in his eyes then turned pleading to the Queen-Mother. Reflected in her eyes was the solemn harsh truth. Evgej crumpled sadly to the ground. After a long period of lament, he released Valam's body. He stood and with his eyes downcast marched angrily from the square.

Seth wanted to stop Evgej and console him, telling him Valam would be happier now, more than he could ever have been here in this existence, yet he could not and did not try to comfort him. Seth hoped that through time Evgej would grow to understand that when it is truly your time you have no choice but to transpire, for it is the Father's wish.

As Seth thought about the new life Valam would find with the Father, old thoughts returned to his mind, thoughts he had thought were long gone; the guilt still remained within him. He thought of a face, bringing a tear to his eye. In the twisting of a fleeting moment he was both elated and sad, angry and glad. He hoped the Father had found special places for the two who were so dear in his heart, and somewhere in the reaches of his mind he knew that they had.

Seth suddenly realized Tsandra had left his side. He scanned the courtyard and spotted her retreating form. He turned to the Queen-Mother and before he could think of what to say, she whispered into his mind, "Yes, go and talk with her. She will need your strength."

Seth hastily departed. He found Tsandra a short while later in her quarters. She did not look surprised when he entered. She had known he would try to stop her from doing what she had already set in motion.

Seth searched his heart for the correct words to say to Tsandra. It was from the depths of his soul that he began. His words echoed the teachings they both knew so well. The entire time he retold Tsandra the teachings of one's passage through existence, in his mind he returned to the pretenses of his youth.

"Brother, what are the basic premises of life we must follow?"

"Not to interfere with its progression. We can guide, but we cannot hinder its natural path."

"Yes, brother, as in all things we must return to the basic laws of life. What is the first law of life?"

"To preserve what Mother-Earth has created."

"Yes, but you have grown beyond the simple teachings. Define preservation."

"It is to allow life to continue along the path that it must follow from one existence to the next."

"Which leads us to the second law of life."

"Yes, teacher. The second law does allow us to give guidance."

"Think not with your mind, brother, think with your soul, wherein lies the will of the Father. Where must one create the border between guidance and interference?"

"When you know it in your heart to be wrong, it is wrong."

"Yes, you are learning well."

Seth returned from his reverie within himself. The words he found were somehow disturbing to him, for they were not what he really wanted to tell Tsandra. Learning from his very words, Seth knew that what he said was wrong. Tsandra was not the one who needed to gain insight on the lessons of life; he was the one.

"Tsandra, I am—" Seth stopped mid-sentence and the remainder of what he was going to say was lost to him. Unconsciously, he took her hand and held it tightly between both of his. As he did, he remembered a solemn pledge he had given that he had long since discarded. A pledge he had given to himself and for Galan.

He recalled the advice an old and trusted friend and mentor had given him. Liyan had shown him the foolishness and futility of his action. Seth set about to show Tsandra the same. After he was finished, there was a long pause. They both sat in silence, contemplating thoughts entirely their own, and then without a word they returned to the courtyard.

When they returned, they found even more people had filed into the yard. Brother Ylad', Brother Nikol, Brother Ontyv, Brother Samyuehl, and the Queen-Mother were all gathered on the platform. The first impression Seth gleaned from their collective minds was one of puzzlement.

For a time before they reached the platform, neither Seth nor Tsandra understood the calamity. When they joined the group that surrounded Valam's body, they understood. Tsandra's heart fell when she looked upon Valam. She did not understand why the Mother had not reclaimed his body; somehow she felt responsible for what was occurring.

"Brother Seth, you amongst us know more about man. Do you know why Valam's body still remains?"

"I am unsure, my queen. Shall I find Evgej? He will know."

"No. He needn't be disturbed. Brother Liyan is just returning from the docks with Cagan. Go and talk with them."

Seth marched briskly to the docks. As he approached, Cagan's boat was just returning. Cagan tossed Seth a line with a broad grin on his face. Seth secured the line tightly. Liyan and Cagan jumped onto the dock, the expression on their faces that of a child being caught doing something he knows he is not supposed to do. Their smiles were rapidly erased by the overpowering sense of confused emotions rising within Seth.

Before the question reached Seth's mind, he responded, "It is Valam. He has passed. It is like a living dream." Further words escaped Seth. He paused and grasped their hands to form a link between their minds and his; then he replayed the scene for them.

The expression that crossed their faces told of the grief and shock they were feeling. Seth broke the link, and the vision faded from their thoughts. "What has transpired in our absence, Brother Seth? How can this be? We do not quarrel amongst ourselves. We do not kill our ow—" Brother Liyan stopped suddenly. His eyes grew wide and then he suddenly yelled, "Come quickly, we must find the Queen-Mother. We must find her now, before it is too late."

Liyan then shielded his thoughts and whispered into Cagan's and Seth's minds what he had felt. Before Seth could shield his mind, he too felt the dark presence sweep by. Instantly he reacted and unleashed all the energy he could gather into a burst of speed as he ran back towards the square.

14

After they walked for some time without incident, Nijal finally dared to break the silence. He whispered to Vilmos, "Why don't we just do that illusion thing again and walk back through the city and get some horses?"

It took Vilmos a moment to snap out of his reverie and realize the voice had not emanated from his mind. "I don't know, but that is a good question." The two broke from their position in the middle of the group and dropped back to talk to Xith, who was taking up the rear position.

"Yes?" asked Xith quizzically when he saw them slow down so he would catch up to them. "We were wondering, why don't we just disguise ourselves and go back to the city or somewhere and get horses?"

"The main reason is that Noman and I fear that it will give away our position and lead the dark forces to us."

"But how?"

"Yes, how?"

"Shh. Remember back in the caves when I made the passage through the wall?"

"Yes, but what significance is that?"

"Noman and I long discussed how they had found us, and the only logical conclusion was the magic he and I used. There was no other way. Vilmos, you should understand. How does one use magic?"

"You reach back into the power of creation and guide it through your center."

"Exactly, but if someone else also understood the workings of magic, they could detect where the energy was being focused, especially since an illusion requires constant guidance and continues for very long periods of time."

"But I thought no one else could use magic?"

"Remember the dark forces that attacked the City of the Sky? Evil like that was created from the wild energies. They are closer to it. That is how they could detect it." Xith had told a partial lie to Vilmos and Nijal, for which he was sorry. He convinced himself it was for the best, and by saying it aloud, it was also based partially on truth.

"How did you create the passage through the rocks? Is this not a good time to talk about it?"

"Oh, it is, all right. I was only lost a second in reflection. What are the two opposing forces in nature?"

"Positive and negative," Vilmos answered.

"Yes, they are the very root of the two forces; the basis for all forms of opposition springs from these two forces. All things in nature contain and are joined by these forces. Some things are truly positive and others are truly negative like raw energy in its pure form. The rock of the wall is no exception to this rule. It, too, contains the energy. To fully understand how the principle works, you must also know that all things are created from the four basic elements: earth, water, fire and air. In all of these four groups, positive and negative exist in equal proportions. In the element earth, the other three elements must also exist to some extent, for it could not exist without its brothers in opposition; thus from the two very basic forms, positive and negative, stem the elements of earth, water, fire, and air. To walk through the stone of the wall, which belongs to the element earth, I relied on those other elements that exist within the stone, the air primarily. I opened the way and guided our friends through it to us."

Many expressions passed across Vilmos' face as comprehension came to him. Nijal's expression remained one of perplexity. Xith smiled as he watched the two. He hadn't expected Nijal to grasp the fullness of what he had said, but he had hoped that Vilmos would. He was most pleased with the results; Vilmos understood.

Vilmos and Nijal returned to their positions in the march, leaving Xith alone at the rear. Noman led them all through the long night. He was very thankful for the overcast skies that enshrouded their movements.

It was almost dawn when they reached a small town far along the northern road. He knew the farming town well. He had passed through here on many a dark night, ages before.

He stopped just short of the village and allowed the others to catch up to him. "We shall rest here for a time. Hopefully, we will be able to get horses and leave just short of nightfall. When we reach the inn, allow Xith and me to do all the talking and follow our lead. We are mercenaries heading to the Barrens. Vilmos, it was you who lost our mounts through carelessness. Do not worry. They will see Adrina as our baggage, nothing more. Remember, mercenaries are a loud lot. We must act the part. We will go to our rooms; I will go last. Amir, you will bring Adrina up to the rooms immediately and remain there."

They all nodded agreement. Noman closed his eyes and formed a picture in his mind. He wasn't surprised that the local inn still stood in the same place along the tiny dirt road. They entered, following Noman's lead of grumbling and complaining about sore feet and the like.

Noman dumped some coins on the innkeeper's counter and demanded some rooms for him and his companions. Amir followed Noman's instructions and went upstairs to the rooms the innkeeper had given them. "And give me four tankards of ale and something to eat—quickly!" said Noman, taking a seat at the nearest table.

Vilmos had never had ale before. He wondered if he would like it; nonetheless, he was looking forward to trying it. The innkeeper soon brought over four steaming pints. "Nothing like warm ale to put me to sleep!" bellowed Xith. He and Noman toasted and brought the tankards to their lips. "Ahh!" they both said at once, setting down the empty containers.

"Stew and bread is all I have at this hour," said the innkeeper as he placed four large bowls of stew and some chunks of bread on the table. No one offered any complaints as they eagerly ate the food. It didn't matter if it was tasty or not, just as long as it was warm and filling.

Vilmos was the first to finish eating. He sponged up the remainder in his bowl with some bread and reached for his tankard, only to find it missing. Xith winked at him and slurped the drink down loudly. "You will learn soon, lad," said Xith, burping and leaving the table.

Vilmos dejectedly stared into the mug. He was surprised to find it still contained some ale. He smiled broadly and drank it quickly. It had indeed tasted good. A warming sensation swept over him, and he felt sleepy. He decided that he did like ale, very much so. He retired a few minutes after Xith had.

Nijal and Noman finished their stew and ordered another round of drink. The second glass went down as smoothly as the first had. The two stomped heavily up the stairs slightly before the first lights of morning appeared.

A chill swept over Vilmos. He awoke cold and frightened. All thoughts of sleep were scattered into the coolness of the air. The dreams had returned again with increased intensity. They ran through all the corridors of his mind. He could not escape their wrath.

He cradled himself tightly, easing away his inner shivers. He looked around the room. His eyes slowly adjusted to the darkness before he could see. No one else was in the room with him. He was alone.

Alone, he confronted the wildness in his mind retrospectively. He closed his eyes and focused on his inner self. He found his center; it could not be denied him. He remembered the lessons Xith had taught him. They seemed like distant memories as he replayed them in his mind.

He saw the conquest of his self from the two. He saw them through the eyes of another, though they were his own. He saw what he had become, what he was.

The battle of the City of the Sky exploded through his soul. The vision ended with the fall of the two, first sons of the Father. They had left his dreams. They were only memories. They existed no longer. Once the summation overtook him, his mind became his own. He had succeeded in controlling the power within. It retreated into the recesses of his intellect.

Vilmos forced his eyes open. As he focused the blurriness away, he thought he saw someone standing before him, a large, hulking figure with a golden locket in his outstretched hand, but when his eyes cleared, there was no one there. He was still alone.

He wondered what time it was. Was it day or night? He felt as if he had slept forever, so it must be night. "But where is everyone?" he asked himself, standing and looking for a window. He found it and pulled back the curtain. It was pitch-black dark out.

"Damn, I wish I could see something," whispered Vilmos. The lamp near his bed blazed alight. He whirled around and stared at it. It had lit by itself. "Strange," thought Vilmos.

He stood there staring at it, wondering how it had happened. "Off," he whispered and the lamplight dimmed and was gone. He laughed loudly, darkly, to himself. "On!" The lamp blazed again. He played with it for a time, lighting it, extinguishing it, back and forth.

Something inside him enjoyed the tiny display of power. Vilmos knew what the something was and forced his mind to quit. It was only then that he came to fully understand how he had subconsciously lit the lamp. He remembered well the skill that Xith had taught him.

He had unknowingly divided his thoughts. All his concentration had been trained on his dilemma. Lighting the lamp required no concentration, so it required little thought. Now that he understood how he could do it, it didn't frighten him so much.

"Wait a minute!" he yelled within. His cogitations were playing tricks on him. As he screamed, all thought came to an abrupt halt. It was then that Vilmos noticed that he had been levitating off the floor because he fell heavily along with all the furniture in the room.

The crash resounded throughout the room. The door opened quickly and Xith, followed by Amir and Nijal, ran into the room. Amir had his blade drawn and cast his eyes frantically back and forth. "Everything is all right. I just fell out of bed," said Vilmos rubbing his head. Seeing Xith's steely stare, Vilmos quickly added, "Yeah, and I hit my head on the corner table and it fell over too. What time is it anyway?"

"Late afternoon."

"Afternoon? Why is it so dark out?"

"The windows are coaled over."

"Oh, why did you let me sleep, if you are all awake?"

"You ask too many questions. Come on, there is food in the other room."

"Great! I am famished."

Vilmos wolfed down two bowls of stew and a loaf of bread before he stopped and caught his breath. He washed it down with a large mug of watered ale. "Yuck!" said Vilmos as he emptied the tankard, "More water than ale." Xith smiled and said, "It is the drink afternoons are made of so one can continue to drink in the evening." "Oh," responded Vilmos, pretending to understand, though he really hadn't.

Nijal and Amir returned to their swordplay. Amir was teaching Nijal how to defend himself better. "You see, your attack is good, very good, but you constantly leave yourself open," said Amir parrying and thrusting. His blade stopped just short of Nijal's belly. "No man can keep up with your speed, Amir," pleaded Nijal.

"No man, indeed!" exclaimed Amir, looking to his ancient compatriot. "Speed isn't everything; skill is."

Vilmos watched the two with amusement for a time and then became bored. He let his attention wander to Xith and Noman. They were in the opposite corner of the quarters, talking quietly. Adrina lay in the bed nearest to them. She appeared so pale and lifeless, thought Vilmos. He felt sorrow for her.

Vilmos joined Xith and Noman. They were so heavily engaged in conversation that they barely registered his presence. He sat with them for a spell and listened. The topic of their words was lost on him; all his attention was somewhere else.

He turned and peered at Adrina's form. Unconsciously, he stood and walked over to her. He sat beside her on the bed. Her warmth reassured him; she was indeed alive.

Vilmos took one of her hands in his two and held it. A tear rolled down his cheek. He pictured the other who had died to save her. To Vilmos, they were both so beautiful and pure. He hated those who had attacked them. He loathed them with all that he was. He wished Adrina were conscious and well again.

He brought her hand to his cheek. The water of his tears touched her hand. Vilmos took her hand to his lips and kissed it gently, then stood and walked away from her.

He went back to watch Amir and Nijal. They were still hacking at each other. Nijal was clearly exhausted; Amir had barely broken a sweat. As Vilmos watched, he could see the frustrations build up in Nijal. He could also see that Nijal's swordplay was improving.

Amir also saw the improvements in Nijal and continued to pummel Nijal's senses. Although Nijal's energy was spent, still he would not quit. He had never been one to give up. Only determination maintained the movement of his arm, his blade blocking and striking.

"Your power is your persistence, my friend. It is good," stated Amir. He held his blade outward and still. "We shall rest now."

"Good. I'm tired," said Nijal sheathing his sword. He wearily sat next to Vilmos, toweling the sweat from his body with his tunic. Amir seated himself across from Nijal and Vilmos with a pleased expression on his face.

"I am starving!" said a sweet voice behind them. All eyes in the room turned to look astounded to the source of the voice, with one exception. Vilmos didn't look, because he wasn't surprised. He knew this would happen. He had wanted it to happen.

Adrina brushed the sleep from her eyes, sat up, and yawned. "Where are we? Am I home?" Her eyes cleared; and as she searched around the room, she knew she wasn't home. "What happened?" she asked, her voice shaking with fear.

"Everything is just fine. Here, eat this, Adrina," offered Noman. He watched her devour the food before he told her anything further. "You do not recollect what occurred? The tunnel, the attack."

"No. I remember Galan; where is she? Is she all right?"

"The 'Little One' has passed."

"No! It cannot be!" yelled Adrina throwing the bowl to the floor and jumping out of bed. Noman was quick to catch her as her leg collapsed under her weight. Noman placed her gently back onto the bed.

Her screams renewed as she looked down at her broken leg. "Where is she? Oh, my leg, it hurts," she cried pitifully. It was then that she noticed the pain in her crumpled hand also. Her tears increased in velocity as they streamed down her face.

"She has passed, Adrina. She has fulfilled her service. She rests with the Great-Father now, in peace."

Adrina didn't offer a reply. She wept in silence, her tears for a lost friend. With her good hand, she absent-mindedly rubbed the dragon mark on her stomach, the food had settled warmly. "Will it be all right?" she said suddenly, wildly.

"Yes, rest easy."

"The pain. It will not go. Please help me," Adrina cried out.

Vilmos could not take her cries any longer. He ran over to the bed where she lay. Without hesitation or thought, he touched her leg with his hands. He ran them along her leg from toe to hip back and forth. Adrina's screams of agony intensified. "Stop, Stop!" she yelled.

"Vilmos, stop! You're hurting her. Stop," Noman, Xith, Nijal and Amir urged. Vilmos did not heed their pleas. He continued his actions. Noman attempted to pull Vilmos away, but he could not. Vilmos knocked him to the ground.

Noman stood, and together he and Xith grabbed Vilmos and tried to force him away from Adrina, but could not. Vilmos latched on to Adrina even tighter as they sought to pry him away. Amir and Nijal ran across the room. Nijal leapt upon Vilmos and knocked him sprawling to the floor.

Vilmos rolled and knocked Nijal from on top of him. He stood and reached for Adrina. He grabbed her broken hand in his and caressed it. Amir gripped Vilmos by the waist with both hands and swung him high in the air with his mighty arms until Vilmos was forced to release Adrina's hand.

Amir carried Vilmos to the opposite side of the room and set him down on the floor. "Are you mad?" he asked. For an instant Vilmos cowered from Amir's towering form, then he stood. His eyes were wild and staring. His body shook convulsively. "You dare to interfere with me? You shall pay for this quite dearly."

Amir watched Vilmos, quite confounded. He was unsure what to do. The others rushed over to his assistance. They all stood and watched. "You dare to interfere?" Vilmos repeated. "Watch!" he exclaimed. He created a bolt of white energy between his hands. It flashed so brightly that they shielded their eyes from it. The light even hurt Amir's senses in a way he could not understand. Xith took a step towards Vilmos. "Don't move again, old man!"

"Vilmos, it is I, Xith. Don't do this. Find the control and use it; don't let it control you."

"Me?" interrupted Vilmos. "Don't let it control me? It does not. I control it, you foolish old man. Watch, as your paltry comprehension of the forces of nature are torn asunder."

In his left hand a blazing blue light glowed. It danced around his fingers. His right hand was consumed by swirls of red energy. "You see, teacher. On this hand we have positive; on this we have negative," said Vilmos madly.

"Vilmos, don't!"

"Don't what? Do this?" cackled Vilmos bringing his hands together. The others gripped themselves for the end they knew would come when Vilmos joined the two forces. The end did not come.

They watched in amazed horror as the two forces dazzled in unison all around Vilmos' hands. The energy spread to his arms and body. It seemed to grow with each passing second until it consumed all of Vilmos, save for his face.

"Vilmos, it is me, Nijal, your friend. Don't do this, please. I beg you."

"Vilmos, you know not what you do! You must stop!"

"It is too late to stop; even you know this, teacher. I now know why you came. Do you think I am a fool? I know why you came. I know all the lies you have told me. I know all the answers to the questions that you would not tell me. What you have feared has already happened. I have learned from the past. I am more than you could ever understand. I am neither man nor god. I am not dead, nor am I alive. I shall outlast time, for I am not in time. I am not held by its boundaries as you are. Even Dalphan or Rapir would fear me though both would have welcomed their creation. Nor do the Father or Mother hold domain over me. I am outside their reach. The Father will kneel and worship me. The Mother will be my—"

"Never!" swore Xith as he jumped upon Vilmos. A tremendous explosion rocked the room. The sounds of hideous laughter resounded from the walls, then all was quiet. Darkness fell over the room for an instant, then the windows shattered outwards. The light of the waning day poured in. When the haze cleared, only Xith lay dazed on the floor; there were no signs of Vilmos.

"Where did he go?" yelled Adrina. She lay in bed, afraid to move. "Is everyone all right?"

"Yes, Xith will be fine in a moment."

Xith stood and shook his queasiness away. Amir and Noman helped him walk to the nearby bed opposite Adrina's. "I'm fine, I'm fine," he said, "I'm just a little dizzy that's all."

A loud knock sounded at the door. "Open up this instant. Are you tearing apart my inn?"

Noman answered through the door, "Just a little disagreement between my associates. You needn't worry about them any longer."

"I heard something break."

"Yes, yes. We will pay for all the damages. Don't worry. Now leave us in peace!"

They heard the innkeeper walk slowly away, stopping every couple of steps to turn and listen for more noise. Noman sighed in relief. "Come, we must leave now! The stables are just down the road. I have already purchased the horses. Let's go. Adrina, are you okay to travel?"

"Yes, the pain is gone. It's funny. My leg tingles."

"Tingles? Can you move it? Try slowly."

Adrina gritted her teeth in preparation for the pain and flexed her leg muscles. The pain did not come. She reached down and rubbed it methodically. The others stared at her, wide-eyed, as she did it. She was using both hands to rub her leg. She felt no pain in the hand that had a short while before been forever rendered useless.

She stood and tested the leg. It was perfect, as if it had never been broken. In glee, she performed a little dance, around and around in a circle she danced, laughing and smiling the entire time.

Xith turned and whispered to Noman, "Well, at least we can go straight to our destination. No place will be safe now, and in the end, none will prove safer."

"Yes, I am so foolish. I should have seen this coming. You know he will return."

"Of that I am certain."

15

"Pyetr, Swordmaster Timmer, may I speak with you in private?" beckoned Captain Brodst. The three retired to the swordmaster's quarters away from the practice room. The captain locked and bolted the door behind himself. He began to speak in hushed tones, "Swordmaster Timmer, can they be ready by tomorrow, the seventh day?"

"Yes, Pyetr made some excellent choices. These are all fine men."

"Good. All the delegates will be arriving later today and into tomorrow. I want your men to take the place of all the inner palace guards and provide personal protection to all palace officials tomorrow morning. Do you know each man by face?"

"Certainly."

"And you, Timmer?"

"Yes."

"Good, I want each man serving under you and only receiving orders from us three, no one else. They will wear no helmets and don our best light mail and bear the blue sashes of honor. I want you always to know of each man's whereabouts, always."

"Why all the secrecy? Is there something going on? If there is, we can be ready today."

"No, I want it to come as a surprise, a last minute thing."

"Is this serious?"

"Very, just keep your eyes on your men. I want you both to keep full inspection on them. Make sure that the man you appointed to a position stays at that position. Understand?"

"Are you saying what I think you are saying? You have seen the changes, too. I am not going mad."

"No, Master Timmer, you are not."

"What? I don't understand."

"This is not to leave this room. No one must hear of this. The first day I returned, I noticed that everything seemed in perfect order, and it was, almost. No offense, Pyetr, you did a flawless job of covering for me, and I thank you. It is just that I know every member of the royal guard by face or can at least recognize their voice. I inspect their posts personally each day. Even with the replacements for those lost I should have been able to recognize them, but I couldn't. Swordmaster Timmer, as the senior trainer, you too should have been able to recognize them, but some you couldn't, correct?"

"Yes."

"I also noticed something odd on that first day. Pyetr, did Volnej check on you each day?"

"Yes, each evening just after I completed final rounds in your office."

"Are you insinuating?"

"Think about it."

"How can you say that? He has served the kingdom his entire life."

"Yes, but until recently, he has served outside the palace. As a member of the council he traveled to many shores. Do you know where he was raised?"

"No, of course not."

"And you, swordmaster?"

"No."

"I didn't either, until I researched his lineage. Keeper Q'yer was most helpful. Volnej's parents were ambassadors from the Kingdom of Vostok.

They enjoyed the capital so much they stayed. Volnej was born before they came here. He did not join them until the age of ten."

"Do you really think he would betray us?"

"Would you, if your allegiance were to another country, another cause? Of course you would, because for all of us our homeland is the most important thing in our lives. It is our life."

"Yes, it is, and if Volnej is a traitor, I shall be very glad to end his life with my blade."

"As would I, but we must wait for him to give himself away. Once he is out in the open, he is ours. Tell no one. I have not even told Lord Serant or Princess Calyin; there is too much at risk. Silently, we can control the situation, but if he knows we have discovered him, he might do something rash and this could end in disaster. We will take them all out at once quietly and safely. I will return tomorrow morning; be ready. We will do this quietly and easily."

Captain Brodst walked back to his quarters, carefully making sure that no one had seen where he had come from. His thoughts wandered to many things. He saw Sister Catrin in the hall approaching in his direction, but he skillfully avoided talking with her. He quickly moved toward the sanctuary of his office, which lay in the opposite direction.

He had just settled into his chair when a page entered with a message for him. He dismissed the page and hurriedly read the letter, already knowing what it would say. The only detail he didn't know was the time the first delegation would arrive. King Jarom's party was going to be the first to reach the capital, early, as he expected.

He was, however, slightly surprised to find King Peter of Zapad and King Alexas of Yug were also with him. As he had suspected, King William of Sever would still arrive separately from the others. The three had journeyed from the South together with a full complement of soldiers each. He had expected roughly 500; he had not counted on there being 5,000.

His plans were being crushed. He would be forced to tell Lord Serant before it was too late. He was hoping to dispatch the few rogues easily and thus quietly retain the union of the kingdom. The plot reached farther than he had ever expected it would. The dispute would not end quietly.

Sister Catrin entered his office just as he finished rolling the scroll and placed it in the fire. She cleared her throat to get his attention, startling him. "Why so nervous?" she asked curiously, wondering if he was hiding something.

"Most sorry, Sister Catrin. It is just that since the attack, I have been on edge. What can I do for you? Is there something you need?" he asked quickly and smoothly, moving her back out into the hall while he talked to her.

"Midori wishes to speak with you."

"Midori, why?"

"I am just the messenger. Please come at your earliest convenience," said Sister Catrin as she departed.

Captain Brodst was curious why Midori would be looking for him yet didn't let it concern him. He had other pressing things on his mind. He rushed from his room to Lord Serant's quarters, only to find that he was gone. Captain Brodst panicked for an instant; where would he have gone? Calyin would not have allowed him to leave. Then he realized where Lord Serant was. He was preparing for the seventh day ceremonies in the audience chamber.

Captain Brodst hurried into the room and whispered into Lord Serant's ear that he must talk to him in private. He looked around the hall. He wasn't surprised at all to find Chancellor Volnej seated across from Lord Serant; and of the many guards throughout the hall, he saw only one that he recognized.

"Would the Princess Calyin like to escort us?" said the captain, offering her his arm. She almost protested until she saw the fierce look in the captain's eyes. The three walked from the hall to Lord Serant's room, which conveniently was close at hand.

Once inside, the captain locked the door and then searched the room. He found no signs of spy holes, so he returned to a seat near the extremely puzzled duo.

"Sorry for all the intrigue; it was a necessary precaution." Captain Brodst was quick to fill them in on what he had discovered, going over each detail completely. When he finished, the shock was evident on both

Calyin's and Serant's faces. It was also evident that they believed what he had said.

They would be prepared if the time came for battle. They sent several runners to all the city garrisons and riders to others close at hand. The message called for the garrisons to rotate in and out of the city for battle dress inspections during the coming ceremonies, keeping the real reasons hidden.

Captain Brodst bade them wait here until his return and he sought out Midori. The more he thought about why she would want to see him, the more interested he became. The question was gnawing at the back of his consciousness for the better part of an hour; now he would have it answered.

Midori greeted him warmly, and readily invited him into her chambers. She wore a light robe, which, if the captain had noticed, was quite revealing. She closed the door and the two were alone. She sauntered back to the rear chamber of the suite, and sat upon the bed. Nonchalantly, Captain Brodst followed her and sat down next to her. "Well?" he asked as she placed her lips against his. "You aim to seduce me. Is that it?"

"Seduce you, yes," she whispered as she kissed him.

"No games?" he asked.

"No games. Is this not your heart's desire?"

"It has been a long time."

"Yes, it has, and I've missed you."

The time raced rapidly by and soon it was well into the afternoon. A heavy rap sounded on the door several times before Captain Brodst opened it.

"Captain, come quickly," the page said. He scrutinized the page thoroughly wondering how he had been found, but quickly followed where the boy led. He arrived in Lord Serant's chamber just in time to see a runner arrive.

"The honorable and mighty Kings of the South, Peter of Zapad, Alexas of Yug, and Jarom of Vostok request admittance into your great city." The small runner announced the message quite brilliantly, then bowed and departed.

"Well?" asked Captain Brodst quizzically. "Shall we? We will be back soon, Calyin, please stay here as we planned."

Lord Serant and the captain hastily ran from the room. They made a short stop to see Swordmaster Timmer and Pyetr to put the captain's plan into effect immediately. Serant ordered the group to go to the palace courtyard, mount, and wait for them.

In the space of a few minutes, the entire company was outfitted, mounted and departing the gates of the palace. They raced towards the westerly gates of the city. Upon reaching them, the column of four parted, splitting into two. Skillfully, they faced each other, then walked the horses backwards forming two neat rows on either side off the road, a very graceful display of horsemanship.

The four lead horses moved from the pack and strode to the gates. Lord Serant signaled for the gates to be opened. Readily the two hulking forms wound outward. "Greetings to the monarchs of the South. Thank you for answering our call. The Great Kingdom welcomes you," announced Lord Serant crisply; then he asked the troops to follow his detachment to the southern garrison.

King Jarom's aide instantly sparked an objection, stating that their guards should be housed in the palace garrison. Lord Serant's subtle diplomacy quickly and decisively won the argument. He still didn't like the high number of extras he was forced to accept as retainers for the kings. He was assured that the men only acted as personal bodyguards and servants and the like. He was quite convinced otherwise but didn't offer further objection. He had them almost precisely where he wanted them.

Once Lord Serant saw that the kings were properly lodged, he and the captain returned to check on Calyin. She flew into Serant's arms and hugged him fiercely. He kissed her gently and carried her over to a chair and sat upon it with her in his arms. Captain Brodst smiled and turned his back for a moment, while Lord Serant kissed Calyin deeply and reassuringly. He chased away her fears, reassuring her that no further harm would befall him.

Calyin moved to a chair beside Lord Serant. "Captain Brodst, it is quite all right to sit down," she said sardonically. The three then discussed their plans in more detail. Pyetr's men had taken the key positions throughout the palace as planned. They had replaced the chancellor's manservant with a planted servant of their own. It had been a delicate maneuver, which Pyetr had quite skillfully managed. The three kings and their servants were placed in the second wing of the palace, which just happened to be nearest the central guard quarters; and the soldiers of the South were tucked away nicely in an easily-accessed position.

Everything was working to their advantage; now they needed only to wait for the opposition to make its move. They would then be able to spring their exquisitely designed trap. With luck, the coming conflict would die just as rapidly as it began.

It was well past the dinner hour when the three entered the great hall. The three kings had eaten long ago and were visibly frustrated by the long wait for an audience. Lord Serant took his place at the head of the table with Calyin to his left. Captain Brodst was the last to enter and he took a place next to his lord.

Servants quickly brought out the main courses and poured drink. Each time one of the guests began to speak, Serant would raise his hand to stop him, offering a toast instead. He was somewhat surprised at how well the royalty retained their etiquette as they watched Calyin, Lord Serant, and the captain drift through an eleven-course meal, which they had already finished earlier.

When the last remnants of food were removed and drink flowed, Lord Serant raised his hand again, signaling it was permitted to talk. King

Jarom's aide was the first to stand and beg a more private audience. Serant snapped his fingers and Chancellor Volnej entered the room. He whispered quietly into Lord Serant's ear. "Ah, yes, Chancellor de Vit, I will permit you this. We shall retire to my personal audience chamber."

The group moved to a smaller chamber just off the hall. Captain Brodst winked at Pyetr, who had just changed the guards around the inner audience hall; as he entered, the doors closed behind him. King Jarom's wolfish grimace grew into a cheerful smile as he studied Lord Serant and his captain.

"You may speak freely in here, gentlemen," said Lord Serant loftily.

"Good," said Chancellor de Vit. He started to speak further when King Jarom silenced him. "Yes, good indeed, we—" said King Jarom, indicating King Peter and King Alexas, "are most concerned about the affairs of the kingdom."

"You needn't be concerned; there is nothing to be concerned over. I assure you."

"We are not so sure. It has come to our attention that since King Andrew's death there have been circumstances regarding the rightful rule of the kingdom that concern us. The kingdom has no true heir. Prince Valam was the only heir, and he is gone."

"You were not called here to debate my position. Princess Calyin is also an heir, and as her husband, I am assuming my rightful place."

"I bet you do!" sparked King Peter.

"I object to what you are insinuating. Calyin is the next in the royal line. It is her rightful place."

"She is a woman. Her rightful place is with her husband, nothing more."

"She is the rightful heir. I will hear nothing more on this subject. We have more pressing matters to deal with tomorrow."

"Just the same, Lord Serant. We wish to make a formal claim to the council to contest your claim. We feel it is a king's place to rule in the absence of the prince."

"Do not forget your place. You come to Great Kingdom as honored guests, nothing more. Great Kingdom has not forgotten the treachery at Alderan and Quashan'. We are not the ones who need to explain ourselves."

"As members of the alliance—"

"—An alliance you honor of your own convenience—"

"What occurred in the south is a separate matter, a matter of lands in dispute," cut in King Jarom. "As members of the alliance, it is our right; it was written into the treaty. We wish an audience with the council in two days' time. I assure you that when Prince Valam returns we will relinquish our rule. You have nothing to worry about."

"Guards! Remove these men from my sight! Now!"

"We are not men, we are royalty, and you will treat us as such in the future. You need to learn to control yourself better. This little outburst will be made known to the council. Good day, Lord Serant—Princess."

King Jarom shook away the arm of the guard that attempted to assist his exit. The three kings walked gracefully out of the room, followed by their aides. Once the door was closed tightly, Lord Serant lost his haughty exterior. "Captain Brodst, would you leave us for a moment, and please send for Keeper Q'yer and Father Joshua. I could use their wisdom."

Lord Serant watched the captain walk stiffly from the room. He turned to look at Calyin and sank down to his knees beside her. "Can they do it? Can they take control?" Calyin understood the pain her lord was feeling. Uncertainty was an emotion he had only recently discovered. He didn't know how to deal with it. Even though sadness filled Calyin, she was happy; her pillar of flawless granite did in fact need her, and that filled her mind with joy.

16

"Keeper, Captain Mikhal's group has arrived."

"Send Captain Mikhal in at once!"

Father Jacob quickly joined Keeper Martin in the command tent. He was eager to get the report from the captain. It had been many days since the scout group had departed. He had feared the worst, his ill omens fading only as he saw the group return safely, and Captain Mikhal stood before him.

"Captain Mikhal! It is good to see that you are returned safe. Here, drink this; it will refresh you," said the newly appointed lieutenant Danyel'. Danyel' was a towering man; his height eclipsed that of most, and his girth was unmatched. His immense size and fierce skill had earned him his title and much respect. Many referred to the former mercenary turned guardsmen affectionately as "Seventh" after his position. He was the seventh to attain the status of lieutenant since they had arrived in East Reach.

Lieutenant was an office that, through Captain Mikhal's advice, had been restored. The title meant much more than Swordmaster First Class or Sergeant at Arms, as it positioned the holder in the ranks of leadership. The captain was still the undisputed leader of the army, but the lieutenants were free to act on their own volition to lead their respective detachments.

During the long journey to the Reaches, Mikhal had been scheming over his plans for the times ahead: the best defenses and the best offenses. The whole picture had been missing one element: a sectional lead, a lieutenant. He divided the entire company into six sections, each section containing ten squads. The sections were led by the lieutenants, and the sergeants or swordmasters led the squads, following the decisions of their leader.

Keeper Martin and Father Jacob were most impressed by the battle wisdom Captain Mikhal showed. His planning was clear and precise. They were quite confident Captain Mikhal would be a potent force when the time came to join the fight.

"Captain Mikhal, are you ready to report?"

"Yes, let's go do it, 'Seventh'."

The two walked toward the tent, the fatigue of the long trek barely showing in their features. Captain Mikhal unfolded their large, roughly formed map onto the table, crimping the edges so it would remain open. Many marks and symbols were newly sketched onto it.

"The report is the same as our last though we journeyed farther out this time; still no signs of anyone. The plains are barren, all homes and farms are abandoned. The mountains appear to stretch across the entire north and west here as we thought. We have spotted two passes, here—and here. They are wide enough for an army to travel through with little difficulty. These marks here and here are two narrow canyons where they could also come through, but we could easily dispatch them from above. In the second one, this river joins the main one here. We could easily block the river. Danyel's group followed the river as far as they dared go and noted the fords. They also spotted a large village here. We did manage to find some salvageable food. This is also where we captured some errant horses, a group of about ten, which brings our total up to thirty four. Here, just the other side of the river, is a small stand of trees, the only trees we have seen on the entire plain. Several times during the night, we could feel someone shadowing us. We would search and find nothing. On the return trip, we did spot a single rider, but he was gone as soon as we discovered him. My group stayed an additional day to try to follow him, but his tracks ended and we could not find the trail again."

"We did not expect you to find anyone. This place is strange, a country at war, and no signs of fighting in any direction. Our first summations must have been correct. The mountains still form an effective boundary, and for King Mark to invade would require a vast amount of troops. We are sitting right in the middle of where he will want to go. I am afraid we return to the same questions. Why hasn't the queen sent her scouts to greet us? Where have all the people fled? Why hasn't King Mark invaded? Our choices are limited with this odd season upon us. I see two options open to us. We can wait here through the coming cold and hope the queen brings us supplies, or we can return home while we still have enough supplies to make the return journey."

"Well spoken, Father Jacob. You know that I fully agree with you as we have discussed this topic all week. What of my other suggestion? Do you think it is worth the risk?"

"I will not hear of it—using the device is too dangerous. You said so yourself. Even if you could trigger it, you don't know if you would survive the teleportation."

"Teleportation?"

"Sorry, Captain Mikhal, Lieutenant Danyel', it's just that Jacob and I have discussed this so often that I had forgotten. Yes, teleportation, the device that is at the command of keepers. Keeper Martin thinks he may be able to trigger it even at this distance through a dream message."

"Is it possible?"

"Anything is possible. It is just that even if I can activate it, I might not be able to complete the journey."

"I don't understand how it works. How could it be possible to carry you that great a distance?"

"Distance isn't the problem if I can trigger it. The device creates a window from one place to another. It is triggered by thoughts reaching it. You picture an image of a place in your mind and it will take you there. It goes through a sphere outside of time and distance. In that space, the kingdom is as close to us as you are to me."

"Then what is the problem?"

"The journey."

"But you said the distance does not matter."

"To teleport from the palace to the hall of the keepers takes place in the span of one or two heartbeats. The problem is the length of time between here and the hall, relative to us. It could be too long."

"If it is outside space and time why does it matter?"

"It is outside our space and our time, yes, but what is the time in that sphere relative to our time; is a minute a minute, an hour an hour?"

"You, my friend, think too much," said Captain Mikhal.

"I understand," added Danyel', "but why would you wish to attempt it in the first place?"

"If I can make the journey there, the journey back here can be traversed with ease. I know this area as well as I know the palace. We will be able to receive word from the kingdom and then form our decision."

The sound of alarm resounded through the camp. A runner ran

screaming wildly toward the command tent. He entered nearly exhausted. "A rider approaches about a half hour's run away."

"A single rider clad in a brown robe on a black mount?"

"Yes. How did you know?"

"He is a friend. You're dismissed. Take an evening's reprieve and an extra serving. Good job!"

"Thank you, sir!"

"That is the rider that has been following us. I know it! Shall we go greet him?"

"Yes, I think we should."

They watched the stranger and his mount grow closer as time ebbed away. They could clearly see his simple brown robe and jet black mount. Captain Mikhal assured them that it was the same rider that had been following them.

A group of nervous guards stopped the rider just inside the camp. Swords raised, they asked him to step down from his mount. A flicker of thought shot searching through the keeper's mind. It was an angry thought. The stranger repeated his demand through the mind of Father Jacob, the captain and Danyel'. None of them could understand his words, only his emotions, so they offered no response in return.

The rider hesitantly dismounted, casting forceful glances at the guards. The guards rapidly lowered their weapons under the weight of his gaze and the keeper's admonishment. The rider stood still beside his horse and solemnly said, "Ne bojtes'. Tol'ko dlya mira ya prikhodil. Slishkom dol'go ya nablyudal za vam. Vremya sejchas! Tsaritsa-Mat' ustraivaet provody privetstvie—i ya tozhe samoe."

His thoughts echoed within their minds. They could not translate them into meaningful words, though they were certain of the dialect. It could only be the tongue of Seth's people. Keeper Martin fumbled the words within his mind searching for any he could comprehend. The only words he knew in the dialect were a greeting Seth had taught him. "Zdravstvujte. Ya Keeper Martin, ehto Father Jacob, Captain Mikhal, i Lieutenant Danyel'."

Teren was abashed at his foolishness. He had forgotten to phrase his words in the tongue of Man. He searched his mind for the terms he had quested from the scouts' minds over the last week. He began to speak weakly; soon his abilities improved, and the warm gentleness of his voice flowed. "Do not be afraid. I have come in peace. Long have I watched over you. The time is now! The Queen-Mother sends out her greetings, and I also welcome you."

Keeper Martin bid them to retire to the command tent. They had many topics to discuss, the most important of which were the whereabouts of the enemy and the progression of the war. They conversed long into the night and the next morning Teren departed the camp.

He had told them many things about the surrounding countryside and of the battle. He assured them that supplies and any horses that could be spared would be arriving soon. Teren also told them an official welcoming party and advisory council would arrive from the capital within the week.

The affairs of the camp in the passing week went well. The spirits of the soldiers remained high, though most wished to be far away in the comfort of their own homes. They had all willingly volunteered their services for a cause they thought just and would wait for the time to defend that cause.

Scouts would occasionally encounter Teren as he roamed across the plains. He would greet them heartily but never stay with them long. Captain Mikhal was still extremely puzzled why Teren was the only one they ever saw. Each time he saw Teren he would mean to ask but never had.

Cold rains slowly crept in. The skies were habitually overcast, and drizzle sprinkled over the camp. They began to make preparations for the oddly cold season. Teren had said the spring in the Eastern Reaches were mild here on the plains, so they were not excessively fearful but it did seem more like early winter than early spring.

A second week passed, and still they had received no signs of supplies or the coming reinforcements. This morning was an especially cold one; Keeper Martin paced back and forth in the command tent nervously. Father Jacob was also slightly vexed, but he hid it better. He sat quietly staring into a map spread fully across the table next to him. They both awaited word from Lieutenant Danyel's scouting party, which should have arrived back at the camp at sunrise.

This day the rains did not relent. They carried over into the afternoon, bringing a chilling northerly wind with them. The rain turned to an icy sheet descending upon them. The camp began to appear dead, as all huddled in the safety of their tents. The only source of warmth was the mass of tightly packed bodies jammed into the relatively small number of dwellings.

Keeper Martin stared out into the sleet. Again he thought that spring in the Reaches was more like winter in the kingdoms. He hoped their idea of cold weather and Seth's were similar, or they would not survive. He also wondered whether their mental stamina somehow shielded them from the chill, and they didn't realize the harshness of it. He evaded any further thoughts on that subject by closing the outer flap and sitting back down upon his chair.

Father Jacob smiled at his old friend. The two had known each other for so long that at time conversation was unnecessary. Each knew what the other was thinking by the way he acted. He knew what the keeper was pondering, and the prospect of the cold settling in did not excite him either.

With the coming of darkness, the last vestiges of warmth disappeared. The sleet turned to hail and slowly to a light snow. The clouds above shrouded the entire sky to form a blanket of early dusk. The only light on this night would be the light from their dwindling fires, which were very few in number, as wood was scarce. Now both Keeper Martin and Father Jacob were extremely worried. The scouts still had not returned, and they could only assume the worst.

Captain Mikhal joined Martin and Jacob after he finished the last of his duties. The three sat wordlessly asking themselves questions with their expressions that none knew the answers to. Mikhal broke out his flask and poured them all a strong-scented ale to keep the chill away; even Jacob partook of it.

"We brought the last of the supplies from the ships today. Good thing. We need to decide what to do with the ships. These storms will soon destroy those in the open. There are some small coves to the west where we could moor the ones that aren't in full cover here," expressed Captain Mikhal, shattering the silence.

"Yes, yes, see that it is done in the morning," answered Keeper Martin distantly. After that, Captain Mikhal kept his thoughts to himself for the remainder of the evening. He knew the keeper well enough to know that he hadn't meant to offend him, though he had.

The group was mounted, traveling down the road just after sunset. Adrina rode comfortably in a richly decorated carriage. Nijal drove the four-horse team splendidly along the sometimes-rough path. Xith and Noman had purchased it from the town's livery owner. He had been building it for his bride, but the sparkle of gold was the miser's real love.

The carriage nicely enhanced their change of guise. They were a group of mercenaries escorting an upper-class lady. With Adrina riding inside the carriage, the illusions really weren't necessary. It had only been necessary to adjust their clothing and armor to fit the image better. From a distance, they were indeed mercenaries.

Noman left the final decision of the direction of their journey up to Xith. The two concluded it was best this way. It kept Noman's mind free for the task that lay ahead. Xith, on the other hand, was left to brood over the choice for hours though he eventually narrowed it down to two routes. They could continue east to Jrenn, on to Eragol Bay and take passage on a ship destined for High Province or they could make their way to the territories, on to Krepost' and then travel to the far north by horse.

Late into the night Nijal was feeling the effects of the day. His eyes began to close and his head to bob, waking him up with a start. Several times, the carriage would veer to the side causing the horses to prance wildly.

When Xith finally saw what was occurring, he called a halt for a few moments' rest. He tied his horse to the rear of the carriage and took Nijal's place at the reins of the coach. "You go crawl back inside and get some sleep. I am sure Adrina could use some company about now," said Xith, in a fatherly tone, his mind still preoccupied.

Nijal didn't argue with Xith. He was tired. He knocked lightly on the carriage door then opened it. Adrina was huddled, frightened, on one side as he climbed in. "It is okay. It is just me, Nijal." Adrina sighed and relaxed slightly.

Nijal had just seated himself across from Adrina when the carriage began to move speedily down the road again. He was surprised at how smooth it seemed to ride from inside. It gave him an interesting sensation. He had only traveled by ship once long ago, so he really didn't remember it, but he likened the movement of the buggy to floating across the water.

He relaxed against the softness of the interior and closed his eyes. It was so warm and soothing. Quickly he began to drift off to sleep.

Xith shifted his thoughts rapidly back to the questions in his mind. He was sure of one thing. Time was the major factor he was concerned about. He mused over which route would be the shortest overall, yet both would take quite some time, more time than he wished to allow.

The storm season was rapidly approaching; by ship they would have to survive the straits, and by horse they would have to traverse the mountains. Both paths were equally treacherous and both had their pleasant sides and downfalls. His ultimate decision was the long trek through the territories; perhaps they would meet the old master, if indeed he yet dwelled in Krepost'.

A large bump caused the buggy to jar suddenly. Adrina awoke again and peered about the cabin. Nijal was still across from her; she wondered if he were asleep. She really needed someone to talk to; her thoughts were in disarray. She just wanted to go home or wake up and find that it was all a bad dream.

"Nijal?" came the whisper from a distance, "Nijal, are you awake?"

"Huh? What? Yeah—I guess so."

"Good."

"Good?"

"You were so quiet I thought you might be sleeping."

"Oh, no, not me. I don't sleep."

"I'm sorry. I didn't mean to—I didn't mean to—" said Adrina as she burst into tears. "Adrina? I didn't mean to upset you. I'm not tired anyway—really."

The sounds of Adrina's sobs did not fade. She tried to hold them back, but each time she did, they only increased. Nijal moved to the other side of the coach beside her. Adrina perceived his warmth and moved up against him, ending up with her face buried in his shoulder, her tears falling onto his shirt.

Nijal was unsure how to deal with such emotion. He just let her lie against him until her tears slowed, instinctively caressing her face with his hand. "Sshh, everything will turn out for the best."

Adrina stopped crying and Nijal wiped the tears from her eyes. The inside of the carriage was pitch black, but both pictured an image of the other in their minds. Nijal pressed his hands warmly against Adrina's wet cheeks, soaking up the pain from within her.

She reached up and touched her hands to his. An emotion began to flow through Nijal that he had never felt before; something strange was happening inside him. His heart began to beat faster and his palms began to sweat. He began to breathe deeper and harder. He felt a shiver come over him, and a knot welled up in his stomach to match the lump in his throat.

They moved closer to each other until they could feel the heat of each other's breath fall upon their faces. As their lips came together, Nijal moved away and just held Adrina tightly in his arms. A tiny voice within his mind told him that was all Adrina really desired from him, someone to comfort her pain.

Besides, he would not have known what else to do. He had never felt emotions like the ones he was feeling. He enjoyed them immensely, but he knew Adrina felt different. They had shared something special, together, as friends.

Nijal's arm was around Adrina and she rested her head on his shoulder. His other arm near her stomach felt the nervous rumbling of her belly and instinctively he moved his hand away.

Adrina released a short girlish laugh, and said, "Oh, Nijal." Teasingly, she grasped his hands and pulled them to her belly. "Not what you think," she said in a hushed tone. "A secret." She lifted up her shirt and moved his hand to the mark and though he could not see it, he could feel the outline of it on her skin.

To Nijal, the mark felt like a terrible scar. "How did it happen?" he asked.

"Not what you think," Adrina repeated. "Tnavres," she said in a clear powerful voice, "Show yourself."

Life grew beneath Nijal's hands and he watched in stunned horror and silence as a dark form emerged from Adrina's belly. In the deep shadows of the coach it was difficult to see but the creature clearly had wings and fangs and then to Nijal's horror the creature turned. His hands wanted to find his sword but Adrina locked her hands around his wrists.

"It is the secret I carry," she told him plainly. "You must not tell the others." She locked her fingers tighter around his wrists. "Promise?" Nijal stared at her blankly. She dug her fingers into his wrists. "Promise?"

As the tiny dragon turned about to face him in the darkness, Nijal said softly, "I will not tell a soul. You have my word."

"Tnavres," Adrina commanded, "return," and so saying the dragon faded into her, leaving only his mark upon her skin.

Unnerved, unsure what to do Nijal tucked his arm around Adrina. Adrina cuddled close to him. The gentle swaying of the carriage acted like a cradle, holding them both safe and secure. They slowly drifted away to the realm of dreams.

The sun was high on the horizon when the group made their final stop. They would stay the rest of the day in a small grove of pines just far enough from the trail to be relatively safe. The coach rocked roughly through the grasses off the road. The first several jolts went unnoticed, but when they continued, Nijal sprang awake. His thoughts were wild with could have only been a dark dream.

He drew his long dagger and popped the door open. The light of the dawning day blinded him for several heartbeats before he could focus. When he did, he found Xith staring back at him. Nijal sheathed his blade and climbed out the door back up to the top of the carriage. He hopped across the short distance to the front and plopped down next to Noman, who was controlling the reins. Noman smiled and passed them to Nijal.

The group set up camp inside the concealment of the trees. Xith told Nijal he had first watch, because he had already had a good night's sleep. Nijal didn't mind keeping guard. He had slept well and wasn't tired in the least, so he offered no objection.

After he made sure the horses were well provided for and everyone was asleep, he went to search their tiny domain. The grove of trees was small and sparsely packed. He skirted the perimeter of their camp, circling outward. He wasn't surprised when he found nothing unusual.

He reached the open ground near the road after completing a couple of spirals. He sat there for a time staring into the dust blowing off the road to the west. He started the walk back to the camp and climbed on top of the carriage. He looked back to the dust pouring off the road, and it dawned on him. "Dust—horses—a lot of horses," spun the thoughts in his consciousness.

He almost fell over backward as he stumbled off the carriage. He turned around and ran back to the road to take another closer look. Astounded, he ran back to the camp. He woke Xith first by shaking him violently. Xith was not pleased to be wakened after such a long night and with so little sleep. He groggily yelled, "What?"

"Horses—lots of horses."

Xith perked up and asked, "Where?"

"Coming toward us down the road from the west."

"Quick, help me cover the carriage!"

"I did that earlier."

"Good thinking. Let's go have a look," Xith said.

The two didn't have to wake up the rest of the camp. Noman and Amir were already fully awake and tending to the horses to keep them quiet. Xith and Nijal crouched in the last tree line, staring down the road at the oncoming riders.

The thunder of hooves echoed closer and closer. "How many do you think there are?" asked Nijal.

"Enough. From the amount of dust they raise and the noise at this distance, there may be several hundred."

"Hundreds?" said Nijal amazed.

"More like thousands," whispered Noman, walking up from behind them.

They watched as the horde grew into a mob of trotting horses. In silence, they watched them pass by. Nijal opened his mouth to say something, but both Noman and Xith quickly clamped their hands over it. Nijal closed his mouth and stared rapidly back and forth along the length of the line of troops.

A full hour passed before the last horses galloped by. Only then did the trio dare to move from their concealment. Nijal didn't understand why Xith and Noman were so calm. He had seen three banners move past and none of them belonged to the kingdom. He decided that if they would not worry, he would worry enough for both of them.

Adrina was also awakened by the noise. She stood next to Amir, looking extremely frightened. "Everything is fine; there is nothing to worry about. Let's get back to sleep. We need to be rested for tonight."

"What?" yelled Nijal.

"Shh!" said Xith, pointing to Adrina. Adrina hadn't heard Nijal's outburst and was heading back into the comfort of the carriage. Amir made sure she was properly tucked in and asleep before he allowed anyone to begin talking.

"Sorry," said Nijal, "I didn't realize—"

"It's okay. She just doesn't need anything further to disturb her right now."

"The banners, whose were they?"

"The banners of the south. King Jarom, King Peter, and King Alexas."

"All three together?" asked Amir.

"Yes, all three, together. I estimated around 5,000 riders."

"As did I. We must reach the territories soon, before it is too late."

"Too late?"

"Do not fret so much, friend Nijal. Had you seen the City of the Sky crumble around you, you would know what is ahead, but the end is also the beginning."

"What are you saying? I don't understand your riddles."

"You understand, but your mind rejects the thought. If you wish, you may return to the Free City. You have no obligation to us."

"No, you are correct. I understand. I have chosen my path, and it is with you, not without you."

Nijal offered to remain on watch throughout the day. No one refused his offer. He watched as they all returned to their sleep. Quietly, he opened the door to the carriage to check on Adrina. He was happy to find her sleeping soundly.

The day turned into night without incident, and the group returned to the road again. Adrina begged Nijal to ride with her inside the carriage so she would have some company. Nijal was hesitant though—afraid in a way. He looked to Xith for advice. Xith didn't offer an argument so he went.

He was tired after the long day though he hid it well from Adrina. When she asked him if he was sleepy, this time he lied and said simply, "No." He enjoyed being with her immensely and didn't want to ruin it. He was also very worried about her. "Sleep is a state of mind," he whispered to himself to stay awake.

Adrina released a tiny cry of pain and then laughed aloud. "What is it?" asked Nijal concerned. "Nothing. Here, feel," she said reaching for his hand.

"He's moving."

"Yes, sometimes he does. Did you feel that?" she giggled. Repulsed, Nijal pulled his hand away. The look in his eye nearly brought tears to her eyes. "You fear me, hate me."

"I fear for you," Nijal said taking her hand in his. "I—I—"

He cut off the rest of his sentence.

"Whaat?" asked Adrina as the coach veered sharply and stopped.

"Shh—listen."

"What is it?"

Nijal didn't have to answer her. The sound became stronger, even as she talked. Nijal peered out through the carriage door. In the darkness it was hard for him to see, but he knew they were moving off the road because of the tall grass striking the sides of the carriage.

All movement ceased again, and Xith jumped down from the coach in front of Nijal. "Stay in there with her. Remain quiet," Xith whispered. Nijal closed the door and latched it. He moved beside Adrina and drew his dagger.

The long wait began. They could hear the sound of voices yelling an alarm. Flickers of light swallowed the darkness as many torches were lit. The trot of horses began anew as riders plunged into the field.

The door to the carriage ripped open; Nijal lunged with his dagger. The man on the other side was much quicker. He snatched the blade from Nijal's hand and pulled him out. It was then that Nijal realized it was Amir. "Come on!" he yelled to Adrina.

Amir grabbed her and readily mounted, fleeing through the fields. Nijal looked around, momentarily disoriented. He saw his escape, and jumped on the horse that was tied to the rear of the coach, but it was too late. He would not reach the other side of the clearing. He made the only choice he could. He decided to hold his ground and give his companions more time. He turned to look at the retreating shadows of his friends one last time, and then released a blood-curdling cry. With his long sword in one hand and his dagger in the other, carefully he maneuvered his mount toward the attack, and charged at the lead rider.

17

"Keeper Q'yer and Father Joshua, thank you for coming so quickly. We have much to discuss," said Lord Serant, as he began to fill them in on the words of the three kings of the South.

After a long period of silence and very careful thought, Keeper Q'yer replied, "I really don't see the harm in it." Lord Serant and Calyin fixed him with a puzzled stare, but let him continue without interruption. "Really. They want a separate meeting with the council to discuss your right to maintain control. We'll give it to them, but on our terms. We will work it into the speeches we had planned for tomorrow. In fact, we will begin on that very topic. We will turn the tide in our favor."

"And with a ruling in front of all members and the council to support us, they can do nothing. Yes, I like your thinking, keeper."

A devilish smile also passed Father Joshua's lips, "Yes, we shall confront them with it before they expect. Our words will be heard first. I, too, approve of it."

The door to the audience hall burst open. Lord Serant was the first to move from the table. In a skillful lunge from his seat as he drew his weapon, he was now only a few feet from the intruder. It took him a moment to relax his sword arm, after he realized it was only Captain Brodst. "Lord Serant, King William is minutes from arriving at the postern gates. Chancellor Van'te of South Province and his aides are just a half hour's ride behind King William's delegation."

"Good. Any word or signs of those from the free cities?"

"No, but if I know Geoffrey of Solntse, he will be late in coming; the governors of Mir and Veter will wait to meet him near the crossroads to the south."

"Yes, that would be like him, wouldn't it?"

After Lord Serant personally greeted King William and Chancellor Van'te, he returned to the audience chamber. Once all plans were set, they retired for the evening. Captain Brodst wasn't tired in the least; he went to check on Pyetr's progress. Only then was he satisfied enough to be able to sleep, but something still burned in the back of his mind. He knew something wasn't right, but he couldn't touch upon it.

Early the following morning, a courier brought word to Lord Serant that Lord Fantyu of High Province had arrived in the coastal city of

Taber on the eastern sea and would regretfully be a day late in arriving to Imtal. "Did Lord Fantyu explain why he was to be late?" demanded Lord Serant.

"Yes, my lord. He told me to tell you, begging your pardon of course, and I quote, 'Tell his lordship if he questions my allegiance by the paltry offense of arriving slightly late that first of all we were delayed by rough seas and bad weather; we rowed our war galleys to a double beat. Secondly, the distance from High Province to Imtal normally takes well over two weeks in fair conditions, and he should be thankful we are here already. Thirdly, I must take into consideration my warships, which are of the kingdom's own fleet. Under no circumstances will I risk my fleet entering the forsakenly shallow waters of his blessed river!' Begging your pardon, of course, your lordship," spoke the courier swiftly.

Lord Serant had to force back a smile; the youngster had imitated Lord Fantyu to perfection. He had even imitated the uncanny nature with which the lord accented his every word with bodily gestures. Lord Serant dismissed the youth, and returned to his morning duties.

Throughout the day, delegates arrived; by noon the High Council was in full count, as was the Council of Keepers and ten representatives from each of the priesthoods. Only the governors of the free cities were unaccounted for. Lord Serant and Princess Calyin were growing nervous. They had fully counted on the heavy support of the governors and Lord Fantyu to seal their approval.

Finally, they tactfully decided to begin the initial ceremonies as planned but to hold off an open meeting until the following afternoon. King Jarom of Vostok was clearly puzzled over Lord Serant's game of intrigue. He and his aides left the ceremony as soon as it was timely. The other kings and their aides were soon to follow his departure.

Lord Serant still didn't approve of the number of bodyguards they retained. In another situation, he would have spoken his opinion; for now, the balance was too delicate to attempt to upset it. All proceeded well for the moment; he hoped it would remain smooth.

He spent the remainder of the day in his study with Calyin, trying to pass the day calmly. He left orders that he was not to be disturbed under any circumstances. Chancellor Volnej assured Lord Serant that he would take care of their guests' every wish. Lord Serant was sure the chancellor would. With Pyetr's men stationed in the key positions throughout the palace, Lord Serant was confident the chancellor would be well watched.

At the moment, however, Lord Serant was not pleased. Sister Midori and Sister Catrin interrupted his and Calyin's solitude. He was busy staring out a window lost to dreams of past and future, while Calyin and the two priestesses were engaged in heavy conversation; the topic of their words was beyond him. His tensions cleared when Captain Brodst informed him that Geoffrey and the other governors of the free cities had finally arrived and eagerly awaited an audience with him.

He seized the opportunity to leave the woman's talk and go greet the governors. He quickly traversed the distance to his private audience chamber. "Geoffrey of Solntse! Well, it is about time, you old wood troll!" shouted Lord Serant embracing his old friend.

Seeing Geoffrey again brought back memories from his youth when the two had first met. Lord Serant had been a cocky young lord and Geoffrey a young but experienced swordsman first class. Lord Serant had challenged Geoffrey to a contest of steel over a simple remark. In minutes Geoffrey had won the duel, leaving a fuming lord. The two had later become good friends.

"I had to make a slight delay, but I overcame the problem."

"What, a stray wildcat? Or a female?"

"Well actually a little of both."

"I knew it!"

"Can we talk freely?" asked Geoffrey looking to Captain Brodst.

"Yes, I would trust Captain Brodst with my life."

"We met a friend of yours on the way here. You know my son Nijal, yes?"

"Of course I do."

"He has left the free city to, ahh, um, travel. I ran into him and his companions near the southern crossroads. He told me to tell you, 'The child is safe'. He said you would know what he meant."

"Adrina? Did you see her?"

"Princess Adrina? I should have known! Why, that little rogue!"

"Captain Brodst, send a message to the garrison nearest to the crossroads. I want Adrina found, and I want her back at the palace! Does he know what has happened? Who was he traveling with?"

"Calm yourself. I know she is safe. Nijal is with her. He would not allow anyone to harm her."

"I know he wouldn't, but in the name of the Father, why haven't they brought her back to the palace?"

"I should not tell you this as I have sworn not to, but if you need assurance this will give it to you. The band that he travels with is quite unique. They arrived in Solntse over two passings of the moon ago. The leader is one of the great ones called 'Noman'."

"Are you mad, Geoffrey?"

"My friend, know that I simply speak the truth and accept it. I would never lie to you. I did not know it was Adrina he spoke of, but again I say she is in capable hands that do no mean her harm."

"I am sorry, Geoffrey. I hope in time I will understand; Adrina's rightful place is here. We will find her!"

Afternoon disappeared into evening and evening ended in morning, which once again became afternoon, although it was very early afternoon, being just past noon. Lord Serant's thoughts drifted from past to present. He remembered how he had stood on the balcony watching the morning sun grow with the birth of dawn. He watched as the old hall began to fill; tension was visible in the air, as was an intermixing of foreboding and relief.

He recalled with fondness the first time he had come to court Calyin. He had fallen in love with her simple beauty and warmth, which time could never taint, only perfect. His eyes fell to where she was seated beside him. She saw his smile and grasped his hand, holding it reassuringly tight.

He watched as the final guests were seated and waited for Chancellor Volnej's queue to enter. Together they stood; and regally, Calyin placed her arm in Lord Serant's. Lord Serant took a last minute look at the guests and then closed the antechamber's viewing port.

They entered the great hall through the antechamber's small, seemingly minuscule door when compared to the immensity of the old hall, which had stood idle during Andrew's time. It had only been used by the Alder, on occasion for which the chamber had been constructed. A similar hall stood in the newer section of the palace, newer being a misnomer since both sections were quite aged, but one indeed had been constructed more recently than the other. This chamber, although it had not the rich design of the other, had, nonetheless, been chosen. A servant behind them drew a tapestry that depicted the sun rising over the far mountains, an omen of good fortune, across the small door as they walked forth.

Calyin's eyes wandered the hall's vast span, which comprised almost entirely the eastern wing of the old palace. They walked past the long, oaken tables behind each of which sat one of the kings of the South amidst their aides, chancellors, and even their bodyguards, with which, even under these most serene and secure conditions, they would not part. Her eyes rose to the high-mounted pews where the High Council sat, only consuming a minute portion of them. In times of old before even the High Council, the seats had been filled with representatives from each city, village, and burrow across the kingdom and all its holdings, but this again had only occurred once, for afterwards there was no need as before.

The great double doors opened wide as the heralds slowly approached. Those gathered rose and remained standing until Princess Calyin and Lord Serant were seated at the foremost position, which took quite some time, as the walk was a long one, especially at a stately pace. The doors were closed as the heralds departed and sealed in accordance with the ancient ordinance. The doors would not reopen until all differences were justly settled and the alliance was secure.

"Herald and Welcome! The few gathered into this great hall represent the trinity that maintains the alliance of peace and prosperity," began Calyin, raising her voice strongly at first to insure that all could hear her voice, but the hall had a wonderful resonance which took her quite by surprise, as her voice carried to even the farthest reaches of the hall at a level that caused some to wince. She continued in a softer, somewhat subdued tone, "In these days of troubled times, it has become commonplace to see a keeper walk the halls of the palace often, forcing us to look back to other days and other times. Now is the time to solve all our disputes. The past is behind us; we have only our future to preserve. There are those that question my right to rule beside my beloved husband in Prince Valam's absence. I hold no reservations; I only wish the kingdom to prosper, so let us begin this session by taking an earnest toll. The majority of you know me personally and know my soul. For those few of you who do not, I understand and welcome your caution in accepting me. Andrew was my father. Knowing him the way I did, I know he would have agreed that I am overly qualified for this honored position. I always remain true to my word, so if you see fit in your hearts to deny me the opportunity to serve my kingdom, then so be it. I will return to High Province without protest. Are there any here who would like to speak before we begin the count?"

King Jarom was quick to his feet; his face showed anger as he spoke. "You are a fool, Lord Serant, if you think you can get by with your trickery! We can see clearly through your paltry words and mocking ways! Let it be known that it was I who questioned Lord Serant's position, and also that I requested a private board before the High Council to discuss this subject!"

Lord Serant shot back, "I think all gathered know of your treachery in the south."

"As I've explained to you previously, Lord Serant, the matter in the south was over long disputed lands."

"The disputed lands are further south."

"The disputed lands include all of South Province."

Lord Serant swept his gaze around the hall. "They most certainly do not and the members of the alliance know this. And now you use the pretense of the alliance to bring an army into the heart of Great Kingdom."

King Jarom looked about the hall, indignant. "You wound me with your words. I demand satisfaction—my champion against yours or you against me. Your choice."

The High Council was charged with managing the proceedings and the chancellors Volnej, Van'te and de Vit stood. Chancellor Van'te spoke, "King Jarom, the High Council is here, and we are listening. Choose your words with wisdom. Do not let them be fueled by arrogance!"

"I am sorry for my outburst, chancellor. If Lord Serant wishes the contest to open, then so be it. I just wish to say to you, those who are gathered here today, that it is our belief that the alliance would be better served if one of higher office held the esteemed position in question. Of those here the only kings are myself, King Peter of Zapad, King Alexas of Yug, and King William of Sever. Of these four, I am the senior and undisputed leader. In the past, my wisdom has been recorded numerous times and is widely respected. I wish it to be known that I would like to honor this position with my wisdom until the day of Prince Valam's return and he is crowned king!"

Lord Serant searched the eyes of the crowd, almost pleading for someone to say something on his behalf. He zeroed keenly in on King William and stared sharply at him. He was sure William did not support

Jarom. He wondered what Jarom had on William to still his tongue.

It was Lord Fantyu who spoke out next. He stood and raised his hands high into the air. "Father, grant us mortal spirits the wisdom of truth," Fantyu intoned in his way of exaggerated gesture. "Why cannot the fool see his prosperity? Is a fool who thinks he is wise, a wise man? Or is the fool who knows he is a fool, the wise man? I have known and respected Lord Serant for a long time. He is an honest man. He speaks no lies, only truth. When a serpent has entered your house and he speaks falsity and lies, do you heed his words?"

"My dear Lord Fantyu. I speak no falsities. My words ring of truth! I ask all of you earnestly, have I ever not held to my word? Have I ever been false?"

Midori spoke, "An aura of darkness enshrouds you, Jarom! You cannot hide the truth from the Mother!"

"Priestess," said Talem, first of the Dark Flame. "I see no such aura around King Jarom. He is a just man who speaks truth."

"Do you speak these words because of his support to your order? Have the priests of the Dark Flame wandered so far from home that they have forgotten truth?"

Father Joshua said, "Quarrelling amongst ourselves will bring us nowhere. As the Great-Father walks within me this day, through the intensity of his presence, I can know the import of this day! Just as the first marked a new period, so will this day. Do we want this day to be remembered as was the first? Or do we want to prove we have learned and grown beyond our past? Lord Serant has my bidding!"

Lord Serant waited through the long silence that followed, hoping both that someone would say something to break the sudden lull, and that it would remain. No one offered any further comment. Princess Calyin edged her hand into his and held it reassuringly tight.

"Well spoken, Father Joshua. Shall the count begin? Are there any who would wish to speak further?" strongly asked Lord Serant. When the silence held, Chancellor Volnej stood and unraveled a long parchment and began to read from it.

"Hence came the alliance of our kingdoms, whence disappeared the strife of the times long since passed. Troubled times have returned. To maintain the stability necessary for our peace and prosperity, a wise and just leader is needed. His Lordship Serant of the West has pledged to us that he will honor this position to the utmost of his ability until our crowned prince has returned to us from afar. Let us begin!"

All attention turned to the rear of the hall, where the toll would start. Two of the primary groups were the priests of the Dark Flame and the keepers. As chief representative of the priesthood, Talem calmly rose from his seat and shook his head a resonate no, then returned to his seat, without the utterance of any spoken word. Keeper Q'yer, who assumed the position as head of the keepers, stood and regarded Lord Serant and Calyin with an apologetic glance. He then turned and fixed several of his fellow keepers with gleaming frigid intent. Slowly he lowered his eyes in shame and voiced, “No.” Keeper Q’yer slumped back into his chair. He understood why the keepers must stand united on their votes; still he yearned to speak his mind and say “yes,” but it was already beyond that.

Lord Serant’s face went livid as he clinched his fists tightly. He turned a scowl towards King Jarom, who returned a leering smile. Calyin interlaced her hand in Serant’s and held it tighter than before.

Father Joshua and Sister Midori each in turn affirmed a jubilant yes, and thus all eyes turned to the tiers on the eastern and western sides of the hall. In a wave, the members of the councils, representatives of all the peoples of the alliance, voiced their individual decisions. In all, only one registered a vote of no.

For the free cities, Geoffrey spoke a definite yes, as did Lord Fantyu. Chancellor Van’te also voted positively. King Jarom, King Peter and King Alexas each followed with a definite no, and lastly King William exuded a yes. As he retook his seat, he smiled broadly at Lord Serant. The smile was short lived and quickly followed by an expression of gloom.

With the final count, the room grew deadly calm. As Chancellor Volnej lowered his quill, he passed the scroll to Chancellor de Vit for his mark. The chancellor read the inscriptions with extreme care, insuring the validity of each word penned. When he was finally satisfied, he scribed his sign and passed the document on to Chancellor Van’te, who represented both South Province and his role as a chancellor at this session.

The chancellor’s face was inscrutable as he inspected the scroll. He turned and faced Chancellor de Vit and Chancellor Volnej. The three retreated to the far reaches of the great hall, seeming to disappear from the sight of those gathered. They sat for over an hour of heated discussion in a second set of high pews on three sides that almost formed a separate chamber, except that they had the same common roof and no walls to divide them. The center tier was only three levels high, but the eastern and western tiers rose to the windows.

Their debate concluded, they sent for both Lord Serant and King Jarom and the two quickly and graciously withdrew to hear the count as it was written, and within the span of a few minutes retook their positions back in the main section of the chamber. The chancellors followed the two and moved to the center of the great hall.

Regally, Chancellor Van'te stood and raised his eyes to gaze unto the throng. Harshly, he cleared his voice and then began to speak these words, "Let it be known that on this day and henceforth all contentions surrounding our most regal office have justly and fairly been settled. All in attendance have been afforded the opportunity to voice their minds and have done so. I hold in my hands the official count, signed by representatives of opposing parties. These words inscribed herein are law, and henceforth will they ring throughout our lands. Lord Serant of the Western Territories rise. King Jarom of Vostok rise."

Chancellor Van'te paused and took a deep breath. "Do you, Lord Serant, understand the law of just dispute?"

"Yes, of course. You know I do."

"Do you King Jarom understand the law of just dispute?"

"Yes, certainly."

"Then do you both agree to the trial?"

"Yes."

"Yes."

"To ensure the absoluteness of the ruling set forth this day, Lord Serant and King Jarom have agreed to settle their dispute according to the rules of the commoner."

***

Hurriedly, the three raced back to the square. All appeared to be normal as the crowd dispersed, but Seth could still feel an overwhelming sense of evil emanating from somewhere within the throng of people. His mind reeled and went back through the past piece by piece, searching. "Had I been so preoccupied with the dilemma that I had failed to notice its source? How could I be so foolish?" he thought to himself as he traversed the maze in his mind.

As they approached closer to the platform, the presence grew stronger. He looked with horror to the platform. The Queen-Mother, Tsandra, Ylad', Nikol, Ontyv, and Samyuehl were all there, circled around Valam's fallen form. He tried to reach out to them with his mind and warn them; he could not. They were all trapped in the enticement as he had been; nothing could reach them.

Seth carefully signaled Cagan and Liyan to sweep around to the backside of the platform. He made the signals with his hands, for now he dared not risk even using the simplest of his powers any more. As one the three jumped onto the dais, they knew the creature perceived their approach and they also knew they were too late.

Valam rose as the vile being spawned within his body. In the single sweeping of its clawed hands it raked through the onlookers. Tsandra, Ylad', and Nikol fell to the ground. Their bodies offered but a single shudder as their threads were released to the winds and as readily as a babe hungrily laps its mother's milk, the creature devoured their waning souls.

Together, Seth, Cagan, and Liyan descended upon the creature, knocking it back to the ground. They held it there only for an instant while the creature mocked their feeble attempt to stop it. It bathed in their anger and then laughed a deep hideous laugh.

"King Mark sends his warmest greetings!" it boomed as it gripped Cagan and Liyan around the throat. Seth battered the being's head heavily onto the platform to no avail. Cagan and Liyan were drawn with it downward, struggling to free the death grip from around their throats as they fell.

Brother Ontyv slowly reclaimed his senses. He saw the struggle and knew the danger, yet his first priority lay with the safety of the Queen-Mother. It was not until after Ontyv had pulled her from the platform that she regained her senses. As she did, the shock of the events hit her and she knew why the creature had won its way into their inner selves. She knew why it had been able to mask its presence from them, and why it had so enticed them. She also knew how it must be destroyed.

Finally, Cagan and Liyan managed to free themselves and now held down the creature's arms. Seth held the dark one's head down with one hand and unsheathed his dagger with the other. He plunged it fully into the being's heart.

The creature only laughed louder and smiled as its strength grew with each passing second. Seth sank the dagger into its chest repeatedly, until he began to feel his energy ebb. He could do nothing except wait as his end came. The creature drank in his soul.

The Queen-Mother rang these words out across the reaches of time and across the lengths of the land, "There is nothing but love in my heart. Only joy and love abide herein, for I am the Queen-Mother. Only love and harmony exist in my mind. Love for all dwells within my heart. My body is one with all in peace and harmony. I hold love in my heart for Valam."

Tears flowed freely down the Queen-Mother's cheeks, as never before, as the vision began to fade and dim. Her whole inner spirit writhed and shouted out to her senses to stop what she had set in motion before it was too late. She wondered at the price the Father had paid to bestow upon her the gift. She understood the wrong that must be corrected and the repercussions if she didn't, but she couldn't force herself to move.

She closed her eyes and replayed the images in her mind; vividly they lingered. They raced faster and faster and in the span of a single heartbeat, she was back on the platform, watching as the creature killed her brethren. She saw Valam run into the crown and watched again as they trampled him. She watched as the life drained forever from his lips.

The Queen-Mother strove to deny the truth of the warning, but it would not be disclaimed. She knew what she must do, and so she did it, as she had done before. In a burst of emotion, she opened her eyes and retreated from the tower window. She ran, faster than she had ever run before, down the stairs.

"Valam! Wait! Oh, please wait! I can find love for you!" screamed the Queen-Mother, as she ran. "I mean. I will honor our union and I will try to find the truth of my heart." She almost bit her lip on the last few words. They had issued from her so effortlessly, without meaning, until she said them. After she said them, she could not deny their truth.

Valam stopped cold as he entered the hall adjacent to the tower. He turned and strained his ears to ensure that what he heard was real. When the words repeated in his mind, he knew they indeed were real and not his imagination. He replied loudly in kind, repeating her words to him.

He raced back up the winding stairs, his hearted pounding rapidly as he did so, and his body began to tremble as he crossed the few last steps that remained between them. He grasped the queen's outstretched hands in his own and pulled her close to him.

They pressed closer and closer together, staring deeply into each other's eyes; the sound of their deep breathing resounded through the tower.

They stood thus, afraid to move for what seemed an eternity but was actually only a moment in time.

Finally the queen inched her lips forward until they touched Valam's, then she pressed them full against his. He returned her caress with equal fervor. Suddenly the queen pulled away as a thought returned to her mind.

She held tightly to one of Valam's hands as she raced down the stairs, almost pulling him behind her. "What is it?" he protested. "We must hurry! Come!" responded the queen.

They reached the bottom of the stairs but did not stop running. The queen raced through several narrow corridors with Valam a pace behind her. As they turned a corner into the central hall, they had to halt to avoid smacking into Evgej. With only a slight hesitation, the queen continued down the corridor. Valam returned Evgej's puzzled look and waved for him to follow.

The queen went straight through the audience hall that Seth and his red-clad followers filled, out the great doors, down the stairs, and into the courtyard. The crowd of brown-clad warriors parted the way as she mounted the central platform in a slow, stately manner, fully regaining her composure.

"What is it? What is happening?" yelled Evgej as he followed Valam and the queen. "I don't know!" replied Valam.

"No! Really, what is it?"

"I really don't know!" yelled Valam as he struggled to keep up.

"Tsandra!"

"Yes, my queen," came the response.

"Come here."

Tsandra mounted the platform and whispered into the queen's mind, "You needn't tell me, I already know what you will say. I, we all, heard your pledge."

The Queen-Mother gazed out into the crowd and knew Tsandra's words to be true. "My daughter, let me look into your eyes and see your heart." Hesitantly, Tsandra obeyed. The queen smiled. "It is I who am sorry."

"This day has been doubly blessed! Our hopes have been fulfilled. Last night the future of two peoples has been insured. The child of East and West will be! Also, I have been allowed the gift of sight and in so doing, the Father has also given his blessing to my greatest wish. I have been allowed to love someone as I have never known before if it is in my heart to do so and I think it may be. Valam and I may one day be as one, but the time still lies in the distant future. We must first win a war! To do that, we must prepare a defense like none has ever seen before. We must continue on schedule with our plans. Today's departure must remain on time!"

The Queen-Mother paused during the loud cheering of the crowd. A chant began to grow; it was the chant of greatest rejoicing for the return of the king, a song that had not been heard in generations.

Tsandra searched for the proper words to begin what she needed to say; unable to find anything she thought suitable, she just stumbled into it, "Queen-Mother, may I offer the services of the Order of the Brown. It will prove my faith to you."

"Brother Seth, it is up to you?"

"Valam?"

"It would be an honor."

"Thank you," spoke Tsandra enthusiastically. She began barking commands to her order to form up and stand ready then excused herself to begin the preparations. "Shall we prepare to depart?" Seth asked Valam. Valam was slow to respond. Hesitantly he turned his gaze from the queen and turned to Seth.

"Ahh, yes. Is there anything that needs to be readied?"

"All preparations are basically set. We need only to find Cagan and Liyan, my queen."

"Yes, Brother Seth, follow everything as planned. You have my permission."

"Thank you."

Valam leaned close to the queen and quietly intoned, "I—I."

"I, too. You must go!" said the queen, harsher than she wished, as she strained to hold at bay the emotions within her. She quickly added, "I think I know where you can find Cagan and Liyan. Try the docks."

"That is what I thought," said Seth as he departed, followed by Evgej and Valam. Valam looked back just before he exited the square, but the platform was already empty. The three walked toward the docks and, as expected, Cagan's boat was just returning. Evgej caught the line Cagan offered and tied the ship to the dock. He held back a laugh when Liyan stepped off the boat after Cagan.

The Queen-Mother watched from a window high above. She nodded her head in approval as they hurriedly moved back into the palace. A man clad in dark-colored robes walked out onto the balcony beside her. He whispered into her mind, "My queen, is it time?"

"No," came the response into his thoughts, "just follow; I will tell you when it is time."

By early afternoon, a large contingent was mounted and waiting before the far gates of the palace with Tsandra, Seth, Liyan, Cagan, Valam, and Evgej at the fore of the group; a mass of brown clad riders filed in long columns behind the lead six. A second formation of riders stretched horizontally across the courtyard.

The queen crossed to her platform, her emotions controlled behind the mask of her face as she looked over the group from rear to front, wishing each rider a safer return. She paused at the last rider and wished him her love. She ordered the central gates opened and bid the group a final farewell.

The brigade slowly strode through the city. A gate in a hillside near the outer walls lead to a wide tunnel that carried them beneath the waters of the great lake. At the exit of the tunnel on the opposite shore they were forced to wait until the supply caravans joined them; then they continued on their way. As they rode away, Valam occasionally looked back toward Leklorall's spiraling towers and mighty walls. His heart was not in riding this day; he longed to be somewhere else but knew he could not.

***

The vision flowed strongly; it would not fade. Vilmos felt the surge of strength within him peak beyond the limits of his mind. The power became him and he became the power. He could not control it, nor could it control him. They were two entities wrapped in turmoil in each other's arms.

"Where will you go now, my friend? Where is it you think you can hide? There is no place to flee to; you only run from yourself."

"But I know where I must go and what I must do."

"Do not lie to me, for you cannot lie to yourself."

"Still your tongue or I will invoke pain within you that will be so great your soul will cry out for death, but I will not let you pass. I will hold your spirit at bay until the pain grows within you to such an intensity that your spirit will wish itself from existence."

"You most of all should know true death, but lest you not forget its curse, I will welcome the day I return to walk through the halls of your memories, as I already have and will throughout eternity."

"Then it is you, old friend."

"Of course it is I, who else could it be?"

"But you are dead."

"So are you; we are both long since passed."

"Yes! Last time we met, I defeated you."

"No, we destroyed each other."

"Correction! I destroyed you both!"

"I do not understand; why, then, am I here?"

"Yes, why?"

"I have brought you back to learn from. I need your knowledge, and I will have it."

"Do you think you can order us, as if we were children? Each of us has the power to utterly destroy you at will and yet you talk to us as if we were token pawns."

"You are quite right. You are token pawns, the fools on the board, and I am your master."

Vilmos received a crushing blow to the head; excruciating pain filled every fiber of his being. He cried out into the darkness of the night. He searched within his mind striving to force the vision away. The two would not go; they could not go. The third spoke in a voice that caused Vilmos' mind to recoil. The image of the last began to clear, and though it was a shadow of himself, Vilmos failed to recognize it. He could not, for he did not want to.

Vilmos watched as the three began to circle each other methodically, each assessing the other. The two old friends smiled cynically at the third. They knew what they must do, and so they did it. Wildly, they attacked each other, creating a vortex of swirling energies.

"Go away!" cried out a small voice, "Go away now!"

The thoughts would not go. They demanded to be heard and recognized. They demanded to be alive. Vilmos clasped his ears and pounded his head into the ground, until the wetness of blood dripping down his face soaked the ground about him. The pain within him was replaced by the pain from without; only then at the moment of unconsciousness did the voices fade from his thoughts.

* * *

Nijal raced his mount toward the leader, his sword and dagger raised ready to plunge. He screamed his battle cry of defiance strong and true; then the two horses collided. The leader had not expected Nijal to reach him; the shock was evident on his face as he was knocked sprawling.

In an instant, the other riders stopped; they thirstily began to circle Nijal. He did not flinch under their scrutiny. His weapons remained erect and challenging.

"Your death will come easy, put down your weapons and we will not harm you!"

"I spit on your offering of surrender; no free man ever surrenders willingly. I am a free man."

"And will die as such!" the words rang out before Nijal could finish them. "The free man's code, where did you learn it?"

"Why, from my father of course," said Nijal spurring his mount into a charge at the speaker. He leapt from his mount, throwing the rider back to the ground. Nijal dropped his sword to free his hand to hold the man, while his other held a dagger firm against the man's throat.

"Tell them to stop the attack. Tell them now or you will die!"

"I cannot. We will both die then."

"Tell them, or I'll slit your throat!" yelled Nijal while he pulled the man's head back by his hair with his free hand. The other stared into Nijal's eyes unafraid.

The light of torches increased about them while the two struggled. Nijal knew his fate was soon coming. He had accomplished what he had hoped for. He had given his friends a chance to escape, and that was all he had wanted. He would die, but he would take this man with him.

"I, Nijal, son of Geoffrey, take your life with that of mine!" said Nijal as he raised his dagger to plunge deeply, insuring the other's demise. The man released a blood curdling cry, "Nijal? No! Nijal, don't." It was too late; Nijal thrust downwards with his blade.

Strong hands grabbed Nijal's arm and held his dagger at bay. Nijal gritted his teeth and cursed, thrusting downward with all his weight, never faltering in his determination. "Nijal, son of Geoffrey—don't! It is I," screamed the other.

Thoughts and sounds exploded in Nijal's mind; with a puzzled frown, he allowed his weapon to be pulled from his hand. "Release him at once! Stop! Stop! Go now and tell them to stop the chase. Go! These are friends!"

Shchander continued to yell and wave his hands wildly in the air until everyone began to listen to him. He helped Nijal to his feet, grabbed the nearest torch and pushed it close to Nijal's face. "Look!" he yelled, "It is Nijal. Nijal, I tell you. Get Geoffrey quickly!"

Several riders raced back towards the main group by the roadside. Nijal instantly recognized the distinguished-looking statesman that raced towards him and embraced him. "It is good to see you!"

"Yes, father it is good to see you also."

"Sorry about the misunderstanding, but when we spotted you and you broke for the trees, we assumed you were bandits."

"Well, maybe I am."

"Yes, you are quite the rogue, aren't you? Have you found what you sought?"

"Yes, father. I am finally content; I have purpose."

"This is good. Tell your friends to return. We shall camp here for the evening and catch up on times past."

"I am sorry. We cannot afford to tarry any longer. We must find our path."

"Are you sure? Do you need anything? Want for anything?"

"No, father. We need only to return to the road. My companions will wish to remain anonymous. We have cargo that cannot be seen."

The two talked, as a father and son do, and quickly caught up on times past. Nijal was very interested in hearing news of the gathering. Readily, he soaked up the information Geoffrey offered so he could re-tell it to Noman. When Geoffrey had finished, Nijal quickly and carefully skirted the details of what he had been up to.

"Ahh, yes, I understand. May I ask where you are headed?"

"North. Tell Calyin and Lord Serant our cargo is safe. The child will be all right. I do not want her to worry."

Geoffrey knew better than to push for further information, so he asked, "Will you be all right, Nijal, my son?"

"Yes, if we leave here soon."

"I will give you an escort to insure your safety."

"We need none."

"Don't argue with me. Shchander is a good man. I will send his detachment with you. They are all loyal men, as you well know. They will receive your orders as they would mine."

"Your offer is kind, but I must flatly refuse it. We need no assistance."

"A few more men can only aid you. It would be for the best."

"We have no need for brute force. Only stealth will save us."

"Then I must accept your words. May the Father watch over you."

"May the Father also watch over you," said Nijal as he remounted. He gripped the reins tightly and spurred back toward his companions.

"Tell your friend, I send salutations. Tell him thanks again for the assistance. I am twofold in his debt."

"I will, father."

Nijal had a wide smile on his face as he raced away, a smile of contentment. His purpose in life had seemed to grow suddenly manyfold. He called out, "It is I, Nijal!" to the bear of a figure that guarded his entrance as he rode closer. "Everything is all right. It was only Geoffrey of Solntse and a group of men from the free city."

"Yes, we know. We heard. We were with you in thought," said Amir.

Nijal didn't understand what Amir had meant by the statement, but not understanding didn't bother him in the least. He simply overlooked the incomprehension and understood. "Is Adrina okay?" asked Nijal, jumping to another subject.

"Yes, she is well."

They waited until Geoffrey's group rejoined the road and the sound of their horses thinned into the night air before they too returned to their path. Hastily, they proceeded along the trail, quietly thanking the Mother for the darkness of the night she afforded them.

Amidst the gloom, they passed the place where it is said that north meets south and east becomes west. Nijal thought it strange that the only settlement was an old rundown outpost. If he were a merchant, this would be the perfect place for a business venture, but then Nijal was no merchant, so he kept his thoughts to himself.

Though the winds were quite calm, the night air held a bitter lash. Xith remarked that the storm season would be early this year, bringing with it an end to the previous year. Noman nodded slightly in agreement with Xith's words. They had been casual in the saying, but each held within them hidden meanings. The future held surprises for them that would not be solved so easily.

As the first light of morning broke, the group stopped for a short reprieve, then took up the trek again: there would be no rest this day. The great road was too well-traveled by patrols and merchants alike. Nijal's mind started to roam as they slowly journeyed down the road. His attention fell briefly to Xith and he smiled, remembering his companion's earlier comments.

"Huh?" Nijal uttered as he recalled their previous conversation.

"Only rogues sleep during the day."

"Well, I guess we are rogues then, are we not?"

"Of course we aren't rogues. Now go help Amir with the horses. We can't afford to have any lame animals on our hands."

"But wouldn't it be better to rest here than to continue?"

"No, it would not be better. Sometimes it is better to be blatantly obvious than to be covert; this is one of those times, and we also need to make up some distance."

"Nijal, watch out! Here give me those."

"Sorry," apologized Nijal as he snapped out of his reverie and pulled the reins to bring the horses to a halt. "What is it?"

Xith pointed to the rider in the distance behind them. "So, what about him?" offered Nijal. "You said this road was well-traveled and so far this is the only person we have encountered."

"Amir marked him last night. He has been following us ever since."

"Where is Amir? I haven't seen him for some time."

"He is there," said Xith pointing again back down the trail.

"Where? I don't see him."

"That is because you see only with your eyes. Look with your mind and you will see him."

"Hocus pocus, mumbo jumbo," thought Nijal to himself. He partially understood the concepts of energies and magic although it was hard for him to accept. Inside, Nijal did not want to admit their truth although he had to confess to seeing some fairly odd things happen since he had joined Xith and the others.

"Okay, I'll look," said Nijal. Once again he was forced to rework his consciousness up to a level of acceptance without comprehension. "Wow!" he exclaimed when a second rider entered the images of his mind.

As the first rider approached it became clear that he was puzzled as to whether he should continue up the path or stop. His horse would speed up and then slow down. Once he even stopped under the pretense of watering and feeding his mount; and when it became clear that he was being scrutinized, he mounted and continued up the path towards them. His face was completely covered by a dark hood, making it impossible to see anything distinguishing about the figure. As the distance between them diminished to a few paces, Nijal couldn't contain the smirk on his face. It seemed so ironic that Amir rode right alongside the other and yet was invisible to him.

"You can dismount now!" said Amir to the startled rider as he appeared beside him and reined in his mount. Obviously shaken, the rider dismounted as he had been told. “Aw, I should have known I never would have been able to pull it off,” muttered the rider as he removed his hood.

Nijal burst out laughing as he recognized the disgruntled man. “You never should have come. This is no place for you, but since you are here—” Nijal paused to judge Xith’s opinion on the subject then continued, “—since you are here—you are most welcome!” Nijal jumped down from his perch and embraced the other.

“Shchander, you are most welcome in our party,” said Noman, “although you have picked a rather precarious time to join us. It would be best for you to rejoin your companions on the road to Imtal.”

“My place is here. I have given my pledge.”

Nijal added quietly, “Now there are two,” saying the last word only in his mind, “misfits.”

“Neither of you are misfits,” added Noman.

18

Princess Calyin's face blanched as the words fell heavily upon her. "What is this outrage?" she cried out. "I will not have it! There will be no test!"

Father Joshua put his hands gently on Calyin's shoulders and attempted to calm her down. Calyin would not calm her tongue for anyone. She pushed Father Joshua aside and rose from her seat. Her face was now dark with anger. Calyin, with eyes cold and fixed, glared around the room, daring anyone to say anything further on the subject. No one with was willing to challenge her, so all remained quiet for a time.

King Jarom, heavily endowed with shrewdness but lacking the better graces of wisdom and good judgment, broke the silence, "Princess Calyin, know your place and calm your tongue!"

"Calm my tongue? I will hold my tongue when I am good and ready to do so; however, until then I will continue to speak my mind! It is you who needs to gain your bearing and remember your place. You are not in your tiny little kingdom any more! You are in my kingdom! In my palace! And furthermore, you are a guest! A guest should know his place!" screamed Calyin as she stalked across the room to confront Jarom face to face.

As she approached, King Jarom's air of superiority modified to become a small, trembling ember, which Calyin devoured. "I demand a recount now! And by the same treatise that brought us here, I am allowed to call for a new count! If there is anyone who disagrees, let him speak!"

Calyin stormed back across the hall and sat down. King Jarom, with a shocked expression on his face, quietly retook his position. Lord Serant, controlling his desire to smile, quickly seated himself beside Calyin.

Chancellor Volnej quelled the growing disorder in the hall. Harshly, he cleared his throat and thumped his scepter several more times to silence the last few murmurs. "It is thus written. A recount is in order. We will pause for a turning of the glass, then begin."

Lord Serant turned to Calyin and smiled with amazement. As their time together grew, he felt his love for her grow with each passing year. He needed her more than she would ever know.

All attention turned back to the rear of the hall where the counting would start. Talem stood and made a symbolic gesture with his hands. Thc other dark priests rose as one and together they intoned a definitive no. Keeper Q'yer smiled and intoned a triumphant yes. Father Joshua and Sister Midori each again affirmed a yes.

Calyin stood and turned to look into the tiers. Keeper Q'yer followed her move, also rising; the other keepers were quick to follow suit. Each individual counselor offered an unequivocal yes and with pride remained standing in salutation. Geoffrey, Lord Fantyu, Chancellor Van'te, and King William completed the movement. The other votes were of no consequence. The vote was clearly changed. Lord Serant would be magistrate for as long as he deemed necessary. Angrily, Chancellor de Vit penned his signature onto the new document Volnej gave him. The vote became fact as the scroll was passed to Chancellor Van'te for his confirmation; there would be no debate this time. The decision was no longer a draw.

"My dear, dear, Princess Calyin. These little games of state do bore me so," haughtily stated King Jarom, "but I wish to thank you very much. You don't know how much I am in your debt."

Awed silence befell upon the hall. King Jarom's crafty smirk widened as tension filled the air. Keeper Q'yer raised his hands to his temples. The intensity of his headache was unbearable. It was as he did this mechanically without thought that he realized something peculiar. The pain of the headache had been as a cloud over his thoughts, but until just now he hadn't noticed it. However, in the back of his thoughts he knew he had been feeling ill since early morning.

His eyes nervously wandered about the chamber. He noted that Father Joshua also looked rather pale. His thoughts began to run wild; he could not concentrate. The pain within his mind was growing, becoming unbearable. He just wanted to rip it out and throw it away.

The keeper strained to clear his mind. Time seemed to be flowing so quickly. He shouted out, "Oh the pain, the pain, it will not go!" but the words never left his mind.

With a snap of his fingers, King Jarom ended the calm. The holy seal on the great doors splintered and fell to the floor. A faint battering noise resounded from somewhere beyond the chamber, followed momentarily by the stifling sound of the crash. The double doors of the room burst open and fell heavily.

A torrent of heavily armored soldiers shouted a gallant cheer and poured into the chamber. In that instant, Keeper Q'yer crumpled unconscious over the table in front of him. Thought returned to him momentarily as he fell; he knew without a doubt that the beginning of the end had begun.

Shock and disbelief paralyzed the gathered throng. The hall was in turmoil even before the enemy warriors stormed into the room. Father Joshua felt with bitterness the anguish in Keeper Q'yer's spirit as it passed. The pain outside his consciousness allowed him to wrench his mind away from the enchantment of the agony within, and thought returned to him.

The dark priests released a mocking laugh as their energies revived. Their mental strength spent beyond their capacities, they could not withstand the impact. The priests had completed their task to perfection, so they gladly did the only thing they could do—they expired. Save one, who sought to flee the turmoil in the chamber.

Lord Serant sprang from his chair and readied for the coming battle. He cleared his mind and prepared for the fight. He would make the traitors pay dearly for this treachery. Once his thoughts were organized, his first duty was to try to get Calyin to safety. Rapidly he assessed the situation.

Jarom had been thorough in his planning; the hall was as an erupting volcano of melee. Lord Serant was grateful that he had foreseen something coming although the treachery had not come directly from Chancellor Volnej as he had expected. He scanned the hall rapidly, searching for Pyetr to signal him to send for reinforcements.

The sentries posted throughout the chamber were quick to react to the danger, and were making a valiant effort to contain the invading horde. Their high-quality light mail gave them a clear advantage over the intruders, who were outfitted in heavy mail beneath large cloaks. Many of the enemies were wasting valuable time removing their guise; although it only took moments to remove the heavy cloaks, it was sufficient to end many of their lives. Their numbers were in no way hindered by the losses.

Captain Brodst grabbed Lord Serant by the tunic and ushered him and Princess Calyin into a far corner of the hall. Lord Serant was offended by the action, but his pride was not damaged. He knew the captain was just looking out for his safety.

Lord Serant cast an angry glare at Chancellor Volnej, who stood nervously beside Chancellor Van'te. The keepers without the leadership of Keeper Q'yer were beset by confusion. The keeper's demise had been sudden and unnerving. They still remained in the tiers along the side of the chamber.

Father Joshua quickly followed Talem, pursuing him into the mass of bodies set before the entryway without thought. He latched onto the dark priest's robe, pulling him backwards, and when the opportunity arose, he pummeled him to the ground. Without hesitation, Father Joshua struck Talem in the face, once for Keeper Q'yer and once for himself.

Their bodyguards, who would at all cost protect the lives of the ones they served, quickly surrounded Geoffrey and the governors of Mir and Veter. As free men, they did not fear melee; it was part of their daily lives. They lived and would die by the sword.

The end came.

End Of Book Two

The Story continues with:

In the Service of Dragons III

The forces of good will continue the fight.

Map of The Reaches

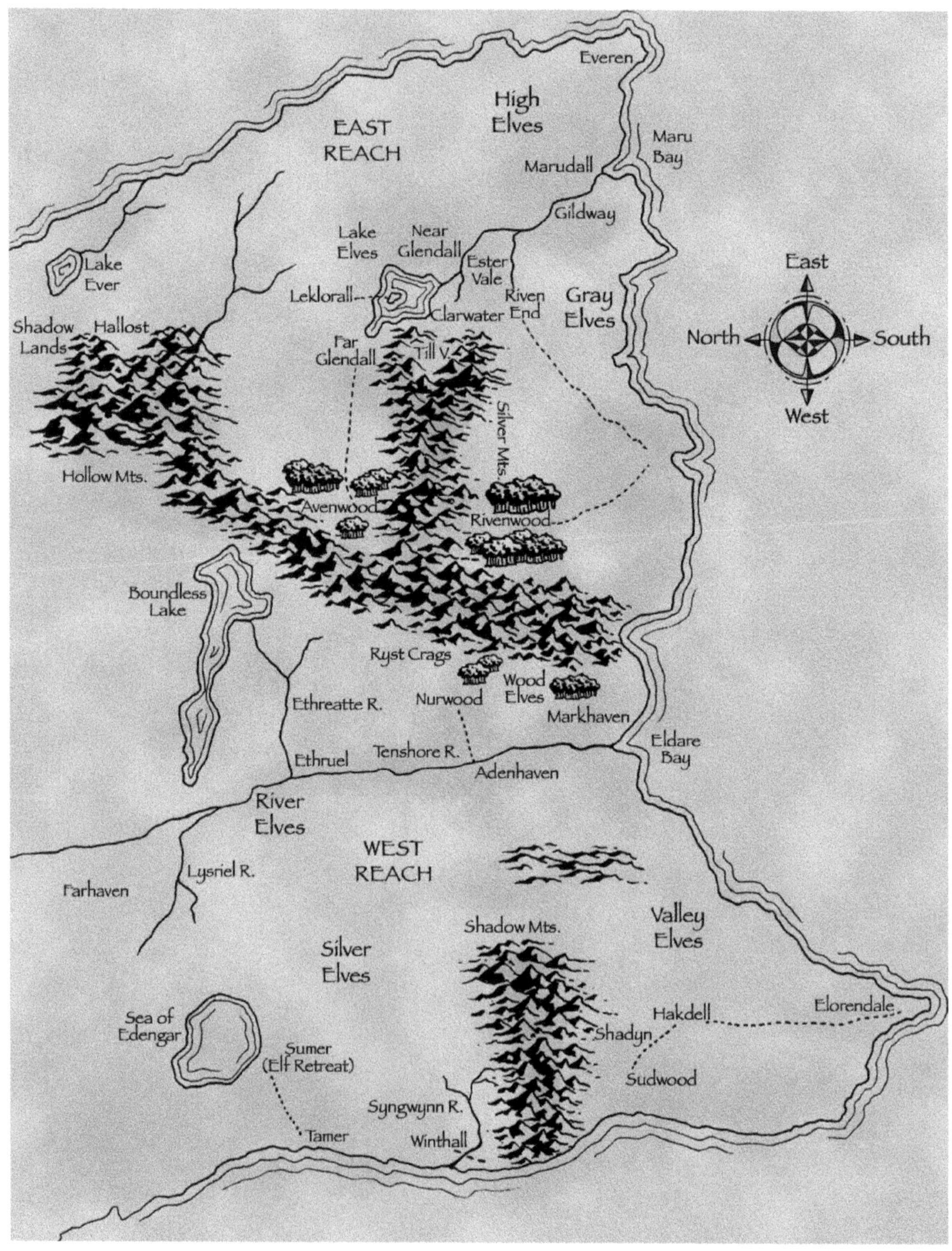

Map of The Kingdoms

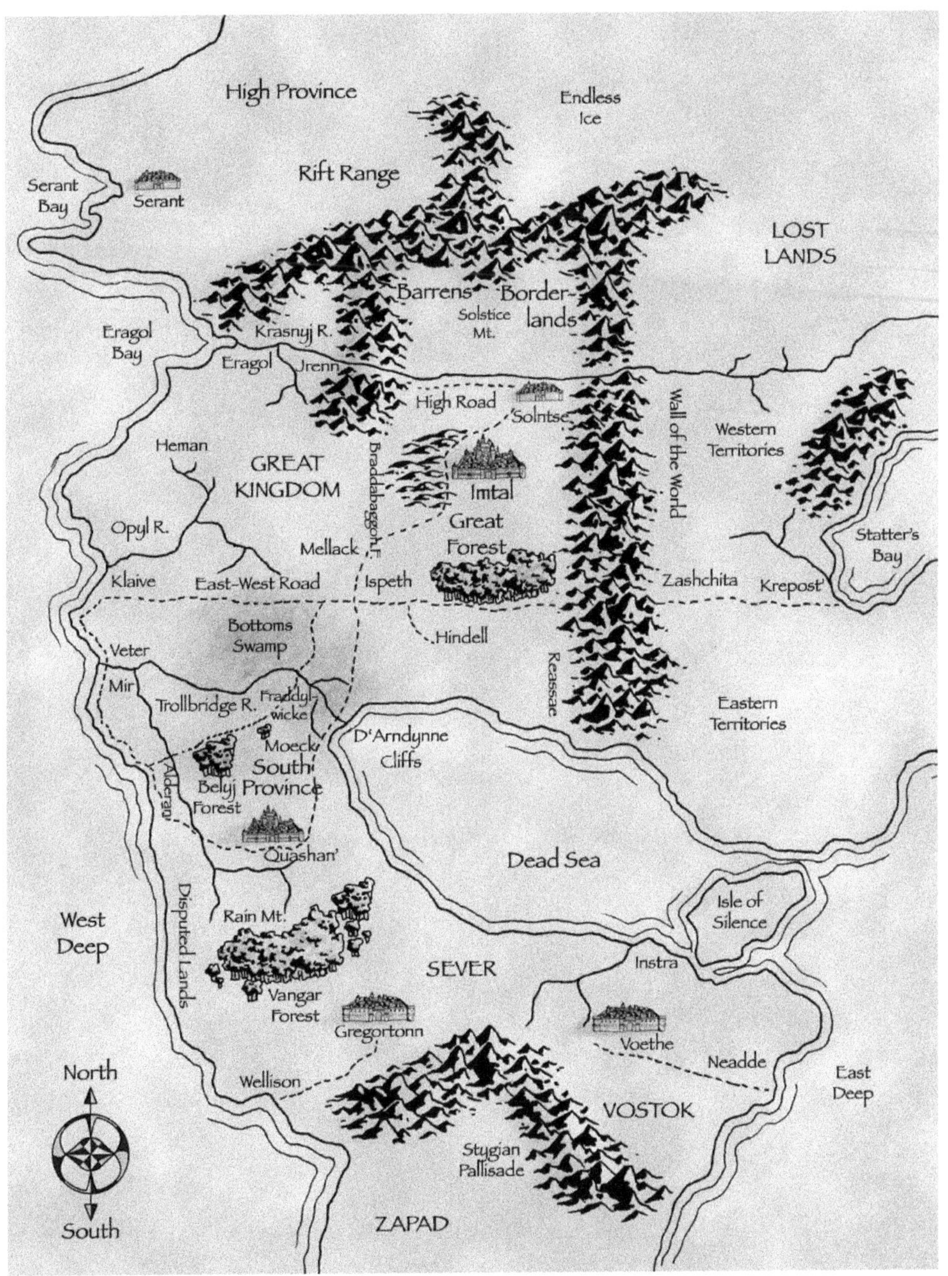

Meet the Characters

Adrina Alder

Princess Adrina. Third and youngest daughter of King Andrew.

Amir

Son of Ky'el, King of the Titans.

Andrew Alder

King Andrew. Ruler of Great Kingdom,
first of that name to reign.

Ansh Brodst

Captain Brodst. King's Knight Captain.

Calyin Alder

Princess Calyin. Eldest daughter of King Andrew.

Delinna Alder

Known as Sister Midori after joining the priestesses.

Jacob Froen d'Ga

Father Jacob. First minister to the king. Head of the priesthood in Imtal.

Jarom Tyr'anth

King Jarom, ruler of Vostok, East Warden of the Word.

King Mark.

The Elven King of West Reach.

Martin Braddabaggon

Keeper Martin. A lore keeper and head of the Council of Keepers.

Noman

Keeper of the City of the Sky.

Sathar

The dark lord.

Seth
Elf, first of the Red, protector of Queen Mother.

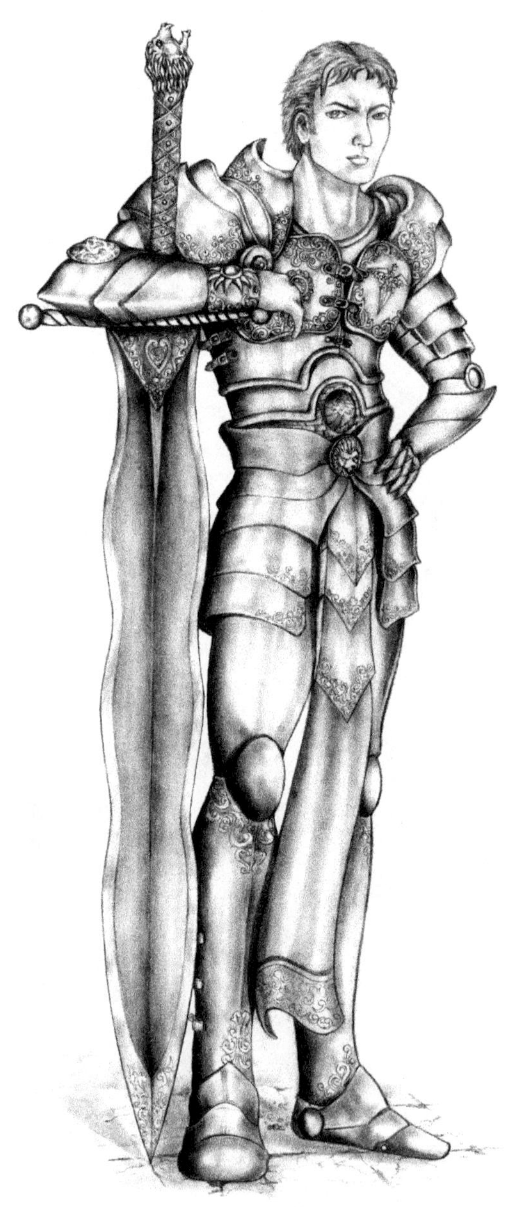

Valam Alder

Prince Valam. Only son of King Andrew.

Vilmos Tabborrath

An apprentice of the forbidden arcane arts.

Xith

Last of Watchers.

People, Places & Things in Ruin Mist

2 (2nd Alliance - 2nd Siege)

2nd Alliance — Alliance negotiated by Imsa Braddabaggon. Under the treaty Hindell, Ispeth, Mir, Veter and Solntse are protectorates of Great Kingdom but outside Great Kingdom's rule. The alliance was originally negotiated to stop the infighting between rival factions in these free city states and end bandit raids that were used to finance the fighting. The alliance includes trade and defense agreements.

2nd Siege — The 1,000-year siege of Fraddylwicke by Dnyarr the Greye. "Dnyarr the Greye, the last great Elven King, laid siege to Fraddylwicke Castle two times during the Race Wars in his attempt to gain the southlands. The first siege lasted over one hundred years, which wasn't enough time for young elves to grow to maturity but was generations to the men who defended the fields with their blood and their lives. Yet if such a thing was unimaginably horrible to endure for those who served, could one possibly imagine a thousand years of such as was the case of the last great siege?" – From the *History Of Fraddylwicke & D'Ardynne.*

A (Abrikos - Azz)

Abrikos — A walled city of Shost. Noble families: Ckrij, Triaren.

Adrina Alder — Princess Adrina. Third and youngest daughter of King Andrew. Her black hair and high cheekbones are from her mother as are the warm, inviting eyes. (See illustration)

Adrynne	A swamp in the southwestern part of Greye. In ancient Greye, Adrynne was a lady of high standing and was also the traitor of Shost.
Adylton, Captain	See Imson Adylton.
Aelondor	Father of Galan, of the Lake Elves of Near Glendall.
Alder	The Royal House of Great Kingdom. A reference to the Alder or the Alder King usually points to Antwar Alder, first king of Great Kingdom.
Alexandria Alder	Queen Alexandria. Former Queen of Great Kingdom; Adrina's mother, now deceased.
Alexas Mytun	King Alexas, ruler of Yug, South Warden of the Word.
Alexia D'ardynne	Champion of the Old World. Kingdom lore says that she was a human slave who seduced the most powerful elf king of all time, Dnyarr the Greye, and later gave birth to bastard twins, Aven and Riven. See Aven & Riven.
Amir	One of the lost. Child of the Race Wars. Son of Ky'el, King of the Titans.
Andrew Alder	King Andrew. Ruler of Great Kingdom, first of that name to reign.
Ansh Brodst	Captain Brodst. Former captain of the guard, palace at Imtal. King's Knight Captain.
Antare	A place of legend.
Anth S'tryil	Bladesman S'tryil is a ridesman by trade but a bladesman of necessity. He is heir to the Great House of S'tryil.
Antwar Alder	King Antwar. The Alder King. First to rule Great Kingdom.
Armon	Said to have been the greatest shipwright that ever lived. His designs for merchant galleys and war galleons are the most duplicated in the kingdoms. He is credited with the discovery of the Mouth of the World during the maiden voyage of Midnight Star, a war galleon constructed for the Alder's fleet. In truth, a misunderstanding between Armon and the ship's captain is more likely responsible for the discovery. During an argument between the shipwright and the

captain, the galleon crashed into the Jrenn Cliffs. The ship was supposed to have been dry docked at Jrenn, transported over the ground to the other side of the cliffs, and put back into the river so as to complete the voyage. The crash, however, broke through the rocks of the cliffs and into an enormous river cave. Being pigheaded, Armon insisted that they go out the other side of the cave the same way they had gone in. Crashing into the rocks a second time crushed the galleon's hull but the ship didn't sink until several hours later—enough time for Armon to claim the discovery.

Armore — Lands to the north of Greye.

Ashwar Tae — The 12th son of Oshowyn.

Aurentid — Ancient stronghold of old.

Aven & Riven — Twin sons of Alexia D'ardynne who rebelled against the tyranny of their father Dnyarr the Greye and helped liberate the kingdoms. Aven and Riven were denied their birthright as one of the Greye, and took no last name that is known. Aven became the great intellectual of his time but as he kept mostly to the affairs of elves, little is known of him. Riven, on the other hand, renounced the throne of Sever though King Etry Riven I, a descendent of his line would later claim the throne.

Ayrian — Eagle Lord of the Gray Clan.

Azz — Village under protection of Daren.

B (Bandit Kings - Br'yan)

Bandit Kings — Rulers of the 12 clans of Oshowyn. Their people inhabit the Barrens, Borderlands and the mountains of the Rift Range. Their lands once extended to Ispeth and the Great Forest before they were driven north by the Alder King.

Barrens — Lands of desolation; desert near the western sea. "Beyond High Road is a vast desert called Barrens, a no man's land. Beyond the Barrens is the untiring Rift Range—ice-capped mountains of jagged black rock that climb perilously into the heavens."

Beast — Dark Lord, enemy of Amir.

Belyj Forest	Vast woodlands to the north of Quashan'. Named after Enry Belyj, the White Knight.
Berre, Captain	See Garette Berre.
Between	A dark, cold place through which realm travelers must go. "That place between worlds where the souls of the dead lingered before they passed beyond this life. That place without dimension that a mage can use to transition between realms."
Beyet	A walled city of Daren. Noble families: Shryth, Styven. War Lords: Lionne, Yras.
B'Him	Village under protection of Daren.
Bloodlord	A Ruler of Right and Knight of the Blood; one of the Nine Sons of the Blood.
Bloodrule	Commander of the blood soldiers, often called Father of the Blood. Less commonly called Tenth Son of the Blood.
Blood Soldiers	King Jarom's elite soldiers, born of the Blood Wars. "Too brutal and uncivilized for the civilized world that emerged after the Great Wars and too many to exterminate, they are all but forgotten about by both the kingdom that gave them birth and the kingdom that conquered them." (See illustration)
Blood Wars	Sometimes referred to as the last great war. It is the war during which Man drove the brother races out of the Kingdoms.
Borderlands	Lands situated between the Great Kingdom and the Northern Reaches. A wild, free country.
Bottoms	Swamplands in northernmost part of South Province. "There's things in there without names, but they'll try to take you just the same. They don't call it the bottom of the world for nothing. Fog rolls in so thick by mid-afternoon that you can't see your hand in front of your face."—Emel Brodstson.

Proper name is Fraddylwicke Swamp. See also Fraddylwicke.

Braddabaggon Hill country around Imtal. Imsa Braddabaggon as Head of Lore Keepers helped negotiate the 2nd Alliance.

Brodst, Captain See Ansh Brodst.

Br'yan, Brother Elf of the Red order. Proper Elvish spelling is Br'-än.

C (Cagan - Ckrij)

Cagan Sailmaster Cagan. Elven ship captain of the Queen's schooner. Proper Elvish spelling is Ka'gan. (See illustration)

Calyin Alder Princess Calyin. Eldest daughter of King Andrew.

Catrin Mitr	Sister Catrin. Priestess of Mother-Earth.
Charles Riven	King Charles, former ruler of Sever, North Warden of the Word.
Ckrij	A valley in the Samguinne Mountains; the founder of the city of Qerek and the first to discover the mystic minerals.

D (Dalphan - Dtanet)

Dalphan	The Wanderer; one of Great Father's first sons; he that created true death.
Damen	First kingdom of Greye; the ruling power of Greye.
Danyel' Revitt	Sergeant Danyel'. Former Sergeant Quashan' garrison.

Danyel' Tae	Son of Ashwar.
D'Ardynne	Cliffs formed where the Fraddylwicke Swamp and the Trollbridge River edge toward the Dead Sea. Although there is a Kingdom Road along the cliffs, the path is treacherous due to frequent rock slides and wet earth. Alexia D'Ardynne, a human slave for whom the cliffs are named, is a Kingdom heroine. Kingdom Lore says that Alexia seduced Dnyarr the Greye and gave birth to bastard twins, Aven and Riven half-elven, who would later help liberate the kingdoms. Sadly, it is also said that Alexia met her end on the very cliffs for which she is named.
Daren	Second kingdom of Greye.
Dark Priests	Also known as Priests of Dark Flame. A sect of priests, officially unsanctioned by the Priests of the Father and the Priestess' of the Mother, that work to expunge magic from the world. They were formed by universal decree after the Blood Wars by the then rulers of the Kingdoms and are not subject to the laws of the land or the rule of Kings. Their decrees are irrefutable laws. According to their law, magic use is a crime punishable by death and all magic creatures are to be exterminated. "Vilmos shuddered at the mention of the dark priests. Their task was to purge the land of magic, a task they had carried out across the centuries."
Davin Ghenson	Captain Ghenson. Imtal garrison captain.
Dead Sea	Lifeless sea to the east of South Province wherein lies the Isle of Silence.
Delinna Alder	See Midori.
Der, Captain	See Olev Der.
De Vit, Chancellor	See Edwar De Vit.
Dnyarr	Father of Daren, Damen, and Shost. The last great Elf King of Greye, creator of the four orbs.
Dream Message	One of the artifacts discovered by the keepers revealed to them the secret of sending messages across great distances (and it is rumored time). The keepers have used this knowledge as a way for the council and keepers spread

throughout the lands to communicate efficiently. In most cases, dream messages are received when a keeper is sleeping and can contain images as well as spoken words. Sending words requires great strength and close proximity. "To begin you must clear all thoughts from your mind and reach into the center of your being. A spark of power lies there that is your soul. You reach out with that power until you touch the consciousness of the one you wish to communicate with. You speak through images and feelings that you create in your consciousness." "It takes an extremely powerful center to create a vision in the form of thoughts that enter another's awareness as audible words. The simpler form is to use images and feelings."

Dtanet — A walled city of Shost.

E (East Deep - Evgej)

East Deep — The great eastern sea.

Eastern Reaches — East Reach. The realm of Queen Mother.

Ebony Lightning — Champion stallion, given to Emel Brodstson by King Andrew Alder for his service to the crown.

Edwar De Vit — Chancellor De Vit. King Jarom's primary aid and chancellor.

Edward Tallyback — A troant (half troll, half giant) and friend of Xith's. Edward would be the first to tell you that he is only distantly related to the hideous wood trolls and that he is a direct descendant of swamp trolls.

Edwar Serant — Lord Serant. Husband to Princess Calyin. Governor of High Province, also called Governor of the North Watch.

Efrusse, Efritte — Rivers; the two sisters. Efritte was in love with a nobleman from Beyet, but her sister, who disliked the nobleman, refused to let her sister wed him. So now as the river Efritte flows sadly down from the mountains, gradually gaining strength, momentum and hope, Efrusse jumps into the river and stops her, and is herself carried away by the river.

Efryadde The last Human Magus. Efryadde perished in the Blood Wars.

Elthia Rowen Queen Elthia. Former queen of Vostok, now deceased.

Eldrick A tree spirit of old.

Emel Brodstson Emel. Former guardsman palace at Imtal; Son of Ansh Brodst. (See illustration)

Endless Ice Uncharted lands north and east of High Province.

Enry Stytt Sergeant Stytt. A sergeant of the Imtal garrison guard.

Entreatte Former Capital of Greye, a city of Shost. Noble families: Jeshowyn, Khrafil.

Eragol Kingdom port town located where Krasnyj River meets the West Deep. Eragol is one of the Great Houses. Family Eragol is headed by Peter Eragol, Baron of Eragol.

Eran, Lieutenant See Tyr Eran.

Erravane Queen of the Wolmerrelle.

Etri Hindell Fourth son of Lord Martin Hindell. Family Hindell has wealth but little power in the kingdoms.

Etry Klaive Knight, husband to Ontyv and father of Etry II.

Etry Riven I Legendary King of Sever. He led an army of peasants and sword sworns to victory against Elven marauders.

Etry Solntse First Lord of the Free City of Solntse.

Everelle, Brother Elf of the Red order.

Ever Tree The oldest living thing in all the realms. It is the tree that helps Vilmos and guides him from Rill Akh Arr. “It was an odd-looking tree perched atop a rocky crag. The roots, stretching over rocks and gravel to the rich black earth a hundred yards away, seemed to have a stranglehold over the land and the trunk, all twisted and gnarled, spoke of the silent battle the tree was winning. Thick boughs stuck out from the trunk and stretched at odd angles to the heavens, almost seeming to taunt those that traveled below as their shadows lengthened with the waning of the day."

Evgej, Captain — See Vadan Evgej.

F (Faryn Trendmore - Francis Epart)

Faryn Trendmore — Captain Trendmore. Imtal garrison captain.

Faylin Gerowin — Huntsman Gerowin, a journeyman class hunter who is perhaps more than he seems.

First Brothers — Council made up of the presiding members of each order of the Elven Brotherhood.

Fraddylwicke — Barony also known as the Bottoms, formerly the gateway to South and home of Blood Soldiers. Fraddylwicke's inhabitants are the ancestors of King Jarom's Blood Soldiers.

Fraddylwicke, Baron — See Riald Fraddylwicke.

Fraddylwicke, Baroness — See Yvonne Fraddylwicke.

Fraddylwicke, Castle — During the Great Wars the castle was a major strategic point for King Jarom the First.

Francis Epart — Father Francis. Member of the priesthood of Great Father.

G (Gabrylle - Greye)

Gabrylle — A training master in Imtal.

Galan, Brother Elf of the Red order, second only to Seth. (See illustration)

Galia Tyr'anth Direct descendent of Gregor Tyr'anth. She is a king cat rider, bonded to Razor since the age of 12.

Gandrius & Gnoble Tallest mountains in the Samguinne. Gandrius and Gnoble were the ancient defenders of Qerek. Legend says that in the end, only the two held the Ckrij Valley from the Rhylle hordes. They are never tiring.

Garette Berre Captain Berre. A garrison captain in Quashan'.

Garrette Timmer Young guardsman, Imtal Palace. Son of Swordmaster Timmer.

Gates of Uver These mystical gates were once used to travel between the realms. In all, there are believed to be 7 gates fashioned by the Uver from a magic substance once mined from the deepest, darkest reaches of the Samguinne. Each gate is fashioned for a different purpose and a different kind of traveler. Two gates are recorded in the histories of Man. The gate in the Borderlands, fashioned for Man, is opened with the following words of power: *"Eh tera mir dolzh formus tan!"* The only other known gate is located in the Twin Sonnets. Both gates are masked from the world by a veil of illusion.

Geoffrey Solntse Lord Geoffrey. Lord of the Free City of Solntse. Descendant of Etyr Solntse, first Lord of Solntse.

Geref, Brother Elf of the Red order.

Ghenson, Captain — See Davin Ghenson.

Gildway — Ancient waterway in East Reach, flows from mouth of Maru Bay to Clarwater Lake.

Great Book — Book of Knowledge, used by Councilors of Sever and other southern kingdoms to relate the lore and the legends of old. The councilors and their families are some of the few commoners who can read and write. "Listening is the councilor's greatest skill. Each tale, each bit of lore, tells a lesson. Relate the lesson through the lore; it is the way of the councilor. Choose the wrong tale, give the wrong advice." "Books are a rare, rare thing in the land. It takes years, lifetimes, to pen a single tome. And only a true book smith can press scrolls into such a leather binding as befits the Great Book."

Great Father — Father of all. He whom we visit at the last.

Great Forest — Extensive span of forest south of Solntse.

Great Kingdom — Largest of the kingdoms, formed after the Race Wars. Referred to as *the Kingdom.*

Great Western Plains — Boundary between East and West Reach.

Greer — Alias for Anth S'tryil.

Gregor Tyr'anth — One of the greatest heroes of Sever and a martyr. Brother of King Etry Riven II.

Gregortonn — Capital of the Kingdom of Sever. Gregor Tyr'anth, for whom the city is named, was the brother of King Etry Riven II.

Greye — Land in Under-Earth where the three kingdoms were formed.

H (Heman - Human Magus)

Heman — Kingdom village; one of the oldest Great Families. The family matriarch is Odwynne Heman.

Although no longer one of the Great Houses, Odwynne Heman does have a sponsor in High Council and does contest the revocation of title at every opportunity.

High Council, East Reach — Represents the elves of East Reach. Its members are the elves of noble families, which include those that are members of the Elven Brotherhood.

High Council of Keepers — 12-member council of scholars that track the lore of the lands and are responsible for caring for the ancient artifacts. The council is headed by Martin Braddabaggon, also known as Keeper Martin. Keeper Martin has an arcane staff that allows him to teleport from Imtal to the High Council of Keepers, which is hidden in a secret location. Although the council is itself neutral, the council has aligned itself with Great Kingdom since the time of the Blood Wars.

High Hall — Meeting chamber in the Sanctuary of the Mother, East Reach.

High King's Square — A square in Imtal where the king's edicts are first delivered to the people. It has been used for coronations, funeral processions and executions.

High Province — Another of the principalities of Great Kingdom, located far to the North beyond the Borderlands. "High Province in the north—the far, far North—where amidst mountains of ice and stone the rivers boil and fill the air with blankets of fog."

High Road — Northernmost garrison town in Imtal Proper. Near the Borderlands on the Kingdom side of the Krasnyj River. "The sole purpose of the elite High Road Garrison Guardsmen is to provide travelers with safe passage along the Kingdom's High Road and to shield the Kingdom from bandit incursions out of the north."

Hindell — An independent state managed by Family Hindell. According to the 2nd Alliance, Hindell is a free nation but most of the lands have been traded back to Great Kingdom over the years.

Human Magus — A mage of the race of Man. The last Human Magus was Efryadde who perished in the Blood Wars.

I (Imson Adylton - Ispeth, Duke)

Imson Adylton — Captain Adylton. Imtal garrison captain.

Imtal — Capital of Great Kingdom. In ancient times, Imtal was the name of a great warrior sword sworn to the Alder, first king of Great Kingdom. In the early days of the Blood Wars, Imtal by himself defended the Alder against an army of assassins. He died with his blade in his hands and is said to have taken fifty assassins with him.

Instra — City built at the mouth of Instra River in Vostok. The Old Kingdom word *inst* can mean either tool or spear depending on interpretation.

Isador Froen d'Ga — Lady Isador. Nanny for Adrina; given honorary title of Lady by King.

Ispeth — Lands of Duke Ispeth, small and swamp-infested but renowned for its apples. Ispeth and her people have been strong allies of the Great Kingdom since the time of the Alder. The apples of Ispeth are the best in the land and often grace King Andrew's table.

Ispeth, Duke — Ruler of the independent Duchy of Ispeth. "Duke Ispeth is not the most trusting of men. I've had the pleasure of his company on several occasions, I know. If he sees plots and spies in the passage of a mere messenger across Ispeth, who knows what he thinks seeing this mob… We'll not be traveling anymore this day."—Emel Brodstson.

J (Jacob Froen d'Ga - Jrenn)

Jacob Froen d'Ga — Father Jacob. First minister to the king. Head of the priesthood in the capital city of Imtal. (See illustration)

Jarom Tyr'anth — King Jarom, ruler of Vostok, East Warden of the Word.

Jasmin	Sister Jasmin. First priestess of the Mother.
Jeshowyn	A road named after a soothsayer who brought the city of Skunne and Pakchek to the same side. Supposedly his spirit still binds the cities together.
Joshua	Priest of the Father.
Jrenn	A floating city located along the Krasnyj River near High Road. It is a Kingdom town, hidden away within the Mouth of the World. Jrenn was previously home to the royal fleet of Oshywon.

K (Kastelle - Ky'el)

Kastelle	A swamp northwest of Beyet. In ancient Greye, Kastelle was a lord and the lover of Adrynne who was a traitor to the king of Shost. It is said the swamp maintains a narrow finger so the two may always touch, even during times of droughts. The two swamps forever protect the city of Beyet's west side.
Keeper	See Lore Keepers.
Keeper Martin	See Martin Braddabaggon.
Keille Tae	Son of Ashwar.
Khennet	Village under protection of Damen.
King Cat Patrol	Legendary defenders of Gregortonn. They ride enormous tigers called king's cats. Few have survived encounters with a king cat in the wild. King cats are fiercely independent but once they bond with their rider, it's a bond that cannot be broken.
Kingdom Alliance	A peace accord signed by Great Kingdom, Vostok, Sever, Zapad and Yug to end the Blood Wars. Also called the Alliance of Kingdoms.
Kingdom of the Sky	A reference to the Dragon kingdoms of old, lost like the Dragon's Keep in the mists of time.
King's Mate	An ancient game played by soldiers and scholars.
Klaive	Small barony in South Province that is rich in resources. Home of renowned shipwrights.

One of the Great Houses. Family Klaive is headed by Baron Michal Klaive.

Klaive Keep Knights — Skilled swordsmen and riders, renowned and feared throughout the Kingdoms.

Krasnyj River — River that flows from the Lost Lands to the West Deep. The river's depth changes dramatically with the seasons and is mostly rocky and shallow. The river's name comes from the Old Kingdom word *kras* (red) as the river is said to bleed in spring.

Krepost' — Walled city in the Western Territories. "Beyond Zashchita lay Krepost' and her ferryman who took travelers across River Krepost' so they could begin the climb into the mountain city and where afterward the gatekeeper may or may not chase them over the cliffs into Statter's Bay and to their deaths." – Jacob Krepost', *Territory Writings*

Jacob Krepost' was ordered into exile by King Enry Alder in 284 KA. It is said that the territory wildmen burned the first settlement to the ground and the only escape for Jacob and his men was to dive to their deaths into Statter's Bay.

Ky'el — Legendary titan who gave men, elves and dwarves their freedom at the dawn of the First Age.

L (Lady of the Forest - Lyudr)

Lady of the Forest — Mysterious woman who helped Adrina and told her she would find help in a most unlikely source. She is of a race unknown and the history of her people is unrecorded.

Lady of the Night — See Lady of the Forest.

Leklorall — Kapital, the capital city of East Reach. Home of the Brotherhood of Elves and Queen Mother of East Reach.

Lillath Tabborrath — Mother of Vilmos.

Liyan, Brother — Elf, presiding member of East Reach High Council.

Lore Keepers — Lore Keepers are the guardians of knowledge and history. Throughout the ages, it has been their task to record history, a mandate written by the First Keeper, known as The Law of the Lore, has kept them independent from any kingdom and outside the control of kings and queens. Their ability to communicate over long distances using dream messages is their true value, though, and the reason few kings want to risk the wrath of the Council of Keepers.

Lost Lands Uncharted lands north of Statter's Bay. According to Territory lore, these lands once belonged to a great kingdom that was swallowed by the Endless Ice.

Lower Council The people's council of Great Kingdom. Handles affairs of local areas and outlying provinces, including land disputes and tax collection.

Lycya Kingdom swallowed by the desert during the Race Wars; now known as the Barrens.

Lyudr Hills at the western edge of the Samguinne Mountains. In ancient Greye, a bandit lord who was the first to discover paths through the hills to Oshio. He led numerous raids into Oshio.

M (Marek - Myrial)

Marek A walled city of Damen. Noble families: Icthess, Teprium. Lords: Ryajek, Ittwar.

Mark, King The Elven King of West Reach. (See illustration)

Martin Braddabaggon Keeper Martin. A lore keeper and head of the Council of Keepers.

Master Engineer Field engineers are responsible for many of the dark horrors used on the battlefields of Ruin Mist. They are the builders of mobile towers, battering rams, ballista, catapults and defensive trenches. Whenever there is a long campaign, you can be sure that field engineers will be deployed along with the troops, and that the master engineer will have many resources at his disposal.

Mellack A small holding of Great Kingdom near the Duchy of Ispeth.

One of the Great Houses. Family Mellack is headed by Elthia Mellack, Baroness of Mellack.

Michal Klaive Baron Klaive. Low-ranking noble whose lands are rich in natural resources.

Midori Sister Midori. The name Princess Delinna Alder earned after joining the priestesses. Her black hair, green jewel-like eyes, and high cheekbones mark her as one of noble blood and a daughter of King Andrew. Since she has been exiled from the Kingdom. (See illustration)

Mikhal Captain Mikhal. Quashan' garrison captain.

Mir A free city state, officially formed under the 2nd Alliance. The name is from the Old Kingdom word *mer* (soil or dirt).

Moeck A Kingdom port town on the Dead Sea, near the Cliffs of D'Ardynne.

One of the Great Houses. Family Moeck is headed by Enry Moeck, Baron of Moeck.

Mother-Earth The great mother. She who watches over all.

Mouth of the World — A natural river cave that cuts under the Rift Range and whose Eastern bowels provide a port safe from harsh northern winds.

Mrak, King — King of the wraiths. One of the dark minions.

Myrial — Cleaning girl who becomes Housemistress of Imtal Palace. Childhood friend of Princess Adrina Alder.

N (Naiad - Nyom)

Naiad — Fresh water spirits of ancient times.

Nameless One — He that is true evil; evil incarnate.

Neadde — The current capital city of Vostok. During the reign of King Jarom I, Lord Rickard Neadde was a Bloodrule, the last Bloodrule.

Nereid — Water-dwellers; sea spirits of ancient times.

Nesrythe — Village under protection of Shost.

Nijal Solntse — First son of Geoffrey, former day captain city garrison, Free City of Solntse.

Nikol, Brother — Elf, first of the Yellow order.

Niyomi — Beloved of Dalphan, lost in the Blood Wars.

Noman, Master — Master to Amir. Keeper of the City of the Sky.

North Reach — Lands swallowed by the 20-year snow during the Race Wars; now known as the Endless Ice.

Nyom — A mountain range east of the Efrusse River named after the founder of Nesrythe. Nyom tried to lead people to safety during the Rhylle/Armore wars.

O (Odwynne Heman - Over-Earth)

Odwynne Heman — Matriarch of Family Heman. Unofficially, a baroness, though the family no longer has the right of title.

Olev Der — 2nd Captain Olev Der of the Quashan' garrison. Captain of the City Watch.

Olex — Neighboring village to Vilmos' home village of Tabborrath.

	One of the three villages in their cluster.
Ontyv, Brother	Elf, first of the Black order.
Opyl	A river near Klaive in Great Kingdom. Opyl Alder was the daughter of Antwar Alder, first king of Great Kingdom. She is said to have fallen in love with King Jarom I, a love that caused her to betray her father.
Oread, Queen	Great queen; first ruler of Under-Earth gnomes.
Oshio	Capital of Damen. Noble families: Ibravor, Glorre, Clareb, Darr. War Lords: Mark, Kylaurieth, Kylauriel, Hettob.
Oshywon	King of Valeria, the unrecognized kingdom. Also refers to the twelve clans.
Over-Earth	One of the three original realms of Ruin Mist. A place of myth and legend. It is said that Over-Earth is ruled by titans, dragons and the eagle lords. The only known gate to Over-Earth was sealed at the end of the Second Age and no one henceforth has ever completed the journey there and back, though many have tried and failed.

P (Pakchek - Priests of the Father)

Pakchek	Capital city of Daren. Noble families: Fiosh, Lann, Jabell, Tanney, Lebro, Thyje. War Lords: Boets, Yuvloren, Lozzan, Ghil, Chilvr, Rhil.
Papiosse	A walled City of Shost. Noble families: Papli, Ivorij.
Parren	Keeper Parren. Member of the Council of Keepers.
Pavil Hindel	Lieutenant Pavil. A sectional commander.
Peter Eragol	Baron of Eragol, head of Family Eragol. The 17th Peter in a line that goes back to the time of the Alder.
Peter Zyin	King Peter, ruler of Zapad, West Warden of the Word.
Priestess' Of Mother-Earth	Serve the land and Mother-Earth. Handle affairs of life, birth and renewal of spirit. Retreat to Sanctuary during equinox ceremonies of autumn and spring. These same times represent the peak of their powers. The Priestess' of the Mother have no known allegiance to any kingdom. Each priestess has a rank with the highest rank

being First Priestess of the Mother. Second and Third Priestess ranks are often offices of contention and there is considerable maneuvering for favor as the second priestess is not guaranteed the highest office should the first pass on or pass her office on before her death. Priestesses are referred to as Sister. Upon earning her robes, a priestess is given a name suffix which indicates her rank and place.

Priests of the Father Serve Great Father. Handle matters of matrimony and death. They preside over the winter and Summer solstice ceremonies throughout the Kingdoms. These times represent the peak of their powers. The highest level of the priesthood is the office of King's First Minister. The office of King's First Minister in Great Kingdom is held by Father Jacob. Father Jacob is charged with ensuring the natural laws of Great Father are upheld in Great Kingdom. The insignia of his office is a white sun with outward swirling rays.

Q (Qerek - Q'yer)

Qerek Village under protection of Daren.

Quashan' Capital city of South Province. Aden Quashan' was a Bloodlord who took and then held the Cliffs of D'Ardynne in the last days of the 2nd Siege.

Queen Mother The Elven Queen. Queen of East Reach, mother of her people. (See illustration)

Q'yer Keeper Q'yer. Member of the Council of Keepers.

Race Wars	The war that led to the Blood Wars. It is a murky time in history that is often confused with the time of the Blood Wars. "When only the five sons of the Alder remained in power, King Jarom the First controlled nearly all the lands from Neadde to River Ispeth. It was his Blood Soldiers that pushed the enemy back to the sea near River Opyl and he with his own bare hands that committed patricide and started the last great war."
Rain Mountain	Majestic mountain in the center of Vangar forest. The mountain is said to be the source of an ancient power but the dark stories about the Vangar keep out the curious.
Rain Stones	The stones. Stones with healing properties that come from deep within Rain Mountain. Other healing stones are known to exist.
Rapir the Black	The spurned one, once a son of Great Father. Also known as the Darkone.
Razor	Galia Tyr'anth's king cat.
Reassae	Barony. Family Reassae is one of the most highly regarded Great Houses. The family and their landkeeps held the East against First and Second Coming, invasions by Territory wildmen. One of the Great Houses. Family Reassae is headed by Gabrylle Reassae, Baron of Reassae, and King's Hand.
Redwalker Tae	Lieutenant Tae. Also known as Redcliff. A sectional commander.
Rhylle	Broad inland plains; an ancient battle place, where the Rhylle invaders were defeated, just short of Pakchek. Lands to the east of Greye.
Riald Fraddylwicke	Baron Fraddylwicke. Low ranking nobleman with holdings in South Province. Keeper of former gateway to South.
Rickard Neadde	The last Bloodrule. Rickard supposedly wielded two great swords, one in each hand, as he went into battle. The swords, named Fire and Fury, are said to have been over six feet in length, a size dwarfed by Rickard's reported height of

nearly seven feet.

Rift Range — East-West mountain range separating High Province and the Borderlands. Ice-capped mountains of jagged black rock that climb perilously into the heavens.

Rill Akh Arr — Home to those that worship Arr. It is a source of dark magic and home of the Ever Tree, the oldest living thing in all the realms.

Rudden Klaiveson — Son of Baron Klaive. Blood relative of King Jarom on his mother's side.

Ruin Mist — World of the paths; the intertwining of Under-Earth, Over-Earth and Middle-Earth.

Ry'al, Brother — Elf, second of the Blue. Heir to Samyuehl's gift.

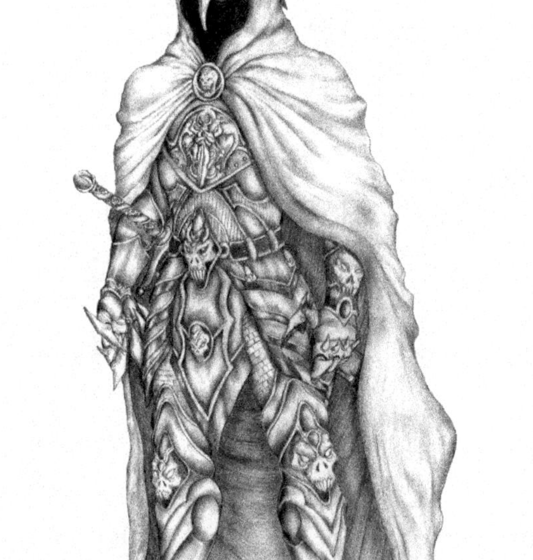

S (Salamander - Sylph)

Salamander — The fire-dwellers; lizard men of times past.

Samguinne — A mountain range dividing the Zadridos and Zabridos forests. An ancient nobleman/war lord who conducted negotiations for Greye with the Armore. Samguinne was an Armorian but served Greye.

Samyuehl, Brother — Elf, first of the Blue order.

Sathar the Dark — He that returned from the dark journey. (See illustration)

Scarlet Hawk — Merchant ship Vilmos and Xith sailed in from Eragol to Jrenn.

Serant	Principle landholding in High Province. Also called the Lands of the North Watch. One of the Great Houses. Family Serant is headed by Edwar Serant, Governor of High Province.
Serant, Lord	See Edwar Serant.
Seth, Brother	Elf, first of the Red, protector of Queen Mother.
Sever	Smallest of the minor kingdoms.
Shalimar	A warrior of Shchander's company.
Shchander	Old compatriot of Nijal.
Shost	The 3rd kingdom of Greye.
Skunne	A walled city of Daren. Noble families: Zont, Adyir. War Lords: Zeli, Ehrgej.
Solntse	Largest of the free cities. Located on the northern edge of Great Kingdom.
Solstice Mountain	Tallest mountain in the Rift Range.
Soshi	Former love of Prince Valam Alder.
South Province	Southernmost lands of Great Kingdom. "South, beyond a forest of great white trees called giant birch, lay South Province with its capital city enveloped by the majestic Quashan' valley."
Statter's Bay	Inlet that cuts deep into the Territories and leads to Eastern Sea. In the Old Kingdom, a statter is the word for a dead man (from Old Kingdom *statt,* meaning still), so Statter's Bay is also called Dead Man's Bay.
Stranth	The most powerful Lord of Greye in recent times.
S'tryil, Lieutenant	See Anth S'tryil.
Stygian Palisade	Steep, rocky mountain range that cuts through the minor kingdoms.
Stytt, Sergeant	See Enry Stytt.
Sylph	Air dwellers; winged folk of times past.

T (Tabborrath - Tyr Eran)

Tabborrath — Village Vilmos was raised in; located in the Kingdom of Sever.

Taber — Ancient name for Eragol, a coastal seaport at the mouth of Krasnyj River.

Tae, Lieutenant — See Redwalker Tae.

Talem — First Priest and Ceremony Master for Priestess Council.

T'aver — Master T'aver. Elder in a small village in Fraddylwicke swamp.

Teren, Brother — Elf of the Brown.

Three Village Assembly — Each village cluster in Sever has a councilor. This councilor is a member of the assembly. Other members include the oldest living members of the village's founding families.

Timmer — Swordmaster Timmer. Swordmaster garrison at Imtal.

Trendmore, Captain — See Faryn Trendmore.

Trollbridge — River runs from Rain Mountain to West Deep.

Tsandra, Brother — Elf, first of the Brown order.

Tsitadel' — Ancient stronghold of old.

Twin Sonnets — Nickname for the free cities of Mir and Veter. The Old Kingdom names, *mer* and *evet*, together refer to windblown earth, which is the common explanation for the enormous delta at the mouth of the Trollbridge River.

Two Falls — Village a day's ride north of Tabborrath.

Tyr — Klaive Knight, husband to Kautlin and father of Aryanna and Aprylle.

Tyr Eran — Lieutenant Eran, sectional commander.

U (Under-Earth - Uver)

Under-Earth — The Lands of Greye, Rhylle and Armore. The dark realm beneath the world of men.

Upper Council — The highest council of Great Kingdom. Handles issues of

	state, issues that pertain to all areas of the Kingdom as a whole, such as roads, garrisons and tax rates.
Uver	A region in the northern part of Greye and burial place of Uver, the founder of Greye.

V (Vadan Evgej - Vythrandyl)

Vadan Evgej	Captain Evgej. Former Swordmaster, city garrison at Quashan'.
Valam	Prince Valam. Governor of South Province. King Andrew's only son. Also known as the Lord and Prince of the South.
Valeria	Once a great kingdom of the North with holdings that stretched from Solstice Mountain to Mellack.
Vangar Forest	Great forest in the Kingdom of Sever. Many dark legends have been spun about strange beasts that hunt in the forest's shadows.
Van'te Duardin	Chancellor Van'te. Former first adviser to King Andrew, now confidant to Lord Valam in South Province.
Veter	A free city state, officially formed under the 2nd Alliance. The name is from the Old Kingdom word *evet* (air or wind).
Vilmos Tabborrath	An apprentice of the forbidden arcane arts.
Vil Tabborrath	Father of Vilmos and village councilor of Tabborrath.
Voethe	A great walled city in Vostok. During the reign of the Summer King, Voethe was the capital of Vostok.
Volnej Eragol	Chancellor Volnej. High Council member, Great Kingdom.
Vostok	Largest of minor kingdoms, key piece of the four.
Vythrandyl	Village under protection of Daren.

W (Wall of the World - Wrenrandyl)

Wall of the World	The Wall; North-South mountain range that separates Great Kingdom and the Territories.
Wellison	Port city in the Kingdom of Sever. Lord Geoffrey Wellison was First Knight of King Etry Riven I and is said to have

fallen on a sword meant for Etry. Prince Etry, at the time, was the sole heir to the throne.

West Deep — Great western sea.

Western Reaches — Lands of King Mark.

Western Territories — Farthest holdings of Great Kingdom to the East.

Willam Ispeth — Duke Ispeth. Ruler of the independent Duchy of Ispeth.

Willam Reassae — Lieutenant Willam. A sectional commander.

William Riven — Prince William. Prince of Sever and heir to the throne.

Wolmerrelle — Shape changers, the half animal and half human race that worships Arr.

Wrenrandyl — Village under protection of Damen.

X (Xavia - Xith)

Xavia A mystic of ancient times.

Xith Last of Watchers, Shaman of Northern Reaches. He is most definitely a gnome though there are those that believe he is a creature of a different sort altogether. (See illustration)

Y (Yi Duardin - Ywentir)

Yi Duardin Chancellor Yi. First adviser to King Andrew. Brother of Van'te.

Ylad', Brother Elf, first of the White order.

Ylsa Heman Bowman first rank. A female archer and later a sectional commander.

Y'sat	Xith's friend of old, dwells in the city of Krepost'.
Yug	Southernmost point of the known lands, one of the minor kingdoms.
Yvonne Fraddylwicke	Baroness Fraddylwicke. Low ranking noblewoman; Baron Fraddylwicke's wife.
Ywentir	Last stronghold of the Watchers; a sanctuary of old.

Z (Zapad - Zashchita)

Zapad	Minor kingdom, renowned for its wealth and the tenacity of its people.
Zashchita	A Territory city that is a defensive outpost.

The Kingdoms and the Elves of the Reaches

Don't miss this bestselling series…

In the Service of Dragons – The sequel series to The Kingdoms and the Elves of the Reaches

Discover what happens when the dragons are revealed…

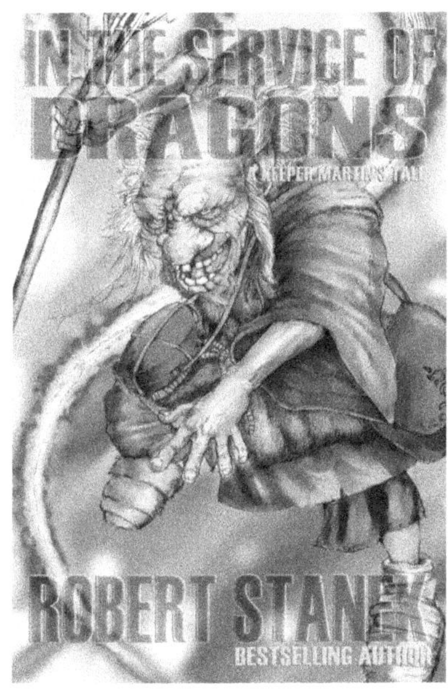

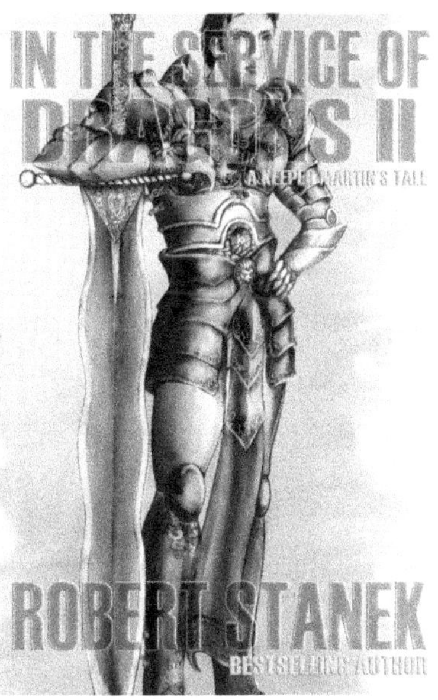

Dragons of the Hundred Worlds – The prequel series to The Kingdoms and the Elves of the Reaches

Discover the time when legends were born…

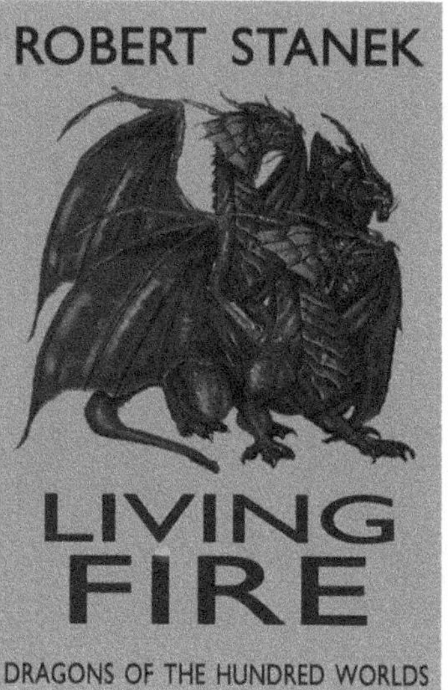

Return to the Kingdoms…

Meet the guardians of the dragon realms